Mafia Playmate

Dark Mafia Romance

Boston Irish Mafia Romance
Book 1

Jamila Jasper

Edited by
Haley O.

www.jamilajasperromance.com

ISBN: 979-8-3303-6247-9

Ingram spark edition.

Thank you to my subscribers for your support with this book.

❀ Created with Vellum

Boston Irish Mafia Romance Series

Mafia Playmate

Mafia Property

Mafia Surrogate

Mafia Possession

Mafia Stalker

Click here for the complete collection:

www.jamilajasperromance.com/catalog

Description

A large pink box arrives on Aiden's doorstep with a woman inside.
His mail-order bride arrives in her birthday suit and tied up in knots
with a pretty pink silk ribbon.

Aiden never requested a dark-skinned beauty...
His family would never approve of such an impure connection.

Who is this woman? What does she want?
A note in the box reveals the truth...
**The woman in the box - *Valentina* - is a gift from an anonymous
sender who wants something dark and twisted in return.**

Thank you to all my patrons for your support with this story.
www.patreon.com/jamilajasper

Thank you to my most supportive readers:

Gwendolyn, King Turtle 22, Jessica Lawrence, Nic, JustChill, Dashauna, Atira, TheeLastHokage, Yvonne K., Chrissy, Janelle, Rian, LaRonda, Deanna, Dlawson382, Jasmine, Haley, Belinda, Sercee, Yvonne, Jadelock, Farah, Tamiya, Quin, J.Payton, Geek Girl, Ashley, Rubi, Pilar, Sandra, June, Anni, Shannet, Joneesa, GlitzyHydra, Amanda, Barbara, Brianna, Jamica, Lyons, Mary Ann, Marketia, SarahD, LoverofHawaiiHearts, Cortney, Yolanda, Monagirl, Dianna, Mary, Amna, Nysta, Fayola, Ty, Shyra, Andi-Mariee, Keisha, Jennett, Fredericka, Candece, Lydia, Sabrina, JM, Jackie, Mo, Ashaunte, Tolu, Lori, Dionne, ZLB, Nicol, Elbert, Jesi, Brenda, Desiree, LaShan, Only1ToniD, Debbie, Tiffanie, Shawnte, Lisema, Christine, Trinity, Monica, Juliette, Letetia, Margaret, Dash, Maxine, Sheron, Javonda, Pearl, Kiana, Shyan, Jacklyn, Amy, Julia, Colleen, Natasha, Yvonne, Brittany, June, Ashleigh, Nene, Nene, Deborah, Nikki, DeShaunda, Latoya, Shelite, Arlene, Judith, Mary, Shanida, Rachel,Damzel, Ahnjala, Kenya, Momo, BJ, Akeshia, Melissa, Tiffany, Sherbear, Nini, Curtresa, Regina, Ashley, Mia, Sydney, Sharon, Charlotte, Assiatu, Regina, Romanda, Catherine, Gaynor, BF, Tasha, Henri, Sara, skkent, Rosalyn, Danielle, Deborah, Kirsten, Ana, Taylor, Charlene Louanna, Michelle, Tamika, Lauren, RoHyde, Natasha, Shekynah, Cassie, Dreama, Nick, Gennifer,

Rayna, Jaleda, Anton, Kimvodkna, Jatonn, Anoushka, Audrey, Valeria, Courtney, Donna, Jenetha, Ayana, Kristy, FreyaJo, Grace, Kisha, Stephanie E., Amber, Denice, Marty, LaKisha, Latoya, Natasha, Monifa, Alisa, Daveena, Desiree, Gerry, Kimberly, Stephanie M., Tarah, Yolanda, Kristy, Gary, Janet, Kathy, Phyllis, Susan

Thank you to my Patrons *for allowing me to use your names to name some supporting characters after you!*

I offer this fun little option for patrons who are at the $10+ tiers behind the scenes.
Thank you also to everyone who helped name the other characters in this book.
🖤

Content Awareness

Read this passage if you require content warnings for sensitive material. I do not give detailed content warnings that will spoil the plot, but be aware of this note.

This is a mafia romance story with dark themes including potentially triggering content of **all** varieties, violence, frank discussions and language surrounding bedroom scenes and race.
All characters in this story are 18+
Sensitive readers, be cautioned about some of the detailed romantic material in this dark but *extremely hot romance novel.*

Chapter One
Aiden

You have one job in the Murray family. You grow up, you get your marks, you listen to Pa, you marry a nice Irish girl, preferably a blond or a redhead with lighter features.
You do what Padraig Murray asks.
You pray everyday and you keep your rosary wrapped in your pocket. You stay loyal. You keep our bloodline strong.

Pa demands a meeting with me now that I'm back in the city. He claims it's important, but it can't be that important if he wants to meet me during the Red Sox game. It feels good to be home. There's something special about Boston, but maybe that's just it – paradise is wherever our family is.

After Pa, I'll go home and see Roscoe, my Rottweiler. Then get my shit together and call my younger brother Darragh to check in on his training and find out if Rian's around. Over the weekend, I'll head to Leominster to visit Callum and then Sunday after church, stop by to see Ma and Odhran. I brought a gift home with me for Tegan, Rian's daughter, and I can't wait to see my niece's face light up when I give it to her.

If there's one thing I don't miss about being home, it's a never ending list of shit to do.

I meet my father at our usual casual meeting spot, Mulligan's, a place where we aren't afraid to celebrate Irish pride. A place where you can catch the Red Sox game and no one can catch your conversation. *It's as much home as anywhere else.*

I spot my father hunched over the bar from the street, his face illuminated by a warm orange bulb as he watches the pre-game announcer talk. I prefer football to baseball, but Pa bets on all their games, so he likes to keep his eye on the Red Sox each season.

When Pa calls, you answer, and he's desperate to know about the affair with the Italians – what the fuck happened, have I found the renegade cousins who pissed off the Italians, and whether I've killed them yet. *I haven't.*

It's all bad news and my ass is on the line if I don't find a way to sort out all the shit that happened in Long Island. At least we're guaranteed peace with the vicious Italians. *Those greaseballs aren't any better than the blacks. 'Trust 'em as far as you can throw them', Pa told me. But for now, we have peace and that's what matters. At least to me.*

I enter Mulligan's and the conversations fall to a hush. *Aiden Murray's back.* I clear my throat and the conversations continue. But there are more phones pulled out than before and two guys sitting in the back leave. I don't hate the reputation I have. Most of the bar fights I earned this cutthroat reputation in were Darragh's fault, but that doesn't change what people say about me.

Darragh, my younger brother, can still throw his weight around in the ring, but he got his practice here, in this fucking place. Our last fight here was over a girl. Darragh kicked some Puerto Rican's ass and a few of our boys jumped him outside… I don't know what happened to the guy after.

My father slides a twenty-dollar bill across the bar to the bartender, Finnegan O'Malley, a one-eared ex-hitman, who in turn fills up two glass pints of amber Sam Adams. Pa's already several drinks ahead of me. *Great. The news can't be that bad then.*

I pull out a bar stool next to my father, who barely acknowledges me, although he must've caught me entering the bar through the reflection on the glass behind the bartender. He shoves one of the pints across the bar towards me. He knows I prefer Guinness, but I don't mind starting with this. I can see my dad's reflection in the glass. He looks older than I remember. He's pushing 70, so I shouldn't be surprised by the large streaks of gray through his slick hair which was once blond, but changed color throughout his life, settling on a dark chocolate brown, like Rian's.

I glance at the television to check the score, but the game hasn't even started yet. I can smell the alcohol coming off of him already.

"You can have a Guinness after you drink this," he says. "I heard you did good work with the Italians."

He sounds raspy, but calm. My tension dissipates. This is just a normal, father-son meeting. Nothing to worry about.

"I didn't find Eoin or Robert. Haven't heard fuck since they all screwed with Vicari," I say as I take a sip of my beer.

"Maybe the Italians killed them," he says. "They're a violent, vicious group of people."

"Yeah."

Like we're ones to talk. Pa's done with his Sam Adams already and waits patiently for me to catch up, as if I could catch up to a man who's been drinking for an hour. At forty, it's not so easy for me to keep up with long nights of drinking. I don't know how he does it.

He waits for me to have a few more sips, his eyes glued to the television. Chris Sale throws the first pitch. It doesn't go so well. My father glances down at his glass and sighs. "It's going to be a long night."

"That bad this season?" I grunt, glancing up at the Detroit batter sliding into second.

I've been too busy to keep up with baseball. My father grunts. Yeah, it has been that bad.

"Any other news?" I ask him, finishing off the Sam Adams. Dad grunts and snaps his fingers for the bartender, Finnegan. The buff, tattooed bartender hustles over as dad orders two Guinnesses without opening his mouth. Bad news if he's drinking Guinness.

"Cops got Rian last week. They're charging him with manslaughter."

Manslaughter?

"What did he do?"

"What the fuck do you think he did?" Dad responds calmly. "He killed somebody, they caught him. That boy's not careful enough and I have to pay to get his ass out of trouble. Maybe some prison time would do him good."

"That's what you said the first three times," I grunt. Sale throws a good pitch and my father's face visibly brightens.

"If it weren't for Tegan, I'd let him spend a few extra years behind bars," Dad confesses. "Your mother won't let me do that to his daughter."

"What's going to happen to her?"

"I don't know," my father says. "No one has seen the kid in a week."

"What?" I growl, sipping at my beer and hoping this is my father's idea of a joke since he sounds dangerously unconcerned.

"What do you mean no one's seen her? Is she with her ma?"

My father shrugs.

Rian's notoriously bad taste in women landed him with a child he should have never brought into the world. She's a sweet girl, but doomed by a mobster father and a whore mother.

Her ma doesn't live in Boston anymore. She wants nothing to do with Rian.

"Where does he say she is?"

"Last time he saw her was the night he got arrested," Pa says before taking a sip of his beer.

"What about the cops? Did they give her to his lawyer or something?"

Chapter One

I don't have a single paternal instinct in my body, but my mind courses with worry over Tegan, despite my father's calmness.

"She'll turn up," he says, pouring more alcohol down his throat.

Fuck, Rian. My brother must be an even worse parent than our father. His daughter's missing and he's behind bars and there's no one else to look for her except…

"I can find out where she is. Once I get Roscoe and take care of–

"It would serve him right if something happened to her," my father says coldly. "Her mother isn't Irish. He keeps fucking up. I'm tired of cleaning up his messes. Now *drink*. This is not why I asked you here."

I bristle at his comment, but it's just Padraig Murray. This is who he's always been and my brother should have had the good sense to keep his dick in his pants. I made it to forty without fathering bastards all over Boston. Rian should have been more careful. I drink a few more sips, but I can't let this go. *Who else will worry about the fucking kid if not me?*

"How the hell did Rian let this happen? Can I talk to him?"

"Best that none of us talk to him. The cops listen to everything. I can get messages into the prison and messages out, but I don't want you talking to him."

"Fine," I grunt, finishing off my first round of Guinness and ordering us another. I try to pay, but my father stops me and then finally answers my other question.

"Your idiot brother trusted a woman," he says. "He wants a mother for that little girl so badly, that he's willing to do anything. He's willing to kill for a woman who doesn't deserve him."

"I didn't know he had a woman," I grumble.

"*Had* is correct," Pa says. "She's dead."

I wish I could tell you a chill ran through me, or I had some other human response to my father's announcement. I don't need a university degree to understand what he's implying. Rian had a woman, she got him locked up, so my father had her killed.

"Will that affect his case?"

"No," Pa says. "It was very clean."

"Who?"

"None of your business, Aiden. You worry about your shit, I'll worry about your brother."

I want to feel sorry for Rian, but he deserves it for crossing our father. This is what happens when he pisses off Padraig Murray. More problems for all of us.

"How much time is he facing?"

"Three years since he's been in jail before. I tried to get that stupid motherfucker to get his life together, but your brother just wants to be a fuck up."

"Who's the lawyer?"

"Someone from Nigel & Bancroft."

At least he isn't cheaping out like he did for Rian's first case. I don't want to push my father's buttons, and despite his outward calm, he must be furious at Rian for drawing more attention to us, but Rian has his uses.

"It's Rian," I remind him. "Crazy fucking Rian. We need him out soon. There are some jobs only Rian has the balls to handle."

Padraig snorts. "He takes after my father. Too proud and too violent for his own good."

We created the monster Rian Murray is. He's our responsibility.

"He needs another woman."

"He needs a woman who isn't a fucking spic," my father spits. "At least the child looks white."

"What about this previous woman? What'd she look like?"

"It doesn't matter," he grunts. "She's dead. Now drink. We have more important things to talk about than your idiot brother and his shitty taste in women."

I drink because Pa commands it. I do everything he commands and have since I was a child. I have the burns and scars to remind me of what happens when you disobey my father. At first, I hated him for what he did to me, but to keep an organization like ours together, you need to inspire fear.

. . .

You have to be cruel to survive – that's just how the world works. I can't let Tegan go. The second I see Darragh, I'll ask about her and track her down.

I drink so I don't lose my temper. He doesn't give a fuck about Tegan. No one does. Maybe he's wrong and one of my sisters took her in. But who would do that? Evie's saddled with her drunkard husband and two unruly kids of her own – Katie and Patrick. Kiara's off at university and Maeve's sixteen, too young to have any involvement.

"I need to tell you something important," my father says somberly, as if there could be something more important than my missing niece right now. I'm burning with desire to leave, but if I get up without my father's dismissal, he'll hurt me. Or someone I care about. Not like there are many of those people yet. It's foolish to get close to people in this life.

"Then tell me."

If he notices my tightening tone, my father doesn't acknowledge it.

"There's a plot against my life. I don't know who. I don't know why but... there's someone out there trying to kill me," my father says, the faded tattoos on his knuckles even more wrinkled than I last remember. He's getting older, but aside from his physical appearance, he shows no signs of slowing down. If anything, he's desperate to prove himself more. If he wasn't ordering more killings than necessary, maybe Rian wouldn't be locked up.

I don't want to dismiss his concerns as paranoid, but he's the leader of our family. There's always a plot against his life. It comes with the territory. My father doesn't have to worry because he has us. *Family.*

"Fuck that," I grunt. "No one would be stupid enough to try to kill you. April 2013, four days after the bombing. An entire decade ago. That's the last time anyone tried."

I was thirty back then, old enough to be the one who ended that war before it started. Back then, we only killed when necessary. I got five tattoos that year, one for each kill. Each a painful release, each representing a necessary act to keep my family safe.

My father smirks and keeps drinking. He shrugs. "That's what I thought. But I'm serious. This time is different. This time the bastards might just get me. I'm getting old, Aiden. Most guys in our line of work don't make it this far."

"What happened?" I grunt, urging my increasingly drunken father to get to the point. His cheeks blaze tomato red with alcohol and his blue eyes swim with tears, again brought on by drinking rather than any emotion. He grunts and knocks his biggest gold ring against the bar's surface contemplatively.

If anyone tried to kill him, surely Darragh would have mentioned it. He's responsible for keeping our father alive.

"I feel it in my bones," Pa replies. "Someone wants to destroy our family."

"Yes," I grumble. "Our cousins. But they're gone and if they were anywhere near this city, we would have heard about it."

"I don't know. Something big is coming for us. I feel it."

"We can make decisions based on feelings now?"

"Cut the shit, kid. You know my instincts are good because you're like me. You can smell shit before it hits the toilet bowl."

"I'm home. If anyone tries to kill you, they'll have to get through me, Darragh, and Callum."

My father smirks. "My boys. I'm proud of all of you. Except Rian. He's a piece of shit."

Ah, Padraig. Honest as fuck, especially when he's drunk.

He might not be proud of Rian, but he still loves my brother enough to spring for decent lawyers and to make sure Tegan goes to the best day school in Boston. Once she's old enough, she'll go to Milton or Dana Hall, or another nice private school where she can meet someone to untarnish her sullied blood, that is as long as I can find her. If Rian's behind bars, she could be anywhere. Hopefully not with her mom's people.

She belongs with us, even if Rian made mistakes. She looks like us and that's good enough to cover up his shameful behavior. I don't know what Rian was thinking with that Puerto Rican chick. Tegan's mother was low class.

Let's hope my brother's behavior doesn't come back to haunt all of us. Let's hope his daughter is safe, sound asleep somewhere and protected.

"Thanks, Pa," I mutter, uncomfortable with even this much emotional closeness between us. I love my father, but trusting him too much is dangerous. Rian found out the hard way that it isn't worth it to defy our family beliefs, and it definitely isn't fucking worth it to screw around with the wrong women.

"And Aiden? I need you to hurry the fuck up and find a wife. I'm getting old and I want to retire, but I need a family man to lead this family. You're the oldest. Why the fuck can't you keep a woman? Do I have to send you back to Galway?"

He wants a real answer.

"Not interested in chasing after girls, dad. All they want to do is take your money and ask where the fuck you're going. I've had enough."

"That old dog won't take care of you when you get old."

"Neither will some Boston snob who could take my ass to the cleaners in a divorce."

He laughs, which is the best reaction I can hope for. He quickly moves along to talking about the game and his plans for the business, and then asks me questions about Long Island. They're a mess out there, but doing better under John Vicari's leadership. We're developing a few buildings together and are prepared to make a lot of money in the real estate game. John does cleaner business than his father. Too bad the old man died of a heart attack... that's the word anyway.

"I need you to find a nice girl," my father reminds me once he's almost blackout drunk. He can barely keep his head up. *Great.* I'm not dragging his ass outta here tonight. If he wants to get so wasted he can't sit up straight, I'll leave him for Finnegan.

"We have this conversation every time we talk."

"This time, I'm serious. I want to retire. I don't want you bringing home no spics either like the Duffy boys."

"Fuck's sake, Pa. You can't talk like that around here anymore."

"I can say whatever the fuck I want. I want Irish children. Irish fucking children and I need you to have a wife so I can retire."

"Retire any old fucking day you want," I growl. "It'll be good for you to stop worrying about who I fuck or marry or the fate of the fucking family."

"The fate of the family matters," he says, taking another sip of his newest glass of beer before rubbing condensation off the sides with his napkin.

"I'm too old to have kids," I growl. "I'm too old to get tied down. You and mom were lucky you even found each other."

That's bullshit and we both know it. They stay together because they're Catholic, because back in the eighties, my dad killed someone for her father and won my mother like a prize. He also put a baby in her quickly and then kept her pregnant. There's nothing romantic about their love story or marriage in the Murray family.

"If you can't find a girl, I'll find one."

"The last girl you found me was a crazy fucking redhead who wanted to bring Roscoe Jr. into the bedroom. No thanks."

My father shrugs. "She was white. Do you know how hard it is to find a white girl around here who hasn't been fucking ruined by some fucking Puerto Rican or black guy?"

"What do you want from me, Pa?"

I know what I want. I want an end to this conversation, and I want my father to give me a fucking break about women and dating. All the Irish and Catholic women in Boston know to stay away from us, and the ones who don't learn their lesson pretty fucking quickly.

"Find a nice white girl with big tits and blond hair and get her pregnant so I know you're fucking serious about family. That's what I want."

"Give me time."

He continues, getting to what I suspect was the original point he wanted to make before the liquor got to him. "And get your ass to the site in Back Bay tomorrow bright and early."

"Why?"

This is the first I'm hearing about something wrong at the Back Bay construction site. I know something's wrong because my father doesn't do anything bright and early unless there's a problem to solve.

"You'll find out tomorrow. You just got back. Go home. Pet the dog. Your mom's tired of walking that big fuck. He nearly knocked her over near Harvard Square."

"How is mom?"

"Pissed off."

"Why?"

"Eh. Upset about another woman. It's nothing."

It's nothing. Dad just got his second mistress pregnant and even if we all know about it, we're all supposed to pretend it's no big deal that our elderly father knocked up a Irish teenager who he supposedly hired to clean the construction company office.

I hate how he treats our mother. What's the point of having a family or a woman if you hurt her? There's no getting through to him, but I have to try for my mother's sake.

"You treat her better, pa. Seriously. She needs you."

He grunts. "Get your ass home kid and get a white girl pregnant."

"Thanks, dad."

"If you can't find one, I'll find a good Irish girl who needs a green card and bring her over to you!"

My father is the last person I want picking my romantic partners. I mutter something to him about cutting back on liquor, then I pat my father on the back and leave the bar. This is the closest we've felt in years, but there's still a wall between us and there always will be. I felt closer to him when I was younger, when it was easier for me to justify the life I led. I know I'm a screw up, I know I don't belong anywhere near a woman or a family or any of the fucking things my father wants from me.

He knows it's wrong to bring a kid into this life, but he did it anyway. He knows that we're villains, but he doesn't care. Fuck, I don't care either, I suppose. I'd just rather not ruin a perfectly good woman.

I drive out of the city listening to rock classics on the radio. Just as I turn down my street – I live at the end of a cul-de-sac – I notice the large box on my front step. There are only five large houses at the end of this cul-de-sac, all of us with wide open well-maintained lawns around traditional New England colonial houses.

The box on my front step is fucking enormous – and I don't remember ordering anything for delivery. My hand moves swiftly to the pistol under my seat. I feel no fear as I reach for the gun and slip a mag out of my pocket. I feel ready.

Leaving the city for any amount of time always carries a risk, especially since I didn't exactly leave the place with a house sitter. The last time my teen brother Odhran house-sat, he trashed the place and had a threesome in my bed. I hop out of my black GMC Sierra with the gun under my coat and approach the box slowly, glancing furtively over my shoulder for anyone who might have eyes on me.

The box has holes in it. It's large. Pink. Wrapped in a bow. I reach for the bottom of the box and try to lift it. *Fuck.* It's heavy. I drop the box and I swear I hear a sound coming from inside it. *Is that possible?* I try to peek through the holes but it's too fucking dark and something's telling me opening this box will be a shitshow. It has to weigh about a hundred pounds. Maybe more. I'm no weakling, but it still takes a measure of back strength to lift a box that fucking heavy.

I open my front door and greet Roscoe Jr., my rottweiler, as he bounds towards the door to greet me. His coat looks shiny, the nub of his docked tail wags back and forth. Pa's choice, not mine. He runs up to the box and sniffs at it a bit.

There's definitely something in there and it gets his attention because Roscoe utters a low bark.

"Roscoe, go lie down."

Once he heads off to his bed, I throw my doors open wider and eye the giant box to decide how to carry the fuckin' thing. I would call Rian if his stupid ass wasn't in jail. I could call Callum, but he's still hung up on some fucking girl and won't answer my calls because I won't sugarcoat my opinion of him. Then there's Darragh… He's probably twice as drunk as Padraig. Not a good option either.

I'll have to carry the box myself. I stretch a little and then grab the edges of the box and grunt as I carry it a few feet inside my doorway. I set the box down more gently. *Is there something alive in there?* If it were an animal, I suspect Roscoe would be barking from his spot in the house, but he's laying down as I commanded, gazing at me curiously and wagging his tail.

He's probably wondering why I'm not taking him for a walk since I'm back. *At least he didn't bite the sitter this time.* I close my front doors and then search for an opening on the giant pink box. Finding none, I start with the ribbon and peel it away. The box comes up to my waist. It's *enormous.*

If it didn't weigh a hundred fucking pounds, I would assume it's a novelty gift or something extra special from one of my brothers. Which of my piece of shit brothers would get me a welcome home gift? It's not like either of them are here with a six pack of Guinness right now…

I peel the top of the box open and there's another box inside it, also pink. I open the second box and stumble backwards as I expose the contents. I don't mean to act like a fucking idiot, but I nearly fall over, because this is the last thing I expected to find on my doorstep. I just got back to Boston… How long has that box been out there?

Holy fuck, why isn't she screaming?

I GAIN control of myself and approach the box again, heart pounding because my second assumption is that the human female in the box might be dead and that's the reason she hasn't made a sound. The sick thought twists my stomach into an unyielding knot.

I slowly approach the box again, ignoring my heavy breathing, focusing instead on taking in as much information as possible about the situation. I move the flaps of the box open and stare at the woman's face.. Suddenly, her eyes snap open before swiveling around and looking me directly in the eye..

Holy fuck, this woman is alive.

"What the fuck is this?" I grunt to myself. Not to myself. I'm not alone. I dry swallow and run my fingers through my hair. She's black. Someone tied up a black woman in a pink ribbon, wrapped her up like a gift and put her in a box on my doorstep. This has to be a sick joke.

I'm almost too scared to reach into the box and touch her, but I have to touch her to get her out of the fucking box. Whoever this woman is, she ran into the wrong fucking people and ended up in the wrong living room.

I have tattoos and vows of loyalty to prove how I feel about people like her. "Don't worry. I'll get you out of there."

I don't know why I'm bothering with comfort. I reach into the box and grab her at the base of her spine before hoisting her out of the box and gently setting her on the ground. My stomach lurches. This is some sick, twisted shit. Whoever did this to her stripped this woman naked, bared every inch of her dark skin, the color of Arabica coffee, and wrapped her in a pink ribbon, contorting her limbs and running the ribbon over her bare breasts, between her thighs and in loops around her body so she's wrapped up like a chocolate present.

My body has an unconscious, primal reaction. I could unwrap her like the present she's been wrapped up to be, but I need answers quickly.

She has a gag in her mouth, a round white ball that keeps her lips spread open and hooks at the back. Her eyes roam around the room in terror as I reach into my pocket for my knife. I've killed people with this knife and now I'm using it to save someone.

Her skin prickles with goosebumps as I touch her. I apologize, but I need to brace myself against her to get her free. I press the serrated edge to the ribbon and make the first cut.

I cut her legs free. She groans as her legs fall in a curled heap. She cries out and tries to jerk them again, but however long she's been in that position was far too long for her to have full control of her legs and hips.

Chapter One

"Don't move," I remind her. I touch her skin again and my stomach lurches. Fuck, her skin is so dark. I look pale as fuck touching her and even putting my hands on her drives guilt through me. She's black. She's the wrong kind of person. I run my tongue piercing over my lower lip as I focus on all the parts of the ribbon I have to cut free.

When I have her limbs mostly free, she rolls onto her side, groaning in pain as her arms and legs curl in an awkward and splayed mess next to her. Even her wrists bend at an unnatural angle. I know she's alive, but the woman still looks dead.

I swallow slowly. What the absolute fuck is this?

"I'll take the gag out, but you can't spit or bite or do anything of that nature. Do you understand?"

She stares at me, but she can't say anything. I approach her mouth slowly and reach around her to find the clasp of her ball gag. I unhook it and take it out of her mouth. She groans again and winces in visible pain as she attempts to close her jaw. She slowly moves her hand to her face and rubs her cheek, groaning.

I crouch next to her, staring at her in awe, knowing that I shouldn't but am completely incapable of taking my eyes off the naked woman in front of me. If her nudity makes her uncomfortable, that hasn't sunk in yet. My cock stiffens inappropriately in my pants and I clasp my hands in front of my dick, refusing to take my eyes off her.

Her breasts are small, but they protrude forward in tiny, dark orbs with nipples that are even darker than her extremely dark skin. Holy fuck, I didn't know nipples came that dark. My eyes widen inappropriately and I pray she doesn't notice my leering. Who sent this woman to me and what exactly did they send her for?

Christ, Aiden. Get a grip. You're staring at her crotch now and it's obvious.

She's waxed completely and my gaze snaps to the bare, dark brown lips. I wonder what this strange woman conceals between those lower lips and what color her flesh is between those thin, toned legs. I clear my throat.

"Who are you?"

"Read the card with the gift," she manages to say, with a raspy voice and an accent I can't place.

"I asked you a question."

"Read the card with the gift," she repeats.

I raise an eyebrow and walk towards the box. There's a large card at the bottom, about 8 x 10 inches, printed on thick paper. I pull it out of the box and read the note, muttering it out loud to myself. *What the fuck is this?*

Dear Mr. Murray,

We hope you enjoy your object. Your task is simple.

Use the object wisely. Have unprotected sex with the object and film a 4K quality video.

Compress the video file and send it to the email address below.

The object may be initially unwilling but both of you will face strong motivation to comply. The object understands that documentation of her existence belongs to us and if she fails to comply enthusiastically, we will destroy her identity.

If we do not receive the video within one week of today's date, you will both lose what's most important to you.

Tegan Murray counts on you to succeed. We have possession of the girl and you would be wise to listen to our orders if you or your family want to see her safe.

Do not call Padraig Murray. Do not call anyone else, or you will both suffer.

It takes less than a second to fire a bullet.

You must comply. When you're finished with said object, it is yours to keep.

Sincerely,

Chapter One

Your Benefactors
OA

"WHAT IS THIS SICK SHIT?" I growl, throwing the card back into the box, causing the woman still kneeling on the ground to flinch. My heart thuds.

These people have Tegan and this woman might know where she is and who they are. I won't be a part of this sick fucking game.

Chapter Two
Valentina

"You have to do what they say," I say to him. *"Please."*

It's not what I want to say, but these were my instructions if I wanted to survive. I never saw the people who put me in the box, but I heard their instructions and their threats clearly.

My throat burns raw as I attempt to plead with the man in front of me, hoping that he'll spare me. *He's involved with the people who took you. He's dangerous.*

The more I talk, the quicker he'll piece the truth about me together. I don't want this man to know *anything* about me. My voice. It's bad enough that he's seeing me naked. It's bad enough that he's about to take a part of me that I never wanted to give to strangers, that I always wanted to *mean* something.

I want to keep a piece of myself to myself. I've never had that privilege before. I won't have it tonight. He's an utter stranger to me and a terrifying one at that.

The gigantic blond man glowers at me, his blue eyes enough to melt me in place. He's 6'4", his hair looks slightly unkempt. Black ink swirls around his pale skin in a variety of Celtic knots, cursive Bible verses and symbols that I don't understand. *Lots of tattoos. He must be a gangster. Something like that.*

I hate that I'm naked, but I'm glad that I'm free. There was nothing but pain in that box. The drugs helped at first, but they didn't last thirty-six hours. That's how long it took to get here from Idaho. Technically, the drive takes twenty-five hours, but I tried to measure time – I have a good sense of it because of the piano – and I know they took thirty six.

There's no getting out of this. Maybe this one won't be as wicked as the first.

"Who are you?" the man growls at me. "Who did this and what the fuck do you have to do with this?"

His anger sends a surge of terror through me as his face reddens with frustration. He has absolute control over this situation and he knows it. I can't afford to freeze and make it worse by proving to him what he already knows – I'm vulnerable, weak and utterly at his mercy.

I position myself to cover my breasts as much as possible as well as my *other* parts, but he's already seen every bit of me. Modesty is entirely pointless.

"My name is Valentina," I rasp out, my voice getting stronger as I tell him my name.

"Is that your real name?" he growls, stepping forward and towering over me.

I'll never know if I had another name. I've been called Valentina since I was a little girl. Sometimes Val, but never anything else. I must've had a life before, but I don't remember any of it. All I remember is Pulsifer. He was my father, my abuser, my everything. I wouldn't call this freedom, but there's still a weight lifted because this is the closest I've ever come to leaving the governor's mansion.

The blond man is even taller than I thought he was. I'm more vulnerable naked and despite wanting to stand up for myself, I shrink back from him.

"Yes," I say as firmly as I can manage.

"Who sent you? Because I'll be damned if I screw around with a n–"

He stops himself, but my skin feels a flush of outrage and humiliation as his lips hover over the n-word. I want to hit him, but I don't know what type of man my new master is yet. A racist. That part I understand. He's not the first racist I've had to deal with. He might be the richest though. *He lives in a mansion.*

"Who sent you?" He roars. His face reddens as he screams and his creepy blue eyes look bloodshot. I shouldn't cross him, but I stopped giving a fuck about what happens to me a long time ago. I've already experienced the worst.

"I don't know. All I know is they want you to do what's on that note."

I don't want that. I have to go through with it, but I definitely don't start off wanting that monster anywhere near me.

"No," he growls, his jaw tightening. "I... This is fucking ridiculous. Tell me who sent you, woman."

His anger mounts and my fear intensifies. I'm no stranger to racism, but for the word to nearly fly off the tip of his tongue like that. *How can someone who looks like that be so ugly inside?*

He reaches into his jacket and I know he's reaching for a gun before he pulls it out. The men who sent me here weren't any better than the man who received me as a gift. My throat tightens and I try not to lose control of my bladder as he pulls the pistol out of his jacket and points it straight at me.

Men are all the same and they're all violent disgusting pigs who will put a bullet in an innocent woman's head if she gets in their way. They'll use us up and spit us out and there isn't a man alive capable of real love...

"If you shoot me, you'll die," I state plainly, trying to sound like I have control of the situation. I'm not lying, but I'm also not stupid enough to mean that as a threat either. "And whoever you love enough for them to threaten will die too."

"I don't give a fuck," he snarls. "Who sent you?"

I don't believe that he doesn't care. I sense a crack in this man beneath his outrage. His anger cloaks his genuine concern. If he wanted to kill me, he would have done it already.

"Do I look like I was in control of the situation? You have their instructions. Are you going to do it or not?" I say to him sharply. Talking to him like this could be dangerous, but he doesn't react to my strengthening voice or sharp tone.

"Am I going to rape you?" He growls, lowering the gun. "Is that what you're fucking asking me?"

He has a thick accent which I can finally place. *Boston.* I'm in Boston, or close enough to Boston that men sound like Matt Damon in *Good Will Hunting.* I don't know anyone in Boston, but maybe that's for the best since I don't know any good people. Never have.

I don't respond to him. He reads the card to himself again and mutters a long string of curse words. I'm already naked and despite his apparent hesitation, the man hasn't offered me clothes. He doesn't know if he's going to do it yet, but I do.

He's going to have sex with me.

"YOU HAVE TO FOLLOW THE INSTRUCTIONS," I say to the terrifying blond man pleadingly. He still hasn't told me his name and I don't know if he will. He might worry I'll go to the police. "At least according to them." Hopefully he thinks of another solution since he's clearly some type of gangster.

I've been through enough shit to know that the police don't care about women like me. The police have *never* cared.

"This is a crock of shit," he hisses, spittle flying from his mouth as his face reddens with pure vitriol. "I have *never*…"

He glares at me like I'm responsible for this. Every inch of my body aches and I have little patience for this bastard acting like I'm the fucking problem.

"Never what?"

He glowers. "I've never been with… I don't… I don't fuck black women."

His voice drips with disgust, but I don't mind because I find this man's racism equally repulsive. He's more bothered by my race than the fact that I arrived on his doorstep naked, wrapped in ribbons, and sent to him in a box.

"You have to follow their instructions. I don't know what happens to you if you don't, but I know what happens to me."

I'll be lost to my past forever.

"Who fucking sent you?"

"I don't know."

I should have expected his next actions. He's a sicko, because the people who sent me only send gifts to sickos. My boss... My *old* boss was probably worse than this man. He was certainly much uglier, but all cruel men are the same.

He quickly racks a bullet in the chamber before re-leveling the gun to my face so I am forced to stare directly down the barrel.

"Kneel," he commands without wavering. I can see in his eyes that he's capable of shooting me. He runs his long pink tongue over his lips. He has a piercing through his tongue, a giant gold knob with a Celtic knot in the center. *What the fuck?*

My knees ache and I can't stop myself from groaning as I obey him. I have no choice but to listen to him despite the pain shooting through me. My stomach turns and if I'd eaten anything in the past 48 hours, it would've come up on this rich white man's hardwood floor.

My head lolls forward and I struggle not to cry out as more pain surges through my legs.

"Who sent you?"

"I don't know," I answer truthfully. If I had those answers, I would disappear in the middle of the night and find some way to get my real identity from the people who own me, or I suppose owned me before him.

"You must've come from somewhere," he says, his finger hovering near the trigger. It never occurred to me that he could do worse than hurt me, that he could kill me. *But he might. The men who did this to me never considered that.*

"My master sold me."

"What the fuck?" he snarls. "What the fuck does that mean?"

"I grew up... I grew up in a house with an older man. He sold me when I turned twenty-five."

"Sold you to who?"

"I never saw. I just know... I know what kind of company he keeps."

"Who was your master?"

"Governor of Idaho. Ezekiel Pulsipher," I respond as calmly as possible, even if just saying his name brings back flashes of horrific memories that still torment me every night. Who needs sleep, right?

"I don't know who the fuck that is," he spits. My chest swells with odd satisfaction that there's a corner of the universe not entirely ruled by Ezekiel.

In any other situation, his confusion would have been confusing. Old Zeke was a king in his universe and I wasn't the only girl in his harem. *He owned me since I was six years old. I don't want to tell this criminal about that, but I wouldn't feel sorry if this psychopath turned on my old master. I wouldn't feel sorry if these modern slave owners met this monster.*

I glare at him. I'm not here to give him an explanation. He's not the victim here, I am, and judging by his accent and other cues slowly coming into view, I'm on the other side of the country with no identification, no proof of who I am...Nobody knows I'm here.

It doesn't matter that I'm alone, I have to survive. I don't know what life will be like on this side of the country, but this is the best chance I've had to escape my entire life. *I can fool this white man. I know I can.*

"Why would someone do this?" He snarls.

"Maybe you're a criminal. Maybe they want revenge," I offer, perhaps pushing him too much with my attitude. His body tenses when I say the word *criminal*. Men. They think they're so careful with their emotions, but they get careless when they're underestimating you. Men get careless when they think they have the upper hand.

"I can't do what they want," he says, keeping the gun fixed at my head. This does little to warm me to him. "I can't screw... If my father found out... he would paint the sidewalk with your brains."

**

Charming. Now I have a definitive answer about the extent of this man's criminality.

He sets the gun on the table behind him and re-reads the card for the third time. His face turns several shades of red.

"This is sick," he spits, glowering at me with familiar, racially motivated revulsion. In most situations, I can't actually know if a man is racist. I have proof about this man.

"You have to. Whoever sent me paid a lot of money. You messed with powerful people," I tell him. "And they have someone you love and if you don't do this–

"I haven't messed with anyone," the man growls, interrupting me. "Get up."

I thought the pain shooting through me would knock me unconscious, but I had too much pride to ask him for relief. I slowly rise, my limbs barely cooperating. I look and feel ashy. I hate that I missed my routine. Spend a any amount of time in a box and you will miss the most damning prison you had before. My body still aches.

He looks me in the eye and I'm too scared not to meet this man's gaze. He's a predator and showing a predator fear gives them permission to pounce.

"My name is Aiden."

Aiden. I shouldn't care what his name is, but hearing it makes me consider him differently. The name sounds forceful and as rooted in his heritage as his Celtic tattoos.

"Great," I reply softly, unclear about what to do with the information.

He clears his throat and speaks again, "I thought you should know before we…"

"So you changed your mind?"

I shake before my body knows I'm shaking. This has happened before. Men have *taken* my body several times. Ezekiel *owned* me and believe me, he made good use of his property. Aiden. The name sounds Irish, but the man standing in front of me is All-American. He's 6'4" tall with *very* pale blond hair, but a thick crop of it. It's nice to see a man who isn't bald and who clearly works out. He's very muscular and the gun is out of the way, which sets me at ease.

"I don't know who sent you, woman. But I intend to find out. Seems like the best fuckin' way to do that is follow their instructions."

I knew it.

Aiden reaches for me and I fight my gut reaction to flinch. I don't want him to know how much I fear him. I want him to worry that I'll stab him in his sleep. I want him to feel like he's risking his life every time he rapes me.

Aiden puts his hand on my shoulder. I expected his touch to be rough, but it's very soft.

"Do they have anyone you love?"

I don't want to tell him, but his blue eyes harden and I sense that I'd better tell the truth if I want him to get this over with. His hand cups my shoulder too gently for me to describe. After the sharp angles and the pain of having my body squeezed into a box, his softness is surreal.

"I... I don't know."

"I don't want to hurt you. I won't rape you."

"If you don't have—

"I know," he growls. "But I won't hurt you. You have to consent. I..."

"I belong to you," I tell him, refusing to look away from him. I want him to gaze into my eyes and see a human being. A part of me desperately wants to shame him. It's hard to stare into those eyes and not feel something. He has intense and expressive eyes.

"No," he whispers. "You belong to yourself and once this is over, I'll have to let you go."

I fight back laughter. He won't let me go. I know men like Aiden better than he can even understand. I've lived my entire life in a world of pain and depravity.

"They'll hurt you if you don't do it. Surely my life isn't as important as yours."

"You're right," he growls. "But I've never fucked one of your kind and I don't intend to rape you either. That's not *my* thing."

He says it with the implication that he knows someone who prefers rape. And there he goes with the race talk again. *One of my kind...*

"You have to do it."

"Then agree to my terms."

"Terms."

I don't phrase it as a question and I don't want to sound too eager either.

"I'll give you money."

"So I won't be a slave, I'll be a prostitute."

His face reddens. "I'll send you away. You said they have someone you love. So you have a family?"

"No. I don't."

His hand drops from my shoulder and I glance down at his crotch. Despite Aiden's assurances that going through with this is the furthest thing from his mind, his dick bulges from his jeans. The bulge sends a deep surge of discomfort through me and my head swims.

There's no escape. All my smart-mouthed comments and my internal pleas that I might be able to survive this... I have to go through with it.

"What do you want, then?"

"A place to rest my head for a few nights. Time to get on my feet."

"Done."

He clears his throat. "I'll film it on my phone. I just... I've never..."

Aiden suddenly leans forward and kisses me. His lips surprise me with how soft they are when they first make contact. I want to scream, but it's a good kiss that draws me into Aiden's world instantly. His smell consumes me. His fingers claw at my cheeks as he holds me suddenly and keeps me still so he can kiss me.

Before Aiden, kisses felt like... cottage cheese. I want to push him away but the kiss is too fucking good for me to break away from it. I don't want to upset him, anyway. When he breaks away, his cheeks are red.

"I'm fucking dirty," he says and the revulsion in his voice tells me that he means it.

He doesn't look like he hated the kiss despite the words coming out of his mouth. He leans forward again and kisses me. This time, he spreads my lips apart and slides his tongue into my mouth. The piercing teases my tongue, sending a shiver straight through me. It's better than the first kiss and I kiss him back. He's the first man I've ever kissed back, the first man who has kissed me well enough for me to even try.

Men have done so many horrible things to me in my life and not one of them has kissed me properly. Aiden pulls away again and he pushes hair out of my face.

"We'll do this in my bedroom. Go upstairs. Third door on the left. Shower first."

Shower first. I don't like his tone, but I can't exactly blame him for it. I've been trapped in a box for several hours in a row and I probably smell exactly like it. At least he isn't pointing a gun at me anymore, and doesn't kiss me like a gross, perverted old man. He kisses me like… he would be a good lover.

That's another experience I've never had, another sad truth about my life that I never want to dwell on.

It hurts to walk up the stairs, but my body revels in the most freedom I've had in days. I almost want to race up the stairs to get to the bathroom quicker, but I walk patiently to the top and follow Aiden's instructions to find his bedroom. I can hear Aiden talking to his dog, telling him to stay on his bed for the next little while while he's busy. His house smells new, even if it's an old colonial that has probably been around since Boston's founding.

The bedroom is *extremely* neat. The floor smells clean and as my bare feet touch it, I feel like Aiden's right to wrinkle his nose at me. I'm the dirty one. *But he's sexually aggressive, and a racist one at that.* I can hear him following me up the stairs. He walks slowly, but he has a heavy gait. That may come in handy later if he tries to sneak into bed with me when I want to sleep. If I need to fight him off. That type of thing.

I had to fight off Pulsifer sometimes. That got easier as I got older. Aiden's a lot bigger than some decrepit governor of Idaho.

Chapter Two

I find the bathroom door open and I walk inside. He has a clawfoot tub that could hold seven people. Judging by the perverts Pulsifer normally deals with, Aiden probably has had seven people in this tub at once. It sickens me to think what other secrets he could have. I flinch as he appears behind me. For a man with a heavy gait, he can apparently walk quietly when necessary.

"Get into the shower. Take your time. I'll set up the camera."

He sounds nervous, which makes me nervous. I imagine him being completely cruel. A monster would be crude and quick. Monsters *really* want you to cry. Aiden doesn't have any of those traits. He glances at my breasts, his cheeks redden and he swears under his breath.

"I can handle the shower," I say to him. He stares at me for a few seconds before leaving the doorway. I relish this alone time. I'm too grateful for my survival to think about escape. I wish I could tell you otherwise, but this is the truth. I grew up being passed around America's dirty underworld. Escape stopped being a real consideration when I turned eighteen and realized this was my destiny – permanent sexual slavery.

I clean myself as best as I can and try to ignore the numb feeling spreading over my body as I anticipate Aiden's actions. Most men are very rough. You can close your eyes and do your best to block out the pain, but nothing stops the dirty feeling of being powerless and having another person use you like an object.

Once I'm clean and have spent as much time in the shower as I think I can get away with, I step out and grab one of the insanely fluffy white towels hanging from the rack. As soon as I put it on my skin, the luxurious warmth spreads through me and the towel is so soft that I get a momentary feeling of safety.

I've carved out a life for myself despite my circumstances. I don't want anyone to feel sorry for me. I've learned how to play the piano. All the men who owned me had books that I enjoyed reading. I write poetry too, though none of it is good enough to share. Who would read my poems, anyway? Certainly not this blond hunk of muscle. His brain is probably the size of a pea.

He returns to the doorway and scowls as he watches me dry

myself, reminding me that he's oversized and perpetually disgusted by me. I'm not shy about him seeing my body. He's seen it all anyway and he's going to have sex with me on camera, so there isn't a point in pretense.

"I took a vow that I would never touch a woman of another color," Aiden growls, sounding angry with me, like it's my fault that I'm black and he's racist.

I don't respond to him.

"I don't know if I can get hard," he says. "You might have to work to get me off."

I purse my lips. I have to ignore his suggestion that I'm too ugly to arouse him. White men. I try not to generalize them, but it doesn't help that all the men who have hurt me have had brilliant blue eyes, just like Aiden's. He has more of a pretty boy look, but he still has those cruel blue eyes.

"Have you done this before?"

"Yes."

I'll respond to his direct questions, but other than that, I have nothing to say. It's not like he cares.

"I'm sorry."

I give him a curious look, but I don't say anything. It's smarter not to say anything.

"If it helps, I'll make it good for you," he says in a gruff and gravely voice.

Don't bother. I want to say something cutting, but I don't want to anger him. Violence and sex are intertwined in the male brain, especially men like Aiden, a giant clearly used to getting what he wants.

This time, not responding to him provokes cheek redness. White men are always turning red when their feelings are about to take over. I brace myself for another racist comment.

"Whoever sent you must know my family. They must know about our beliefs and I want you to be clear about mine. I know my history and my heritage. I believe firmly in the superiority of my people over all others. This will not change because I stuck my cock in you," Aiden says, his voice trembling with rage as he stares at me.

I drop the towel. I'd rather him finish this than continue listening to his racist tirades.

I don't flinch, even if I want to. His words cut me deep, but Aiden, for all his complaints, still reacts like a man. His gaze drops decisively to my breasts and his teeth instinctively sink into his lower lip. His supposedly difficult to rouse cock bulges forward in his pants. *It doesn't look like he's struggling to get hard at all.*

He's even redder than before and his left hand clenches into an angry fist. I hope he's not the hitting sort. Those are always harder to deal with.

"Get on your knees," he commands, asserting power over me as my naked body renders him powerless to continue his racist little speech. I don't defy him. Despite my complete disgust with Aiden, pleasing him represents my best chance at survival, so I consent to his commands.

Any position on my knees still hurts. If Aiden cares, he doesn't show it. He walks towards me and crudely thrusts his hips into my face. His trousers smell like cigarettes and beer. His pants pockets bulge with car keys and a few other objects I can't identify. A simple, brown belt cinches over his dark blue denim.

His thighs are thick and muscular, barely held back by his pants. My heart quickens as he shifts his stance to his left side, cocking his hip. I glance down at his shoes. Brown boots. The tips are probably steel, so I don't want to do or say anything that could provoke him to kick me. I'm in enough pain as it is.

"The camera's over there," he says. "We'll have to move. I just wanted to see if you would obey me."

He leans forward and kisses the top of my head. *He's fucked up. It aches down here on my knees and I'll have to get up again.*

Aiden commands me to my feet and I follow him back out into his bedroom. He shows me where he has his cellphone set up on a bookshelf right in front of Sun Tzu's *The Art of War* and an extremely tattered copy of *The Holy Bible.*

"Kneel there," he commands, pointing to a spot in front of the lens. "It's already recording."

I obey him and quietly kneel before Aiden, facing away from the camera. He walks into the frame and commands me again, "Look up at me. I want to see your face."

When I gaze at him, he frowns with that mixture of revulsion and disapproval I already recognize as his gut reaction to me. Despite his cruel facial expression, he's still hard. I can still see the bulge in his jeans and it's terrifyingly huge the closer he gets to me.

"I don't cum from getting head," he says. "But I doubt you can arouse me without it. Take my dick out."

He's so full of shit. This man has the biggest erection I've ever seen. *He doubts I can arouse him? Something is making him unbelievably stiff and there's no one else in the room but me.*

Taking my time to remove his cock from his jeans is the only way I can postpone it. I've seen dicks before, and most of them are completely unpleasant to look at. Many of the ones I've seen are shorter than my pinky finger. The governor called some of the world's most depraved men his friends.

Aiden remains resolutely planted in place, glowering down at me as I unbuckle his belt and then slip the jean button through the loop before unzipping his pants. Because of his muscular butt, I can't rely on his jeans to fall off on their own. I hook my fingers through the back, making contact with Aiden's ass as I pull the jeans down. As I ease his jeans over his ass, I can't help but notice how deliciously round and muscular his ass feels. My hands fight the urge to cup his firm glutes and focus on the required task - getting his dick out of his jeans.

His breath catches as the jeans slide down, revealing an equally toned and muscular pair of thighs. He has tattoos everywhere, but the thigh tattoos are the most alarming. *Choose death.* He has a skull, several Celtic knots, Bible verses, and intricate designs woven together in a tapestry of a criminal's life.

A pair of crisp white boxer briefs cling to Aiden's thighs. More details of his bulging cock become apparent to me. The monster curves slightly in his briefs, the thick head oozing fluid that creates a wet spot where the tip touches the fabric.

The elastic waistband of his boxer briefs sticks to his hips and as I remove his underwear, I expose more tattoos and worse. He has scars and partially healed wounds all over his body, not to mention more muscles. He's the most muscular man I've ever seen this close and it feels wrong to notice.

All the men who fucked me were ugly and cruel with bodies and tongues that failed to arouse me. This man might be a sick mother-fucker but at least he's handsome. It's a small comfort, but I've never touched a man with such well-defined muscles, and the least I can do is appreciate it.

His cock springs free and juts forward with all the arousal Aiden claims he doesn't feel. His body doesn't lie. I haven't even touched him yet, but his cock already protrudes with pure enthusiasm. Once I get the briefs over his ass, they remain taut and stretched around his thighs.

I can't help but stare at Aiden's dick. I've never seen one as big as this. His dick is nearly the length of my forearm and it's thick, with a dusky pink color. The tip reddens immensely, like he's sore from how hard he is. *His dick is so red.* Tufts of trimmed dirty blond hair cover the base of his cock and his shaft is so heavy, his erection leans to one side.

Clear fluid oozes from the tip.

"Don't just stare at it. The camera's rolling."

He probably doesn't mean to be insensitive. He's nervous about this too. It's not like he wants me in this position. I grasp the base of Aiden's cock to hold it up and he makes an uncomfortable grunting sound. He pulses with heat and saliva pools in the corners of my mouth against my will.

He's huge. I run my tongue over my lips so I can get them wet enough to stretch around Aiden. I lean forward and he grunts, nearly jerking back.

"I can't..."

I grasp his shaft tighter. It's too late to back out of this. Before Aiden can pull away from me and deny both of us a chance at survival and escape, I run my tongue over the head of his cock and lick up every drop of the clear fluid emerging from the tip. Aiden's next groan sounds more like an uncontrollable moan of pleasure.

Pleasing him is good. Pleasing him will bring this to a quicker end and I'll have a much greater chance at survival if I please him. The thought occurred to me that once my use has run out, he'll kill me, but I can't dwell on that. If pleasuring this man ensures my survival, it's what I'll do.

I tighten my lips around the smooth, bulging head of Aiden's big cock. He makes an ungodly pleasurable groan as I get his dick head wet with my spit and prepare myself to take the length of that enormous thing down my throat. If I gag, he could hurt me. I have to make him like it. We're being filmed, aren't we?

I tighten my lips more and get Aiden's dick even wetter. His next groan is even louder than the first and he touches the top of my head instinctively before remembering himself and jerking his hand away from me.

Men enjoy having lips around their cocks, but this man really likes it judging by the moans coming out of his mouth. I flatten my tongue along the underside of Aiden's shaft and then slide the full length of his dick into my mouth.

Tears prickle in the corners of my eyes as I stuff every inch of Aiden's dick in my mouth. He groans with pleasure again and I tighten my lips around the base of his cock as I feel the tip tickling the back of my throat, threatening my gag reflex to erupt. I squeeze my eyes shut and focus on breathing slowly through my nose.

As the tip of Aiden's cock touches the back of my throat, he moves his hips slowly with one thrust, and then he erupts. His climax happens so quickly that we're both equally surprised. The tears threatening to pierce the corners of my lids fall freely down my cheeks. I make a gagging sound as Aiden pumps thick ropes of cum into my throat.

The first warm gush fills my mouth and as Aiden tries to remove his cock from the sticky deposit of fluid between my lips, even more spills from the tip and he leaves my lips, face and mouth a mess of cum as he stumbles away and gains his composure after a few steps, making the conscious choice to put as much space between us as possible. There's surprise evident on his face, especially his eyes. *They're terrifying.*

I cough once and try to swallow the cum in my mouth, but that does nothing to remove the thick ropes coating my face and lips.

"Fuck," he says. "I've never…"

"I'm fine…" I whisper, leaning forward, trying to wipe the cum off my face and not wanting to look Aiden in the eye out of pure humiliation. I look ridiculous, I'm crying and there's cum all over me. I worry he won't go through with the instructions on the card. Then what? I'd rather stay here, thousands of miles away from the governor than to *ever* return. If Aiden doesn't finish this, I don't know who might come looking for him.

Aiden crosses the room, standing straight in front of me with his cock hanging limp. My body tenses with uncertainty. I can't predict how he'll react. He crouches in front of me, forcing me to gaze at him with concern. *Is he going to hit me?*

We're face to face and Aiden takes his finger, places it beneath my chin and turns my face so I'm staring him right in the eye. We're still on camera, but it doesn't feel like it. This moment is just for the two of us.

"That was the best head of my life," he whispers. "Once we make this fuck tape, I'll pay you back for that with my tongue. I owe you."

The touch of his finger and the intense blue gaze feel romantic, but Aiden's words emerge with a business tone. There's no romance here. I nod slowly and he rises to his feet.

"Get up," Aiden commands. "Get on the bed and face the camera."

He won't look at me as he commands me this time. I don't want him to look too closely. He's seen more than I would show a stranger, if I ever had control of my life enough to make the choice not to. I avoid gazing into the camera lens directly, but I obey Aiden and position myself in all fours on the bed.

I feel lewd on display like this. I tilt my head downward so my hair falls down over my shoulders to cover my breasts from the camera's view. It's not exactly modesty, but it's the closest I can manage given the circumstances.

I glance over at Aiden through my peripheral vision. He's hard again, with barely any time between this and his previous orgasm. The way he spoke about his ability to cum, I expected a man with some type of sexual dysfunction, not a seconds-long refractory period.

My throat tightens as I imagine my body stretching to accommodate that thing. I nearly choked on Aiden's dick in my mouth. That enormous thing could make me bleed if he isn't careful.

"Arch your back," Aiden whispers. "I want to see your ass."

It might be my imagination, but I swear his voice shakes like he believes the words emerging from his mouth represent the worst taboo. He approaches the bed slowly with that gigantic cock jutting from his hips.

"I've never filmed something like this," he murmurs as he draws closer. Aiden presses his large hand to my lower back tentatively. His hand is so fucking warm. His warmth spreads through me and I squeeze my thighs together to avoid any biological reactions to his touch.

I can't control my response to him. Aiden moves his hand down my lower back over my ass cheeks, his palm curving around my soft cheek. He makes a low growling sound in the back of his throat as he touches the inside of my thigh and discovers my wetness.

"That will make it much easier," he murmurs in response to my wetness. I think that'll be it, but Aiden slides his finger through my juices, swirling his index finger in slow circles through the juices on one thigh before moving to another. "But this is the only time. I don't fuck around with black women. Understood?"

I don't answer him. I just nod. If I'm going to have sex with this racist, I want to get it over with quickly. Judging from what happened before, maybe this won't last long. That's my best hope.

Chapter Three
Aiden

My cock stiffens instantly at the sight of her in this most unholy position. I can't stop myself from gaping at this *thing* that I've never seen before. She has the darkest skin I've ever seen up close and that I've ever touched. Blood rushes to my cheeks and it's too much and it's everywhere...

When I place my hand on her back, goosebumps erupt over her skin. I can't see them, but I feel soft hairs prickling my palm. She's afraid.

"Don't be afraid," I whisper.

"That thing will hurt."

Yes. Probably. She's not the largest woman I've seen. Valentina isn't petite either, but she's not very big. I press my knee into the bed and position my body behind her. I glance at the camera and then down at her...

I've never been this hard in my life. I ought to be spent, but staring down at Valentina's exposed flesh arouses me beyond my control. I touch her smooth ass and my cock jerks forward eagerly.

"You're soft..."

Fuck. The words escape my lips without consent. I stiffen my body and bite my tongue. This isn't the time to blurt out every raw thought that enters my head. I need to make love to this woman. *No. I need to do something much worse...*

I slowly run my fingers between her lower lips, spreading them apart to expose her gooey pink center. She has different colors down there and wisps of thick, textured hair in a strip over her mound. I don't need her bare. Valentina shudders as I take juices from her inner thighs and push them into her tightness, sliding my finger inside her by surprise.

"Easy..."

Holy fuck, she's tight. Valentina's perfect pussy wraps around my finger and I can't help myself. I push deeper inside her. *She's soaking and she's so tight.* My attention to her heightens. I slide my finger over her inner walls until she moans. Her moan surprises me, but it's genuine and it seems to surprise her too because she bends her head.

I add a thumb to her clit as I thrust my finger between her legs to ready her for my cock. Valentina emits another unwilling moan and her pussy clenches around my finger. I can't stand this...

I withdraw my fingers quickly. Even in the heat of my desire, I keep my head on straight.

It wouldn't do me any good to get this woman pregnant. I'll have to pull out. That would be more problems than it's worth. Padraig isn't like the Italians. He doesn't want half-breed children running around Boston laying claim to our inheritance.

The blacks didn't want us here any more than anyone else. I don't give a fuck what they say they've been through. That isn't our problem, is it? We didn't do that shit to them, but they rob our neighborhoods, they rape our women... We don't fuck with those people, Aiden. Never. Ever.

Those thoughts distract me from her until she shudders at my touch again. We have to finish this. She's right — anyone who can afford to send a human woman to me and make the threats they've made must have enough money and power to back those threats up.

I have to sleep with her. I'll willingly break vows, regardless of the fact that doing so could get me killed. All to get Tegan back and avoid getting killed. It's not as pleasant as it sounds.

Her hips move as she pushes backwards, getting closer to me and enticing me to enter her. *I want to watch her cum.*

Holding Valentina's hips for balance allows me to experience the softness of her curves for the first time. She's perfectly soft. I bend over and kiss the center of her back. I wouldn't call her a classic beauty, but her physique gets me *very* hard.

I push the head of my cock up against those spread lower lips. The angle she holds herself makes it easy, or at least it ought to. She's so tight that the first forceful push from my cock meets resistance from her flesh. Valentina's too tight to take me with one thrust, even if she has a soaking wet pussy, eager for my entry.

I position my cock at her entrance again, slowly sliding the head against her lower lips to get my dick nice and wet before I enter her. She makes an unwilling moan as I progress. She moans as my dick spreads her entrance open and I push the head inside.

Oh fuck. The wet, slippery feeling against my cock head nearly makes me want to cum again. I have to enter her. I have to go through with this if I want to save both of us. This isn't just for me. I push forward a little and her pussy yields to my cock head. *Finally.*

Valentina emits an ungodly moan as the head of my cock spreads her wide. Her tight pussy resists entry from my cock again and I can sense from the way she trembles that I'm hurting her.

I don't know anything about her except how fucking tight she is. I don't know if I should be careful, or if I should let myself go and just take what I want. Claiming her feels like heaven.

I grunt as I thrust inside her, yielding to her tightness and reveling in the pleasure of her pussy around my cock. I want to stop myself from feeling anything with this woman, but my cock has other plans. *She's not my kind, she's not my type and I can never be with a woman like this.*

Enjoying this is out of the question, but I can't help grunting with pleasure as I bury my cock to the hilt in Valentina's softness. Her pussy squeezes my cock and I feel how tight and silky her pussy is.

Every cell in my body begs me to cum inside her, to fill her with my seed.

"Fuck, you're tight."

She whimpers, stifling a moan of pleasure that I'm sure she doesn't want to feel. She doesn't know the first fucking thing about me. She can't possibly enjoy this. I move my hips at a steady rhythm. The least I can do is try to make her cum. It's impossible to tell how long I'll be able to hold back.

I feel around the front of Valentina's thighs and slide my hands up the length of her thighs towards her perfect wetness while I pound into her. Her whimper turns into a moan when my finger touches her clit and I slowly massage her nub. Valentina moans again and glances over her shoulder at me.

Her face nearly causes me to erupt. *No. Not yet.*

"Look at the camera," I growl. "Look at the camera."

I don't know why my body nearly rushes over the edge at the sight of her dark brown eyes. They're deep, dark, impossible fucking pools of brown and I shouldn't get rock fucking hard from gazing into them.

Valentina obediently faces forward as I slide my cock all the way out of her and then enter her again slowly. The slow withdrawal allows me a brief few seconds to regain control of myself. My fingers continue rubbing her soft clit and I feel her tender lips getting wetter as I slide back into her slowly.

She can't disguise her moans this time and Valentina thrusts back against me, sliding her tight sheath over the full length of my cock. *Holy fuck this is impossible to resist.*

Bursts of pleasure make it impossible to hold out much longer. I feel Valentina's tightness squeezing around my cock and she thrusts backwards slowly and nervously, like she doesn't *want* to enjoy herself, but she can't help it.

"Cum for me," I growl. "Let go, Valentina. Let go..."

My cock stiffens as I feel her cumming around it. She moans and collapses her weight onto her elbows, arching her back further so the tip of my cock rubs her inner walls better with each thrust. A gush of warmth surrounds my dick and then wetness trickles out of her tightness, coating her thighs with a thin layer of her clear, sticky juices.

The sound out of Valentina's mouth forces me to burst. I grunt and lean forward, burying my cock inside her as deeply as possible before I finish. Cum is cum after a point, and I've never cum in a way worth noting until now. It's different. Copious. It's intense. I squeeze her so hard that she screams as I cum inside her. *Shit.* I didn't mean to do that. But I've done it and my regret feels forced. I'm still a man and this is still the most natural thing in the world. Stupid, but natural.

Despite myself, I imagine filling her with my seed, pushing my fingers between her perfect brown legs and pushing more of myself inside her. *This could get me killed. Fucking her could get us both killed, but I still did it, because there are worse things than dying.*

I withdraw from her slowly, out of breath and utterly worthless. She collapses onto her stomach, her thighs trembling from either her climax or the cold. I pull a white sheet over Valentina's bare legs and walk over to the camera with a spent cock. *What the fuck did I just do?*

I turn the camera off and my throat tightens. I need to send this to the address beneath the note. No edits, no thinking about it. I hit the 'new email' button and type in the address. I send it and instantly want to throw my phone across the room. I toss it in a dresser drawer and turn to gaze at the woman on my bed.

Maybe I should kill her.

I don't want to kill her. I don't want to hurt her at all. I just had the best sex of my life with a complete stranger, and words escape me. She's rendered me completely fucking weak.

Valentina's curious dark eyes gaze up at me from a pile of limbs and the white sheet on my bed.

"You sent it?" She asks.

I nod. I'm not in control here and I hate it. Now that I've cum, now that I've obeyed this filthy demand, I have to do something about her, about this... about the future. I'm fucked.

"Yes. You came."

Her face knits together with disapproval.

"Yes."

"Lie on your back."

She adjusts her body so she's seated on the edge of the bed. I can't help myself. I stare at her nipples. They aren't pink. She doesn't have pink nipples. I suppose it makes sense that they're darker than her deep brown skin, but I didn't expect them to be quite this dark. I know I'm staring inappropriately, but I don't feel shy.

I'm hard again. Fuck, Aiden. You can't screw her again.

"I'm not sleeping with you again," she says. "If you want that..."

Her voice trembles. She doesn't want to say this, but she does.

"If you want that, you have to pay," Valentina says.

I smirk at her.

"I'm not paying to eat your pussy. I could get killed for eating your pussy. But... it's only fair."

"You don't have to do that," she protests. Valentina squeezes her thighs shut. Her pretty dark brown thighs have just enough flesh on them. They're perfect for squeezing. Perhaps the women I've been with have all been too thin, too boring, too predictable. Every part of this woman is a fucking mystery to me.

"I want to."

She wrinkles her nose in disgust. "Why?"

I've already broken my vows to my family and to my people. I don't want to explain myself to her. I can feel her eyes on me. She's suspicious of me and she definitely loathes me. I want to say that the feeling is mutual, but it isn't and that's the fucking problem. She's black, and I want to hate her for it, but I can't help wanting her more than I've ever wanted another woman.

"Because... I hurt you."

Valentina's mouth drops open in surprise and she quickly responds. "Don't say that. The people who sent me could kill you and they could kill me and anyone they wanted to. You did what you had to."

"I have to do something for you."

I close in on the bed. I stand right in front of her. What's the plan,

Aiden? Do you really think you can intimidate her into having your tongue in her cunt?

"Listen, white man. I don't need you to do anything you don't want to do. You've made it quite clear how you feel about me."

I smirk again, but it's a conscious mask. For the first time, I'm embarrassed about what I've said to her.

"This isn't about feelings."

"Then why do you want to do that?"

"Stop asking questions. Spread your legs if you want a place to sleep tonight."

Valentina scowls. "You scared me more before we slept together."

Isn't that how it always is? We show them our weakness when we cum, when they see us spent of all our energy, that's when women understand the power they have over us.

I grunt in response and to my surprise, Valentina slowly lies back on the bed, using her feet to push herself up further, so her legs don't dangle off the edge. She spreads her legs and my cock jumps to attention.

No, Aiden. Not now. Focus.

Her thighs are still soaked with her juices and her spread cunt drips magnificently over her thighs and outer lips all over my bed. Her scent intoxicates me as she spreads her legs.

I bend to my knees and prop her thighs up on my shoulders. She doesn't look at me and I don't blame her or expect her to gaze into the eyes of the man who owns her. Despite myself, I kiss the tops of her thighs.

Valentina shudders as my lips touch her. She doesn't smell or feel dirty or wrong to touch. I know it's wrong to touch her, to take a risk like this, but I can't and don't want to stop myself. I just want this to continue.

I spread her lower lips with my fingers and run my tongue over the length of her slit. I taste her delicious, salty skin, and then her cum. Fuck, her cum tastes good. Her lower lips smell like coconut and sex. I run my tongue over her outer lips again and rub my tongue piercing over her clit. *She loves it.*

Valentina moans and my tongue fixates on her clit. This is the golden treasure. Her back arches, thrusting her pussy into my face. It's delicious. I grab her ass and pull her closer to my face. It's the first time I've properly held her ass and felt the globes of flesh spilling into my hands. She has a much rounder and softer butt than I expected.

The excitement causes me to drag her so hard that she nearly flies off the bed. I pull her to my face and kiss her pussy slowly before focusing my attention on her clit. She whimpers as I roll my tongue in slow circles around her little nub.

She's getting close. I squeeze her perfect ass and keep teasing her until Valentina can't take it anymore. She cries out loudly and then she cums all over me. It's fucking glorious. Her pussy drips a constant gush of clear, sticky juices which I coat my face with.

I lick every drop of her juices off her legs until I feel Valentina's hands push through my hair. Her fingers touching my scalp so gently gets me rock fucking hard. I pull my face away from her pussy and run my tongue over my lips to get the last taste of her on my tongue.

My stomach lurches as she pulls herself to the edge of the bed and gazes down at me on my knees. I feel like a fucking puppy looking for a pat on the head. I shouldn't expect anything from her and I know it. My body between her legs keeps them spread. I could enter her again… *but I shouldn't.*

"No man has ever done that for me before," she says. Her face transforms from stern to gentle. I allow myself to think the two words I've avoided thinking about Valentina since the second she tumbled out onto the floor of my foyer.

She's beautiful.

I grunt as a response. I don't know what she expects me to say.

"WHERE SHOULD I SLEEP?" She asks. My stomach lurches again, but for a different reason.

"Stay here," I grunt. "Just for tonight. I'll set you up wiht a room of your own in this massive fucking empty place. It's better if I keep you close. Do you need a shower? Food?"

Chapter Three

She bites her lower lip and then reluctantly utters, "Food."

I CAN HANDLE FOOD. What comes next? I don't have a fucking clue
how to handle that.

Chapter Four
Valentina

He orders food for delivery, and as we wait he instructs me to take a shower. I obey him and when I emerge, he's shirtless in the bedroom with a pair of New England Patriots themed sweatpants. I knew he sounded like he was from Boston.

I have a towel around my body, but that doesn't stop him from staring at me. For a racist guy, he sure enjoys looking at me. I suppose it's just because I'm his captive or his property or... whatever.

He glances at me and then shuffles around some items in his dresser before grunting at me.

"The pizza will be here soon."

He has a nice body for a psychopath. I shouldn't stare at Aiden, especially knowing that he's racist, cruel, and involved with I don't know who – the sort of people who would give a human being as a gift. In bed, he was... different from other men. I can't allow that to fool me.

He was just afraid for his own life and his niece.

That's the main reason he's keeping me here. He thinks I can help him find who sent me and get to the person he really wants to save. My life means nothing to him as long as he thinks I'm useful to him. Well, let him think I'm useful.

I won't help him for nothing or give him just anything that he wants. I have to be smart about this. There are things at stake for me too. I want things out of my life, despite what all the men around me seem to think.

With just that pair of gray logo sweatpants cinched around his waist with a knotted shoelace, I can take in every detail of his physique. His bare, muscular back has a few dark brown freckles. There's not an ounce of body fat on this man. He's disciplined. *Controlling, that's what he is. You know that from going to bed with him.*

His natural musculature hints at a lifetime of athletics, but he doesn't have any sporty tattoos – they're all Celtic or religious. He's covered in them, except his back. That's mostly bare, except for the freckles.

He looks about forty, which makes the full head of hair especially surprising. It's a nice shade of blond – a very pale gold.

The thought of how his hair felt between my fingers sends an embarrassing thrill between my legs. I understand that thrill, but I've only felt it for one other man before – none of my owners or abusers, obviously. I never actually touched that particular man, but he was the last time I felt anything like what I felt with Aiden.

Aiden's handsome, but he scowls too much and it's strange that he has a tongue piercing. The slightest thought about his tongue reminds me of that thing he did with it and I struggle against an uncomfortable throb between my thighs again. *Why did he give me an orgasm? He's racist... Why would a racist guy do something like this?* I shouldn't think too much about trying to understand him. If information about Aiden won't help me get out of here, it's useless.

Perhaps he's not as wicked as he looks. Maybe he'll help me just to save his own ass. He hasn't hurt me yet – not beyond what my captors asked him to do and even then... I don't think he wanted to hurt me at all. He was too gentle. *He made me cum. I've never been with a man who made me cum first.*

I don't want to stare at him, but he's not as cruel as he looks, so I don't feel afraid. The tattoos make him look like a criminal, which I suppose he is but...

The thought slides out of my mouth before I can stop myself. "Why do you have that piercing?" I mutter, then snap my mouth shut before saying something more stupid than that. I know my big mouth will get me in trouble one day. I glance nervously at Aiden to gauge his reaction.

Aiden turns to look at me and he almost smiles. It's not like his other cocky smirks. This one is different.

"I've never tried it on a woman," he says. "Did you like it?"

I nod, immediately regretting that I brought it up. He doesn't exactly answer my question either, so there was nothing gained from my embarrassing comment.

"Good," he whispers. "I don't know…"

He finally looks at me. His eyes are so blue, they're terrifying.

"My family would kill you if they knew what happened," he says plainly.

I don't know how Aiden expects me to respond to that, so I don't grace him with a response. "You would die too."

"I don't want to hurt you," he says after a few awkward seconds. "But I'll need you to stay here. I can't let you leave this house. I can't risk anyone seeing you until I figure it out."

Figure it out. He cares about who sent me, but I don't. This country is filled with sick people who move in the shadows, trade and traffick women and children, and then there are people who buy us, people who rape and assault for pleasure.

I don't care who sent me. I just care that this is the closest I've ever come to freedom. If he's a good man… eventually, he'll let me go. He didn't buy me, someone else did, and that's the closest I've come to a good person in all my years on earth.

"Who are you?" I ask him. "If you want me to listen to you, I need to know more about you."

"I'm Aiden."

He walks like a cocky bastard, but he has to know that won't be enough for me.

"There must be a few million Aidens in America."

He smiles again. "Yes. Aiden Murray. I'm not one of the special ones."

I ask him bluntly, "Do you sell women? Maybe you have enemies from shady business deals."

"Fuck no. That's not our kind of business."

"So you're a businessman?"

"Yes. Murray Construction."

"I see."

"I'm Irish. I have business all over this city, and possible enemies, who are racist fuckers who want all Irish people dead. But… that's not important," Aiden says. I don't know what he means by racist fuckers and I've never heard anyone talk about abolishing Irish people, but I listen quietly.

"What do you mean by business? Are you a hitman?"

He raises an eyebrow. "You're no dummy."

"Is that an answer?"

He draws close to me. He smells like beer and clean laundry. Aiden shrugs and then pulls away. I don't know why I thought he was going to kiss me. I'm glad he didn't. I need to get information, not fall prey to his lust again.

"It's not important," he continues. "Unless whoever sent you tries to hurt you or take you away. I have to keep you prisoner, but I promise I'll keep you safe from other people."

"You kill people, don't you? So you do something that might have angered someone else."

"This is none of your business," he growls. "You're a stranger and you don't have the capacity to understand my life and what happens in it."

Emotional. It's far too easy to get under this man's skin. At least he doesn't reach for his firearm or raise his fists, or do anything else that might suggest that I'm in real danger.

"You must have enemies."

"So must you. I wasn't the only person they threatened."

"I grew up as an object in a rich man's house. They threatened me because I'm nothing. I don't matter. They just want me to comply to get to you."

"You seem to know a fucking lot about their motivations for a woman who claims ignorance."

"I'm not stupid," I tell him forcefully.

"No," he growls. "But you have a big mouth."

I scowl at him. "I suppose you prefer your sex slaves quiet?"

"You are *not* my slave," he snarls. "You are… in my custody. That's all."

The fierce redness in his cheek pales a little more. I shouldn't push him too hard. I still can't trust this man and he has absolute control over my life.

"They'll want more from you. I don't know why you listened."

"Despite your disdain for me, I'm not a complete monster. We don't hurt women. We don't rape them. And we don't interbreed. Whoever did this wanted to sully me and my bloodline."

"You think a lot of your bloodline for an admitted criminal."

"We are not criminals," he snarls. "We came to this city when nobody wanted us and we made it ours. Boston bleeds Irish because of us."

"You're full of yourself," she says. "Maybe your people have a proud history, but it doesn't make you better than me."

"Just like your history doesn't make you better than me," he snaps. "Now, enough. You will stay here and listen to me until I discover who sent that letter. If I find out you're holding anything back, I want you here."

"So you can kill me?"

"You don't seem to care if you die or not considering your tone."

I hate that he's right. A part of me died a long time ago and it will take more than this brief respite from Pulsifer to revive my hope for my life. I've spent my entire life as a slave to a sick man. I have no identification or job experience. Although I did receive some education, I have no evidence of it. Pulsifer was right when he said I couldn't survive in the real world.

"You don't know what I've been through."

"Hell, by the look of you," he says. "But you seem well-fed."

"I suppose that justifies slavery in your world?"

Aiden shifts uncomfortably. "That's not what I meant."

"I had an owner. He cared for my physical needs. But he was brutal and violent and he stripped me of any will to live before I turned eighteen."

Aiden's throat tightens and redness returns to his face again. His flushed cheeks are a soft pink that contrasts the harsh contours of Aiden's angular jawline.

"A sick man hurts a child."

"He wasn't sick," I respond. "Calling him sick implies he could change and he could heal. Now that I'm gone, he'll only find another little girl to hurt."

"I'm sorry."

"I don't need your pity."

"You do," Aiden responds callously. "Otherwise, you'll be out on the streets. Once I discover who did this, that's where you'll be anyway."

Message received, but his threat won't force me to hold my tongue. Every woman has her limits and I think I reached mine the moment mysterious captors drugged me and twisted me into a pretzel to ship me in a box to a monster clear across the country.

"Don't expect me to be too grateful."

"I don't," he says. "This benefits both of us and it doesn't change anything," he says. "Understood? This is just until I solve my fucking problems."

"Then I'll be out on the streets?"

"Something like that."

I fold my arms across my chest, drawing my towel tighter around me. He seems determined to keep me here which suits me well enough for the time being. I need to get my bearings. Escaping Pulsifer had never been a consideration for me. I watched him react to me growing up. I knew he was losing interest in me... but I didn't think he would cast me out like this.

I didn't think he would sell me to the highest bidder without a care in the world for what happened to me.

Aiden can't be a worse man than him though.

I ask as politely as I can, since I've already sassed him plenty. "Do you have any clothes I can wear?"

Aiden grunts and nods, the pink returning to his cheeks. I shouldn't care that he's seen me naked, but I do. He's still a stranger, even if he's a very attractive one, and what we shared seemed both unusually and inappropriately intimate.

I hope he doesn't try to sleep with me again. Currently, he doesn't seem to have any interest in that and he barely looks in my direction. He hates black people and he's not even ashamed to say it to my face. I don't have to worry about him crawling into bed with me.

Aiden drapes me in a pair of oversized black sweatpants and a giant black sweatshirt with *Murray Construction* printed on the back. The sweatshirt smells like him, but it also smells like beer and asphalt, maybe a bit of coffee. It's an XXL and insanely comfortable.

I wonder if he's cold without a shirt on, but he doesn't seem to mind. I try not to think about how his body felt on top of mine or how despite the circumstances, he was gentle... *That was strange.*

Once I'm dressed, our food only takes a few more minutes to arrive at the front door. When the doorbell rings, the sound echoes through Aiden's entire house along with his dog's barks. It's a large, colonial house and he hasn't forbidden me from exploring, just leaving. I follow after him downstairs, careful not to trip on the slippery staircase.

"Stay out of sight," he warns me gruffly, pointing to a small round dining table in the center of his kitchen where I suppose he wants us to eat. There's a fake sunflower in a vase in the center of the table, so I move it to the counter to make room for the pizza. I hear a soft growling sound and glance back at the hallway we came from.

A pair of beady, yellow eyes nearly cause me to scream until the mass of black fur emerges into the light and I see the source of the growl. Aiden's at the front door and there's nothing between me and this massive Rottweiler. My heart quickens as I grab the arms of my chair.

"Please don't lunge at me and bite my neck."

The dog lets out a deep bark that causes me to emit an unwilling yelp. I hear Aiden chatting away with the delivery boy and I want to scream. *Get the hell over here before your hellbeast tears me to shreds.*

His conversation only lasts a few more seconds and Aiden emerges with a pizza in hand. The dog relaxes its stance once Aiden enters the room.

"Roscoe, sit."

The dog sits. I can't take my eyes off the thing.

"Don't worry, he's friendly."

"He didn't growl like a friendly dog."

"You're a stranger. You can't expect him to like you right away."

For all of Aiden's commentary about my sass, he has one hell of an attitude himself.

I can smell the pizza from where Aiden's standing in the doorway, and head over to the dining room table to take a seat. He slides the box into the middle of the table before taking a seat himself.

"I hope you have a big appetite," he says, opening the box.

We eat together, and I work on getting as much information out of Aiden Murray as possible. *A businessman.* After a few minutes of conversation, his secret becomes apparent. He's in the mob.. His tattoos, his piercings, the way he talks... and his obsession with race.

Once we're done eating, I sense Aiden doesn't know what to do with me. He checks his phone several times and makes indecisive movements towards the fridge, then towards the sink and then back towards the kitchen island.

"Do you have a piano?"

"Huh?"

He seems confused.

"White and black keys? Music?"

"Yes," he growls. "I have one. Don't know the point of the fucking thing, but it looks nice."

"I play."

He raises a skeptical eyebrow. What trick could involve pretending to play the piano?

"Oh really?"

"Yes. Would you like me to play for you?"

"What do you play?" He asks. "Rap music?"

I ignore his racist and quite frankly, stupid comment.

"I can play anything you want. If you play me a song on your phone, I can play it back for you... and improve it.."

Aiden smirks. "Where did a little thing like you learn to play the piano?"

"I'm not little."

"How old are you?"

"Twenty-five."

Aiden grunts and shrugs. "As long as I can bring a slice of pizza with me."

"Sure," I tell him. "You'll like it. Trust me."

He still seems skeptical, but I'm not. Men are soothed by food, music and sex. They're simple creatures despite their insistence otherwise. Aiden leads the way, irresponsibly dripping pizza grease on his hardwood floors.

I try not to stare at all the art and furniture in Aiden's living room. Ireland came alive in here. There's a large Irish flag framed above the mantle, an enormous fireplace, ivory couches covered with blankets and Celtic knots of different flavors decorating almost everything.

On one of the walls, there's a hand-painted wooden sign with the Lord's Prayer printed on it in swirly black script. Then, there's the piano. She's who I've been waiting for.

"You didn't mention you had a grand."

"Whatever the fuck that means..." Aiden grunts. "A beer would help wash down this pizza."

"After the song."

I have to stop myself from running to the piano bench. Once I sit, my body feels at home. Aiden opens the keylid before turning to open the lid of the piano itself, and I run my hands over the keys without pressing them.

This is the most beautiful piano I've seen.

"Where did you get this?"

"The old country," Aiden says. "It was my mother's but she has no use for it now. Evie thinks it looks nice. I dunno. I guess it makes the place look fancy."

"The old country. Ireland?"

I guessed easily because of his tattoos and Aiden's name was another clue, but his Irish ancestry is pretty obvious otherwise looking around the room more closely. It's cozy and warm in here, surprising because Aiden seems so cold.

"Yes," he responds gruffly.

I've never seen one so beautiful before. I hesitantly place my hands on the keys of the C cord. I can play my scales. I play through C and then D before glancing over at Aiden. He's staring at me and his gaze makes me uncomfortable.

"Sorry," he grunts.

I nod, but I don't say anything. I play something easy, *Frere Jacques*.

"I know that one," he says, grinning. "What else you got?"

He has a nice smile. He runs his tongue over his lips unconsciously and my mind wanders to what he did with that tongue and the gold ring pierced in the middle of it. Aiden's eyes sparkle.

"What kind of music do you like?" My fingers playfully tease the keys. Someone keeps this piano tuned. Aiden's cheeks redden as he considers his answer. He shrugs after a few seconds of careful thought.

"I dunno. Hip hop."

I fight back a smile. Of course. He hates black people, but he loves hip hop. It's a tale as old as time. I know he'll have something smart to say about my response to his request.

"I don't know any hip hop," I admit to him. Pulsifer would have never allowed me to listen to that type of music growing up and when

I got older, I guess I never grew a taste for it. I listen to black classical music. Aretha. Tina. Whitney. Nina. Etta. Billie. *All* the greats.

He snickers. "That's funny."

I knew he would say something smart. I play a few bars of Claire De Lune.

"What's funny about it?" I ask him.

"Nothing."

He wasn't shy about his racism earlier. I wonder why he's holding back now.

"I can play jazz," I tell him, choosing a genre for him in the end. The governor enjoyed jazz music. Perhaps a little too much.

Aiden smirks and his response doesn't surprise me. "I don't like jazz."

I bet he doesn't like disco either.

"You don't know any jazz," I say straight back to him without a moment's hesitation. All those years with the governor and I still lose the ability to hold my tongue sometimes.

It's risky talking back to Aiden like that. He's still a stranger and capable of hurting me if he doesn't like the way I breathe, sit or look at him. He has ultimate power over me and that scares the crap out of me, despite my frequent attempts at verbal rebellion.

"You're right," he says. "I don't know any jazz. Impress me."

I learned to play by ear, so it's easy to start up a Nina Simone song. I learned straight off her records. The governor had a vinyl collection that any music lover would envy.

He loved Nina Simone. She was always my favorite out of Pulsifer's favorites. *She's so dark, he would say. Beautiful negro woman. Not as pretty as you though, Val...*

Aiden doesn't stop staring. I sing and play *Don't Smoke In Bed*.

"You have a pretty singing voice," he says. "It's deep. It's..."

He trails off. Pulsifer said I sounded just like her, but he was just flattering me, trying to get me not to hate his guts. I don't need Aiden's guilt to cause him to say anything he doesn't mean.

"I can play classical music too," I tell him.

"Better not," he says. "We should probably talk about your future here... If you would like to stay."

"Stay here?" My heart races. I can't stay in this man's house.

"I mean... You have nowhere to go. No identity. I suppose I can't put you out on the streets."

I don't have a future here.

"Oh."

I don't want to hope that this man would give me a place to stay and not expect anything from me. I guard my emotions carefully as I wait for what he's going to say next.

"I can give you a job until you get on your feet. Six months," Aiden says after a few minutes of consideration.

"Six months? And what job would that be?"

"Housekeeper."

"HOUSEKEEPER?"

The place is spotless. It looks like he already has a housekeeper. He doesn't need another one.

"Yes. And... I'd like you to play every night."

"For the next six months?"

"Yes."

"I see. How much are you offering for this job?"

"Enough to get you on your feet. $4,500 a month."

He's crazy. You can't agree to this, Val. Why should you trust this man?

"THINK ABOUT IT," Aiden says. "You don't have to answer now. I just got back in town and need to bring my brother here. He can't see you. Go upstairs and don't come out of your room until I call you."

I don't like the tone of his brusque instructions, but what choice do I have but to listen to him? I nod. "Okay."

"He can't see you here, Val. If my father finds out I'm keeping a black woman here, he'll kill us both. Now go."

Chapter Five
Aiden

I'm in over my head. Callum's the one I would normally go to about this stuff, but he'd run to Pa and then we'd both be fucked. There's only one motherfucker in Boston who can handle this level of monumental bullshit. I know he's fucked around with one of these women in the past, even if he thinks none of us know about it.

Darragh strides into my kitchen drunk. He smells like Wild Turkey and blood.

"What's the fucking problem?" He says, while Roscoe Jr. leaves his bed to come greet him as if he hadn't just broken into my house.

"How did you get through my *locked* front door?"

"Picked it. What's the fucking problem? I drove all the way over here from Harrison Ave."

Harrison Ave is one of dad's strip clubs.

"You drove drunk?"

"Yes," Darragh says, without a hint of guilt or shame. "But I drove quickly so I'd get off the road faster. You're welcome."

I hope my brother never breeds.

"Tegan's gone."

"What do you mean gone?" Darragh asks, straightening up from petting Roscoe. He asks as if there are several other meanings for the word.

"Rian's locked up and Pa has no idea where she is."

"With her spic mother," Darragh says, the slur rolling easily off his tongue. *She's not there or these bastards would have never sent me that note.*

"You're just like dad. You don't give a shit about anyone other than yourself."

"She's eight. She can look after herself."

"She's missing, you fucking idiot and I think... Someone took her."

Darragh snickers. "Are you joking? Who the fuck would take one of our kids? Someone who didn't want their fucking life, apparently."

I would have thought the same thing if I hadn't received the note.

"I've done something stupid and I need to know if you can keep your mouth shut."

"It'll cost you."

"I'll get someone to kick the shit out of Mickey Donahue before your next fight, then I'll tell you his weak spots."

Darragh grins. "I'm not a cheat, Aiden."

"Maybe not, but you're a damn drunk and if you lose another fight, dad's out $50k."

"What the fuck?"

"He has a problem. And now, I have a problem. I got a weird fucking package."

"Tell me about it..." Darragh grumbles.

My BROTHER IS the most impossible shit head alive. It's a miracle he's made it this far without all the blows to the head turning him to complete mush.

I explain what I can, leaving out the part where the girl I fucked is black. He doesn't need to know everything. The less he knows the better.

"Where's the girl?" Darragh asks.

"Upstairs."

He raises his eyebrows. "Tied up and everything?"

"No, you idiot. I'm not a monster."

"Wicked."

"It's not fucking wicked, it's messed up."

"Do you have the tape?" Darragh asks. "Maybe if I watched…"

"You'd watch your own brother sticking it to someone you fucking pervert?"

"That's not what I meant," Darragh says, but he doesn't explain what he meant, which doesn't inspire much hope.

"What did you mean?"

He does not elaborate.

"You sent a fucking sex tape without knowing anything about the person? What the fuck is wrong with you, Aiden? Do you not know how the internet works?"

"Not really."

Darragh's one to act like I'm a fool. He's been hit in the head so many times his eyes changed color.

"Fuck's sake, Aiden. This is bad. Did you tell Pa."

"You can't tell our father. Fuck, Darragh. Do I need to put a bullet in you?"

"Chill out, bro. Chill. No bullets. Why can't we tell him?"

"It's blackmail. And the woman… they have her identity, everything that proves she exists and possibly more. She's in a vulnerable position."

"What do you need from me? Want me to look into the email address, see if I can't find who's behind the screen?"

"Look into it. And we'll wait for further instructions, I suppose."

Darragh might be an idiot, but he's loyal. We've been through too much together for him to screw this up and he understands far more about technology than I do. It's better for the bastard to have something to do aside from bashing heads in. He needs something to keep him sane. Whatever happened to Katie? He needs to stay away from that little skank Kamari and find himself another Katie...

Once he's gone, I approach Val's room upstairs with Roscoe at my heels. My cock throbs in my trousers as I get closer to her. *Easy, buddy. Nothing's going to happen. You don't stick your dick in those people. You just don't.*

Only, I've already done it and there's nothing I want more than to shove that door open and see Valentina naked in bed with her legs spread and her fingers between her beautiful, brown lower lips. *I want her so fucking bad, it's sick.*

I knock on Val's door and she answers with a smile that makes my cock lurch.

"I'm free," she says with a hint of sarcasm. Her verbal quips are her only way of fighting back, I suppose. I don't mind sharp tongued women. Wild, sharp-tongued women are way more fun than women who do every fucking thing you say without a little fight in them.

"Yes. You are. Have you thought about my offer?"

"I CAN'T STAY HERE DOING nothing but cleaning and playing the piano. I'm not stupid. I have an education. Is there anything more complicated you need help with?"

It's not more complicated, but I can think of a thing or two I need help with. First, I want to know how the fuck a woman with skin that dark can be so gorgeous to me. I feel like I've never even *seen* a colored woman before her. She's just... special. Different. She can't be unique, can she? She's just a girl in a box. A pretty girl with a fucked up life.

"I'm in the construction business. That isn't women's business."

She scoffs. "I suppose sex is women's business?"

"No," I respond quickly. "I can't have you for that. That was only for–

"The blackmail," she says. "I get it. But just because I'm black doesn't mean I'm only good to scrub the shit out of your toilet."

The anger in her voice surprises me, although perhaps it shouldn't.

What the fuck do I expect her to think about me? I haven't exactly given the impression that I'm a saint, have I?

"Listen, this isn't about hatred. It's about keeping my bloodline pure. My *Irish* heritage," I explain. She doesn't seem impressed. My cheeks grow hot.

"Hm."

"I'm not some racist," I snap at her. I don't appreciate her judgment of me. She has no right to judge. The Irish have been through things too. We've been looked down on. We've been pushed to the edges of Boston, given the shittiest jobs, judged for drinking, judged for our faith. Judged for everything.

"I never called you a racist," she says. Her gaze fixes fiercely on me and I think I'd better take this one seriously. I can't underestimate her. She might have been trapped in a box and tied up, but that woman's mind is sharp.

"Right. If you don't want to clean, maybe you can cook and help me watch Roscoe. I don't cook much."

She smiles. "Really?"

"It's the only thing I need around here."

"No kids? You don't need a nanny?"

"No. Just me."

"How old are you?"

"How old do I look?"

She smirks, like someone who knows better than to answer that question honestly.

"I'm forty," I tell her after a beat. "Forty with no wife, no kids. Just me and my dog," I say, glancing down at Roscoe who's sitting at my feet.

Val runs her tongue over her lips, and watching that pink tongue dart out of her mouth gets me hard as a rock. Fuck, this is impossible.

"Are you sure there's nothing else you need?"

"Cooking. Cleaning. Watching Roscoe. And... that's it."

. . .

I KNOW I want more from her, but I can't debase myself by asking for it. No. Weaker men ask for sex like this. I've been weak with her. This isn't like me. "I'm not less than you," she says softly. "I'm not less than any man who has kidnapped, trafficked, or raped me."

"Will you stay, Val?"

"Yes. But I'll do honest work. Despite what you think about me, I'm not a slut and I'm nobody's whore. Not by choice. I'm also not lazy, stupid, incompetent, or anything like that."

"As long as you put dinner on the table in time for the Patriots game, I don't care. I probably owe you."

"Thank you, Aiden."

"I'll leave you be, then."

AND SO I DO THAT. I leave Valentina alone for two painfully quiet weeks. I introduce her to Roscoe Jr. She seems afraid of him at first, but he lacks company and wants to play with her the second he senses her willingness. At first, Valentina is skeptical of his deep growl and his loud barks but I catch them cuddling on the couch after a few days. He refuses to settle after his morning walk until he sees her. *She's even winning over the damn dog.*

Val does exactly as I ask. She cleans everything spotless, she cooks delicious food and she plays the piano every night when there isn't a game on. She plays a little earlier when the Patriots play. I don't care much for classical music, but there's something about the way she does it that I fucking live for. She loses herself in the music.

She lets her hair down sometimes in those long strange braids that I can't stop myself from longing to touch. I'm sick in the fucking head and if Darragh can't fix this for me, I'll have her for six months and then what? I'll have to spirit her out of here and leave her to the streets where the man who raped her and held her captive could find her again.

I can't allow that to happen.

. . .

Chapter Five

BUT FOR TWO WEEKS, there's nothing until I get a big letter in a pink envelope, the same color as the box Valentina showed up in. She's chopping celery in the kitchen when the envelope arrives. She stays away from the windows when the mailman comes per my instructions.

When I bring the letter inside, she freezes.

"Anything important?"

She knows damn well this is important. If there's one thing I know about Valentina, she's no dummy. She's turned on the charm while she's been here, but she never lets me get too close. She entertains me, she makes me laugh, but she won't tell me a single thing about her past – about the woman she really is.

I shouldn't want to know and I shouldn't care, but it gets lonely here. All I do is work and when I come home to hot food on the table and Valentina walking around in my clothes...

"A letter."

"I see."

She eyes me carefully, continuing to chop celery and feigning disinterest.

"I think it's from..."

"Open it and find out," she interrupts. "That's the only way you can know for sure."

Her hands shake so much that she has to stop chopping the celery. She doesn't want me to see how frazzled she is, so Valentina heads over to the sink to wash dishes. She nearly drops the first plate she touches.

I open the letter, leaning over the counter and watching her to make sure she doesn't faint from fear.

You never respond to blackmail, Aiden... What made you do this? A simple fucking threat?

Dear Aiden Murray,
We appreciate your compliance.

Unfortunately, we have found this insufficient.
Within 4 days, Tegan Murray will die.
If you go to your father, we will send him the video.
...

I CAN'T READ the rest of the letter out loud. They want me to do something so shameful… so hurtful… *I can't.*

She stares at me expectantly.

"What is it?"

"Nothing."

I pretend I don't notice her rolling her eyes. She stops what she's doing and strides over to me as fiercely as possible. *Beautiful. Why the fuck do I find her so beautiful?*

"You're lying. They want something else, don't they," she snarls at me. She meets my gaze with ferocity I can't ignore. There's a thump in my chest and then my stomach drops.

"If you would tell me what you know, I could've had my people stop this a long time ago."

"I don't know who he sold me to," she says. "I told you already. Why would I lie? Why would I protect these people? What do they want this time, Aiden? Tell me."

She wants me to trust her, but how the hell can I do that?

"THEY WANT us to sleep together again," he growls. "But it's not just that. They want more."

She tries to hide from me, but we've already slept with each other, which changes everything between us fundamentally.

Her head tilts to meet mine, her eyes betraying none of her emotions. I feel exposed in front of her and ashamed. I don't want to touch her again. I don't want to hurt her but… *I must.* My cock rises in my pants and my shame heightens. Thinking about sleeping with her gets me hard, even if it shouldn't. I feel sick in the head.

"What do they want?"

"No, Valentina. This ends here. I'll call my brother and–

"This isn't just about you," she snaps at me, the tension in her voice rising. I want to be angry with her for her tone, but I can't blame her.

Valentina comes closer to me and my fists clench. I smell her skin as she moves and I feel my body growing weaker as she approaches. This is madness. Her effect on me is madness.

"What do they want, Aiden?" she asks, her voice sounds like honey and she's so close that I can see her smooth dark skin and remember what it feels like to touch her.

"They want me to fuck you in the ass. I could *never*. I would never do something like that to you. It's disgusting."

A strange expression crosses her face. She stifles a laugh.

"I don't see what's so funny?"

"We've already had scx. What's the big deal?"

"Are you saying you've been fucked in the ass?"

I can't imagine it. She's so tiny. It's such a small part of her and if she's spent her life the way I imagine... *Fuck, I can't imagine anything so cruel.* The smile on her face disappears. Valentina's face contorts into a raw, but confusing expression. I don't know if I'll ever understand her, but I don't want to look away and stop trying.

"I spent my life as a slave. The men who held me didn't care what they did to me. You can stop gaping. It's what you racists want, isn't it?"

Heat prickles across my neck. It's not what I want. I didn't realize that was how she saw it and the way she's looking at me fills me with shame. I would never want something so horrible to happen to her. She's just as much of a woman as any other. She deserves protection, not pain. My mind jerks back and forth. I want to just believe her view of the world, but I can't just switch my opinion so quickly, not after a lifetime of what I've been taught. She isn't the problem. I can make an exception for Valentina.

Not all of the women are the problem, naturally. But there are some problems...

"I want to protect my family from ruin," I say sternly. "I don't care to steal women and rape them."

"You don't get to have it both ways. We either have equality, or we have slavery."

"Slavery's over, princess. That didn't stop some monsters from hurting you and that has nothing to do with me and my beliefs."

I'm pushing her away. I'm making this worse than it has to be. If I have to touch her and hurt her like that... I don't want her to hate me. It's absolutely foolish. Her opinion shouldn't matter to me, but I can't bring myself to truly believe that Valentina's less than me. She's smart, gifted at the piano, and she's quick with her tongue. I shouldn't like that, but I do.

"Pulsifer believed what you believed," she says. "So pardon me if I don't see the difference. You both think I'm subhuman, you just act on it differently."

Subhuman. Where does she get those words? It's nothing like that. It's... It seemed so easy to explain before Valentina dropped into my life. I want to wipe the frown off her face and kiss those pursed lips until she stops giving me that mean, unyielding look.

I didn't mean to fight and I definitely didn't mean to offend her.

"I don't mean..."

"You would rather lose something important to you than sleep with me. Your hatred means that much to you."

"There's a difference between pride and hatred," I growl at her, grabbing her wrist and pulling her against me. It's rough and my violence surprises me, but I don't want her running off. I want her to give me a chance to explain myself. *I'm not a bad person. I've spent my entire life serving the needs of my family. Because of me, there will always be Murrays in Boston. I'm building a legacy that remains strong and unbroken from the 1800s to now.*

"I wish you knew the difference," she whispers venomously.

"I do," I whisper. "And I'm not too proud to sleep with you. I just... I don't want to hurt you."

Chapter Five

"Then let go of my wrist," she says. I'm gripping her too tightly and I know it, but it's too enjoyable to feel Valentina's body against mine and if I'm not going to sleep with her, I at least want to enjoy this. She smells amazing and her thigh brushes against my cock, sending a shiver straight down my spine.

"Valentina…" I whisper. "We can't. There has to be another way."

"Let me see the message."

"No."

"You have no reason not to trust me, Aiden. We're on the same side and I'm not too stupid to look for clues."

"I never said you were stupid."

Her gaze narrows again and I loosen my grip on her wrist. If she wants to read the blackmail note, at least I can guarantee that she won't run. She reads through it.

"They still have your niece. She must still be alive," Val says.

My niece has never had enough protection. My father hates her mother. The only reason he forgave Rian at all for breaking his rules is because the girl has blue eyes and a complexion that conceals her heritage.

"I suppose you haven't bothered with the police."

"We don't deal with the fucking cops," I grumble. "We're not those kinds of people."

"Whatever that means," Valentina mumbles, scanning the letter again. "I don't think you have a choice, Aiden."

"I could accept my fate. Let them send the video to my father," I tell her. "But if something happened to you, it would be my fault."

There's a flicker of confusion in her eyes.

"Why do you care? I'm just an object."

"You're not. I might not agree with the degeneracy of my heritage, but I don't consider you an object. It's clear that you're intelligent and…"

And despite myself, my cock can't help but remain constantly stiff in her presence. I don't want to describe her as beautiful but… not even the most beautiful women have this effect on me, so she must have something different. Something more than beauty.

I bite on my lip to stop myself from saying something stupid. Valentina sets the note down and gives me a disappointed look.

"What other options are there, Aiden?"

"I don't know. I... I have to find Tegan."

"Why would someone take your brother's child? Why would they want you to hurt me? It seems like a lot of trouble to go through. Do you have enemies?"

I scoff.

"It's not a stupid question," she snaps. "Although coming to think about it, I struggle to imagine you getting along with anyone."

"Hmph."

"The question is... do you have any enemies with enough money and power to do this?"

"Only if they had support from another family. We rule this city. We own it. There are no enemies strong enough to stand up to my family."

"How humble of you," Val responds crisply.

I understand her very existence depends on what we do with this letter, but I can't figure out why she's pushing me to do this with her. Contrary to her opinion, her color isn't what keeps me away from her. I've already done the deed. I just can't stomach the thought of hurting her. She might be black, but she's still a woman and it's hard to ignore how womanly she is up close. Women are angels, all of them, and this woman is sensitive, soft, and everything that I want.

It hurts, but it's an uncomfortable truth budding up.

"I don't want to hurt you, Val. That ought to be enough."

"It's not."

"Do you have to argue with everything I say?"

"Yes. Because you let me."

"Hm," I grunt. "Perhaps we should stop arguing and... strategize then."

"That doesn't sound appealing at all. Your strategy probably involves planting a bomb or shooting something."

"And yours involves...?"

"We make the video and then... you tell your father the truth. You need a way to trace where these emails are coming from. But you can't do that unless you play their game."

"How am I supposed to trace emails?" I growl at her. "This isn't a fucking movie. I can't do that."

"People can. Don't you have a team? Anyone who can help? You can't be completely useless."

The mouth on this woman. I raise a threatening eyebrow in her direction, but Valentina doesn't appear perturbed. She thinks this is all so simple, but it isn't.

"I am not *useless.*"

"Then think of something," Valentina chides me as if speaking to me like a Catholic school nun will make our situation better. *Let's hope Darragh does what I ask without screwing up. Who knows how much time we have before Tegan gets hurt.*

"I don't know."

"Aiden... This is important. It's not just about me. They have someone you care about."

"I know that. I don't need any more pressure."

"This isn't about pressure. You have to be strong."

She takes my hand. The gesture surprises me because it's not like Valentina to reach out and touch me. She reflexively pulls her hand away, but then she touches my forearm again.

"Think, Aiden. I don't know you very well, but I know you love your family. If you're so proud of your heritage..."

My body stiffens as her fingers linger on my biceps. A part of me wants to beg her to stop, to command her to stand still and stop touching me, tempting me and fucking with my mind. But her hand... She touches me so gently and for the first time since she's come into this house, she wants to.

Or she wants something else – not me. It doesn't matter. At least I'll get to have her if I go through with this. It doesn't matter if it's immoral or fucked in the head. She smells delicious and I've wanted her since the first time. It's twisted. It's wrong. But that makes me want this black woman even more.

"I love my family, but that doesn't change our situation."

Aiden

"I have an idea, but you won't like it..." she says, a strange glimmer in her dark eyes.

"Should I be worried?"

"Yes," she says. "But this might work. So I need you to do exactly what I say."

I TELL Roscoe to stay downstairs. He whines, but listens and rests his head on his paws. *What the fuck am I getting into, big guy?*

Chapter Six
Valentina

Aiden sets up the camera in a similar position. He gives me a stare that darkens his baby blue eyes considerably. He has a cruel, intense gaze that softens when he notices me watching.

"This is a foolish idea," he growls. "I don't know how I let you talk me into this."

I know exactly how I convinced him. Aiden might be a racist, but at the end of the day, he's a man and they all work the same. Light touch. Gazing into his eyes. He might deny his feelings for me, but I can feel them when our skin touches, even if it's something light and casual.

Aiden grunts and presses the record button on his cellphone. He gruffly strides over to the bed where I await him, clothed. We thought it would be better if we started this time with clothes on. He pushes me back onto the bed. Our bodies press together with familiar urgency.

Despite himself, he's stiff, completely erect and his hardness rubs against my thighs. Aiden presses his warm lips to mine and although a part of me wants to freeze and push him off me, fight against this situation, Aiden's lips unravel me. I whimper as his tongue slides along my neck, filling me with heat.

"Aiden..."

"Sh," he whispers. "You can't act like you want it. You can't."

He forces my legs open and I press against his chest. He's right. This was my idea and I can't change my mind now especially without any other alternatives. It's either this or something far worse. Aiden caresses my thighs through my clothes and steels himself for what we both need to get through.

"Are you sure?" he murmurs. "This is your last chance to stop me."

"Take control," I mouth back to him as quietly as possible. Our eyes lock and Aiden rips part of my clothing away from me. I'm exposed before him and gasp loudly. His rough hands grasp at the fabric as he tears it away from my skin, significantly darker than his, a contrast probably visible on his camera.

My back arches and my body rises to meet Aiden's as he yanks against the fabric, and then slides his hand in the large rip he just made.

As his rough palms rub my legs, a guilty surge of pleasure rushes through me. He can't help himself. He's too good at this and even when he ought to be rough, his hands and lips are all too gentle.

He rips away my shirt before turning his attention to my thighs. I don't know if I can handle him touching me more. I have to, but I don't know if I can. Cool breeze tickles my thighs and Aiden's hands follow the flow of air. His tongue presses against my neck and I emit an unwilling moan again. Aiden grunts and adjusts his hips against mine. His cock juts forward, stretching the fabric in his pants as Aiden surprises me by cupping my cheeks and kissing me even more slowly.

I kiss him back, closing my eyes and accepting my fate. My heart quickens. *He'll start soon. He's acting sweet like this because he feels guilty I want him to do something completely fucked up.*

But it will work.

If they wanted me dead... they would have killed me. I'm the only chance

Aiden has at a bargaining chip. I'm the only thing that could sink him. He has to do this.

He slides his hand over my underwear, cupping my mound with one hand as he continues to hold my cheek with the other and kiss me like we're lovers, not strangers tangled in a blackmailer's twisted web, fighting for our secrets.

Aiden's breath quickens as he slowly rubs my lower lips through my underwear. His pale cheeks turn a shade of red that looks like it's going to kill him. His flush spreads from the high points of his pale cheekbones to his full lips. Aiden's pupils tighten into black points and his eyes are so blue they're almost clear. There's no hate in his previously cruel gaze this time. I wriggle beneath him, flashing my gaze away from his. Hate feels more comfortable coming from him compared to whatever I'm seeing in his eyes now.

I can't fool myself about this man's identity. He wears his pride all over the large biceps caging me between his firm physique and his king-sized mattress. His bed smells more like him than before. If he were any other man, I would want him to wash his sheets, but Aiden's scent comforts me. I close my eyes, ignoring my own heart quickening.

An urgent index finger pushes the fabric of my underwear aside and his chest tightens before Aiden plunges his finger inside me. I bite down on my lip so I don't cry out in pleasure but I gaze back into his eyes, the moment shared privately between us. Aiden's back faces the camera as he clutches me towards him.

"You're soft," he growls. "I shouldn't be... I... fuck..."

He plunges another finger inside me, distracting himself from whatever sentiment he nearly uttered. I bite my lip so hard that it nearly hurts. His fingers wriggle inside me until Aiden finds his rhythm, searching for the spot between my legs that provokes the strongest reaction. His lips tease my neck as he rubs my inner walls and the fire between my legs becomes difficult to ignore.

I don't want to beg him to hurry again, even if I should. This should be painful, but it's total bliss to have his capable hands stroking my inner walls. My core tightens and I feel my body responding too hastily to Aiden's touch. There's no way a brutish white guy should be able to make me cum like this.

I bury my face in Aiden's bulging shoulder muscle, sinking my teeth into his well-developed deltoid until Aiden's dusky pink skin flushes darker red. I cum hard, thrusting my hips hard against his fingers and taking him deeper as I bite him. *Yes...*

As a flood of pleasure surges through me, Aiden's face slowly returns to a normal color. His cock continues to press lustily around my thighs, but the tension in his shoulders and torso slowly yields.

"You're welcome," he grunts. "Now I'm very sorry, Val... but I need you to do your part. You can stop me. Any time, you stop me and I'll accept the consequences."

I wrap my legs around him and dig my heel forcefully into Aiden's thighs. He can't keep talking and risk betrayal. The overhead fan might not cut out all evidence of our conversation.

"Scream," he growls. "I'm going to pin you down and fuck you, Val, so I need you to scream."

Yes, Aiden. I know. It was my plan.

The change in his demeanor shocks me, even if I know he's acting and that this was all my idea. He grabs my arms forcefully and pins them above my head. I cry out in genuine pain this time as Aiden twists my arms uncomfortably and holds me down with a firm grasp and the weight of his hips.

Aiden rips the rest of my underwear away and rushes his pants over his legs. I emit another convincing scream and he nearly hesitates, a flash of genuine worry crossing his face. *Aiden, it's a game. It's our game. Don't stop.*

His breathing gets heavier as he leans back into the moment, ripping the rest of my clothes off and exposing my breasts as his bare cock rubs against my thighs. I push back against Aiden's grasp with realistic force and he pushes me harder into the bed.

I feel the soft round tip of his cock searching for my entrance. He scoops me up and adjusts my body so our skin presses together more and I can feel the head of Aiden's dick moving closer to my wetness.

Chapter Six

The tip slides between my lower lips and I sink my teeth into his shoulders again to stifle a moan.

As the head of Aiden's cock runs along the length of my slit, his reddening continues until he finds my entrance and pushes inside me. The pain spreads through me immediately and I let out a very real cry in pain.

"Shut up," Aiden yells. "Shut the hell up while I fuck you…"

I DO what we agreed to. I scream and fight against him as Aiden fucks me harder. He grunts with pleasure, occasionally making eye contact with me to check on me. It's the only way he can tell if he's really hurting me, but gazing into his eyes as he fucks me hurts. *I can't look into his eyes and stop myself from feeling something. He might be inhuman, but I'm very human. The things that happened to me never killed my spirit completely. There was always something to live for – music, books, and the idea that there could be love waiting for me out there somewhere, far outside of Pulsifer's compound.*

Aiden thrusts his large cock too deep and I cry out with genuine pain. He notices the shift and tries to move slower. The change in pace inadvertently pushes me over the edge and to my great humiliation, I cum, unable to stifle a very real moan of pleasure when I ought to pretend that Aiden's hurting me.

He clamps his hand over my mouth and growls, "Quiet, whore. My property doesn't get to cum until I do."

This he says loudly enough for the camera to pick up. He effortlessly continues pinning me to the bed with one hand over my arms and the other pressed to my mouth. I breathe slowly through my nose as my pleasure gushes around Aiden's cock and more heat spreads through me. I can't stop myself from cumming again.

Aiden thrusts into me harder, determined to appear rough and violent, but the secret shared between us and the pleasure of his hardness between my legs forces me to cum again. A rush of fluids coat my thighs and Aiden's face turns so red it looks like he's going to burst.

We have a plan for this.

My fear rises again, but I can't back out, even as Aiden pulls out of me roughly and flips me onto my stomach.

"I'M SORRY," he murmurs as I feel the lubricated head of his cock smack my tender asshole.

This is what we agreed to. The pain needs to be real. He wants to make this good for me but... it's a dick in the ass and a blackmail video. I feel lucky that I have the momentary bliss of an orgasm to make this just slightly less painful.

Aiden thrusts his hips forward, but it takes more than a gentle thrust to get the head of his enormous cock into my asshole. He pushes harder and I cry out. He hesitates. *No, Aiden. They can't notice you hesitate.* I thrust my hips back to meet him in quiet acquiescence to our agreement. The pain is temporary. I could save a little girl by going through with this.

It's worth it...

Aiden's cock successfully pierces my back door. The pain is worse than anything I've experienced previously. He has such an enormous package that I never had a shot at taking the entire length of his cock without suffering. I can't see him, but I feel his weight as he pushes his hips forward again and the initial pain intensifies.

That wasn't the full length of him and now, I have him buried deep in my ass, a thick thatch of golden brown pubic hair tickles the round flesh of my butt as our hips fit together with tight precision. He's too deep inside me for me to move and I'm frozen in agony.

"Fuck," he growls. "I love your tight ass."

That's genuine Aiden. But his next action isn't. He holds the base of my neck and thrusts my head into the bed. My body tenses again as Aiden slowly withdraws his hips. More agony as my tight back door adjusts to the movement from his cock. There's lubrication, but it isn't plentiful.

I cry out as Aiden pushes my head into the bed and slides his dick back into my ass. Holy fuck, he's big. It seems impossible that my body could accept the entire length of his hardness, but I can feel him moving inside me, so impossibly close to me that I don't only feel the ache in my backside but deep in the base of my stomach.

He grunts and moves his hips again, attempting to pick up a rhythm. He has to plunge himself into my ass slowly, but I sense his impatience as his body tightens and he grunts like a beast with his firm body hovering over mine. This won't feel good. I have to accept that.

Aiden pushes into me deeply again and I cry out in pain. He finds a rhythm that hurts at first, but slowly, my body yields to his and the tender beginnings of pleasure begin in my core. *Oh God, this ought to hurt. This should be painful but…*

He slips his hand around the front of my naked body, spreading my lower lips and giving my clit attention as he takes my ass. Agony gives way to pleasure and his movements come faster.

Aiden forgets himself and instead of pinning me to the bed and giving all appearances that he's hurting me, he clutches my hips, forcing me into that familiar, possessive grasp of his. *He's unbelievable.*

I want to fight against him properly this time to disguise his softening demeanor towards me, but I can't because of Aiden's hips moving faster behind me and his cock plunging even deeper into my satiny heat.

Having gained a tight grasp on my hips, his fingers return to my clit and he rubs me to an orgasm which forces my ass to grasp his cock even more tightly. Once I cum, he can't hold back and I feel the gigantic man press his weight into me. I cry out again and feel Aiden's cock erupt in my ass.

Holy fuck, that's a lot of cum.

A strange pool of warmth builds in my forbidden depths and Aiden loses his grip on himself. His weight collapses on mine, his cock pushing deeper into my ass as he releases more of his seed. His cock feels so deep that I almost wonder if he can pull out of me without ripping me in two.

"We're not done," he growls before pulling out of me and getting off the bed, unceremoniously dragging me to my feet completely naked and his pearl-white cum sliding out of my asshole and down the back of my thighs. I glance at the camera lens, my fear convincing.

Aiden wraps his arm around my throat, and grabs my hair, tilting my head back so I scream as he holds me prisoner and drags me closer to the camera lens.

"Listen motherfuckers," he growls. "I played your little game but after tonight, I'm done. If you don't release Tegan Murray in 8 hours, this bitch is dead. You hurt my niece, and I'll do worse than kill her."

He reaches forward for the phone and quickly stops recording, throwing the phone on his bed as he catches his breath. Aiden thrusts his hands through his messy crop of brown hair. The golden hair sticks out in untamed spikes, slick with his sweat. Aiden's flush settles into a dusky pink again instead of that urgent red.

"THAT'S IT THEN," he says, his gaze resting on my naked body and then unconsciously flashing to the thick ropes of white cum dribbling down my thighs. A self-satisfied smile crosses Aiden's face, but his smile only infuriates me.

"Send the video. We don't have time."

"You don't know what you're asking me to do," Aiden grunts.

"It's my life on the line," I snap at him. "Not yours."

"You don't know my family," Aiden growls. "My father... my people have killed for less. We've killed... *for amusement.*"

He hides an uncomfortable smirk that I force myself to ignore. My heart thuds uncomfortably in my chest. Trusting him could be far beyond foolish, but this foolishness has become my only hope of freedom.

I NEED MY IDENTITY.

HE SENDS the video and then tosses his phone onto the bed like before. Unlike before, he gazes at me after, his eyes wandering to my leg, covered in a thick stream of his cum.

"I didn't like hurting you," he says.

"You came pretty hard for someone who didn't."

A grimace replaces the smirk on Aiden's face.

"I came because…" he glowers at me, as if I'm responsible for the emotional confusion his own bigotry rises in him. "It doesn't matter."

He touches the underside of my chin with his finger and draws my face close to his for a kiss. The tenderness behind the kiss surprises me, but his inability to communicate with actual *words* does little to impress me. He can't kiss away his bigotry if he won't even admit to it. It's not just that. Aiden won't admit that despite his so-called beliefs – he cares about me.

"I'll get my clothes on."

His eyes gleam with further outrage.

"You will not," he says sternly. "Not until I've examined you to make sure you aren't hurt."

"I can examine myself, Aiden. I don't need you poking around down there."

White men. Their constant reddening completely thwarts their attempts to hide their emotions. Aiden's lips tighten as he struggles to hide his frustration with me.

"You will do as you're told," he grunts, posturing his body in a broad, intimidating stance. "Follow me to the shower. *Now.*"

Aiden can't stand anyone saying no to him. I fold my arms and stand firmly in front of him with the fiercest glare I can muster.

"Fuck, you're stubborn," he says before wrapping his arm around me and flinging me over his shoulder like an expensive handbag.

"AIDEN!" I screech, my legs kicking fiercely, spreading around the liquid dripping down my dark brown thighs. I hit his back muscles as hard as I can, but he's too strong for that to do anything.

"Stop fucking fighting," he growls, carrying me towards his bathroom. My ass hurts as I move my legs, but I kick him again for good measure. Aiden grunts in frustration as I knock the air out of his lungs, but none of my attacks are nearly powerful enough to stop him from dragging me off to his bathroom completely naked to examine my sore and swollen ass. *He doesn't need to see that.*

Aiden sets me down and I shove him as hard as possible once my feet land on the ground. The cold tiles send shooting pains up my legs. I'm still sensitive from my days in the box, but not too sensitive to tell Aiden off.

"What the fuck is wrong with you?" He snaps. "I'm trying to help you."

"By picking me up like an object?"

"I'm trying to... oh fuck..."

"You're not even man enough to admit you care about me, Aiden. I don't need you on your knees pretending to be a nice guy for me."

AIDEN PURPLES with anger and grabs my forearm tightly, wrestling my body against his as I fight his unruly attack.

"Aiden, let go of me!"

"No," he yells back. "I'm quite tired of your attitude. You don't need me to tell you how I feel. Talking about my *feelings* if there are any left in my cold fucking heart is the fastest way for me to ruin my life. So no, Valentina. I won't be ruining my life for you. But that doesn't mean..."

He releases his tight grip on my forearm, but before I can escape, Aiden wraps his hands around my hips and drags me against him. He kisses me before I can call him an idiotic brute again. Aiden's forceful yet romantic kiss knocks the sense out of me. I flick my tongue over his piercing and Aiden makes a low growl in his throat.

I can't explain why I'm kissing him back, but the low growl in Aiden's throat provokes me to kiss him harder and tease the stupid golden Celtic knot piercing his tongue. It's cruel how good it feels for him to have his tongue between my legs.

Chapter Six

After a few seconds of indulging my unreasonable desire to kiss Aiden Murray, I try to break away from the kiss, but he moves his hands from my hips and grabs my cheeks, dragging my body back against his.

This is how he feels about me. He wants to show me.

We kiss until I forget I want to kill him. He breaks the kiss, but clearly has no intention of letting me go. Aiden's hands move back to my hips and I'm so close to him that there's nowhere to look but his eyes. At first, they were hard as ice, but the longer I look at Aiden, the softer his eyes get, like I'm melting the coldest parts of him.

Not enough for him to say how he feels, and you know you need the words, Valentina. You'll never believe him unless he says it.

"Will you let me look at you," he asks in a less domineering, more concerned tone before dropping to his knees. I'm naked, so this puts Aiden's face very close to my crotch. My chest heaves nervously as he rakes his fingers through a thatch of my wet pubic hair before spreading my lower lips apart to examine them closely.

Aiden clears his throat. "You look swollen down there. Does it hurt?"

"A little."

He runs his finger in a small circle around my clit, coming away with my moisture. He puts his finger into his mouth and then resumes his slow examination, stroking my lower lips in a search for abrasions or sensitive spots. This isn't the part of me that aches the most, anyway.

"Hm," Aiden says. "You look hurt. In desperate need of repair."

Before I ask what he's talking about, Aiden flattens his unreasonably large tongue and presses it between my legs, running it over my clit until his tongue ring flicks my sensitive nub. I moan loudly and Aiden chuckles against me. "That's what I want to hear."

He grabs my butt and then drags my face close to his lips, thrusting his tongue between my legs again.

. . .

Oh God... Yes...

Chapter Seven
Aiden

Her cunt tastes delicious. I rub her little nub with my tongue until Valentina produces that lusty little moan again. She has the softest, most innocent moans. It burns me up inside that anyone could have hurt her, that they could have hurt her since she was a little girl.

It kills me that I've hurt her.

Once I go to my father, I know what I have to do. It's not a part of our agreement but... I'll set her free. She wants her identity, I understand that, but I can give her a new one. I can set her free and give her the life she wants away from monsters masquerading as men.

It's best I keep her right where she is, confused about my feelings so she never has to feel the guilt I know she'd feel, regardless of all the cruelty I've brought into her life. She allowed me to hurt her just to save Tegan, someone she doesn't even know.

I can't keep her my prisoner. But before I can think about setting her free, another compulsion drags me forward. My tongue spreads

Val's lower lips and I enjoy her clit growing between my lips as I suck on her pussy and tease her to a heightened state of arousal. More clear liquid dribbles down her thighs, mingling with my dried cum.

I'll make her cum before I probe her ass for how much damage I've done. As my tongue returns to Valentina's pussy, she spreads her legs further and surprises me more by curving her fingers around the top of my head, sinking her hands into my hair and touching my scalp gently.

She moans again, tightening her grip on my hair. I push my face deeper between her legs and Valentina's thighs squeeze together.

"No," I whisper. "I want you to cum. Don't stop yourself."

She pushes her hips forward and her warmth envelops me. I don't want to stop kissing her and tasting her, so I lose myself in her delicious juices. Even her moaning becomes background noise. I'll stop when I want to stop. I cup Val's ass and feel her shudder as she cums for the first time.

Not enough. I'm not done.

MY FACE IS red and my hair stuck to my neck with a thick layer of sweat once I'm done with her. I pull away from Valentina and she stares down at me with utter shock on her face.

"What is wrong with you?" she gasps.

"A lot of things."

"You've been down there for…"

Hours maybe? Every inch of my bathroom smells like Valentina's pussy and I want to drown myself in the scent.

"Turn around," I grunt before she comes to her senses and remembers to give me that perpetual disapproving expression she has on her face. Orgasms apparently have the effect of making her very obedient. Val turns around. Her ass is fucking perfect. There are scars on her butt and the tops of her thighs from what looks like a belt buckle. She doesn't flinch as I touch them and to my surprise, she doesn't flinch as I spread open her cheeks to examine her asshole.

· · ·

<h1 style="text-align:center">Chapter Seven</h1>

My stomach lurches.

"I hurt you." I hate myself. This won't be worth it.

"I told you not to look. It's too late."

"I'm sorry," I whisper, releasing my grasp on her butt and wrapping my arm around her waist. I kiss the small of Val's back and then her butt cheek, then I press my face into her ass, just holding her, cradling her as if this small comfort could force all her pain away.

She doesn't respond.

I kiss the top of her ass again. "I'm so sorry, Val."

"Stop, Aiden," she says, her voice catching. "I don't need your pity."

"I'm not showing you pity, Val. This is my fault," I murmur, stroking her soft brown skin and wishing I was a different person for the first time since she showed up in my home. "I'll make it up to you. I promise."

She sleeps in my bed at my request. I can't tell if she's there because she fears me or if she genuinely wants to be there, but I don't care. We're running out of time together and I'm a selfish cunt as it is. What she wants shouldn't be my concern.

As Valentina sleeps, I fight my desire to hold her. She finds sleep much easier than I do, which surprises me. She's been through hell and the best thing I can do for her is to put an end to it. Valentina grunts and rolls over, facing me with her eyes closed. She's close enough to touch me and when she reaches a hand out, my body warms instantly.

She's a woman. She's just a woman.

When she's asleep, I don't have the same reactions I do to her waking form.

"It's so much easier to admit I care about you when you're asleep,"

I murmur to her. "My whole life, I was taught to hate people like you. To never look at women with your complexion. You were the first... How can I ask you to stay with me, Val? You're right. I'm a monster. A racist. And I have to let you go..."

She's asleep, so she doesn't respond. I kiss her forehead, but that still doesn't stir her. Some sick part of me wishes she would hear me, but she doesn't. I move my body beneath her arm and let my thoughts run wild.

She can never be mine, but fuck it feels good to hold her.

IN THE MORNING, I leave before Valentina awakens and drive straight to my father's house. There are too many cars parked outside. *Fuck.* Darragh's obnoxious lime green Hummer blocks Callum's beat up olive green Chevy Colorado, and my sister Orla's Mini Cooper. *Great. Orla.* If my sister's here, it's for the sole purpose of chewing someone's ear off about something. We don't get along.

I don't see my dad's car in the lot, but Odhran might have it, so that doesn't mean anything. I park at the end of the driveway and walk up to the front door. It shouldn't feel weird going home unannounced, but considering the last three fights I've walked in on, I wonder if I ought to have brought my gun.

Darragh and Callum can hardly be in the same room without a fight breaking out, and Callum's normally on the losing end...

Orla throws open the door to our parents' house before I ring the doorbell.

"Did you know our fucking niece was missing too?" Orla yells at me without so much as a greeting. She smells drunk, despite her comfortable position on her high horse.

"Yes."

"Fuck's sake, you're all a bunch of useless bastards," she yells, calling half the sentence over her shoulder, to my brothers, I presume. "What are you doing here, asshole?"

"Visiting my loving family. What does it look like?"

Chapter Seven

Orla rolls her eyes. "Are you doing something about your missing niece?"

"Yes."

She relaxes and opens the door wider, as if the wrong answer would have prevented her from allowing me into my parents' home.

"Where're mom and dad?"

"Mom's upstairs, dad's probably out with one of his whores. Don't you know them at all?"

Orla convinces herself that because I work closely with my father, everything is my fault. She won't listen to reason and she doesn't give a fuck that I'm the reason she has a nice three bedroom house in Brookline where she can be a huge bitch away from the rest of the family and stay out of trouble.

"I need to talk to dad."

"Well he's not here. Darragh's drunk and Callum's being a cunt about Tegan. Rian sent me a letter and he wants to know what you're doing about it, so tell me because I can't believe you would lose track of your own fucking niece."

SHAME BRISTLES the back of my neck. Darragh clearly hasn't told them about the blackmail and I can't say I don't appreciate his loyalty, but my sister's low opinion of me bothers me. She twists her face in disgust at my lack of a hasty response.

"Do you know where she is?"

"I can't talk about this with you."

"Like fuck you can't."

Orla pushes me out the door again and slams it behind both of us. My fiery sister pushes her thick mass of blonde curls out of her face, blue eyes tense with outrage.

"What the fuck is going on?"

"I can't talk to you about it. It's business and it's getting pretty fucking serious, so I'd much rather you go back to your side of town and stop getting involved in these issues."

"Unlike you sick fucks, I care about Tegan. If she's safe..." Orla's voice breaks. If we had a better relationship, I would wrap my arms around her and promise her that I would take care of my niece.

"Orla," I interrupt her before her sadness can turn into an attack on my character. "I care about Tegan too, but I don't know where she is. You're right that we need to find out."

Tears well in Orla's eyes.

"You don't know? No one knows?"

"Listen, there are people who hate our family…"

"Like how our family hates everyone?" Orla snaps.

"We do not hate everyone," I respond to Orla, trying not to let her get under my skin. "We look after each other and we are the only people who matter."

Orla scoffs and shakes her head. "Maybe our family's racism has provoked someone to steal Tegan off us and teach us a lesson."

"What kind of lesson would that be to steal a little girl?" I ask. She angles her head towards me with marked suspicion. Ten years younger than me and that woman can strike the fear of God in me. She was always a spitfire, and far too much of a tomboy to please either of our parents.

She might not play softball anymore or cut her hair in a tight crop that mirrors mine, but Orla still throws a wicked punch and she isn't afraid to slam her fist into any of her brothers' nuts if we cross her. I angle my body away from her just in case she picks up the teenage habit again.

"You have more information than I do," Orla snaps. "But judging by the stubborn look on your face, you won't tell me anything else. Is anyone close to finding her? Are there clues? Can I go out there and look for her myself? Rian's worried sick."

If Rian gave a crap about his daughter, he might have been down here himself instead of doing shit to end up in jail.

"I can't trust you with this, Orla. You've shown your loyalties before and this is more than you need to be involved in."

Orla's thin, over-plucked eyebrows form an outraged arch.

"My loyalty is to the missing girl in our family that none of you assholes give a fuck about," she says. "Did you come here to solve this fucking problem, or to bitch about your personal problems like Darragh and Callum?"

"I came for Tegan. But there's no one at this house with the capacity to help," I growl.

"How long has she been gone that you're just showing up now?" Orla complains.

It's been two weeks, but Orla doesn't understand... I can't do anything about the time passing. I've done the most that I can without causing any more problems than our family can handle. I want my niece safe just as much as my sister does.

"I care about Tegan, but not everything works quickly in our world, Orla. I can't just snap my fucking fingers and unleash disaster on Boston. I have to be careful because I'm not the only person who gets hurt if I'm reckless."

Orla scoffs. "Is there another person you care about aside from yourself?"

"Didn't you just hear me say that I'm here for Tegan? I need Darragh or somebody useful and I strongly doubt that useful person is you, so go home, Orla. Go back to the house that your family you hate so much pays for and leave me alone to get this done."

"You are such an asshole, Aiden," Orla says. "I am not useless and just because I don't kiss Pa's ass..."

"I don't have time for this, Orla."

"Let me help you."

"We can't talk here. This is proof you aren't ready for this. We need privacy to–

"Then let's go into your fucking car, asshole," she interrupts. *Fuck, Orla.* My wild sister walks down to my truck and clambers into the passenger seat before promptly putting her feet up on the dashboard. She doesn't care if she gets mud up there or if her filthy shoes will piss me off. I slide into the driver's seat and wait for the onslaught I expect will be coming from Orla.

"So," she says. "You know where Tegan is, but you haven't told anyone yet. What the fuck is going on, Aiden?"

"I told Darragh. He's been looking for my blackmailer."

Orla snickers. "Blackmail? You've barely left your house the past year except for that trip to Long Island, and Callum told me you barely left the warehouse then. What could you have possibly done?"

Don't tell her. She's your family and even if you all love the fuck out of each other, we're petty fools, desperate for our father's approval. Even Orla with her uncontrollable temper wants and needs this family to love her.

But she's my sister. And she's a lot less useless than Darragh despite what I've just said to her. Orla's greatest problem has always been that she has a mind of her own. My father hates that about her almost as much as he hates her love life, which Orla's had the good sense to keep private for quite some time.

"I did something recently," I grunt. "Something foolish in an attempt to get Tegan back. I should have known that negotiation would lead nowhere."

"Can you get to the fucking point?"

"Can I trust you not to run mouthing off to the entire family?"

My sister looks more disgusted with me than deceptive. There isn't a chance of winning her approval again. She's bailed me out of jail after one too many bar fights and knock downs. She's seen my white t-shirts caked with Sam Adams flavored vomit and worse. There's no glamor to this life and Orla knows it.

"I don't care about the family. I just care about Tegan. She's an awkward, defenseless little girl and it's not her fault everyone hates her father."

Ouch. Leave it to Orla to "tell it like it is", both bluntly and offensively. It's easy to see how she's made it to thirty without ever having a boyfriend… At least I assume she's never had one, because I surely would have had to beat one up a couple of times growing up. I'm her older brother, so yes, that would have been my job. *She pisses me the fuck off.*

"When I got back from Boston, I received a strange package with a message and instructions to perform *certain tasks* if I didn't want harm to come to Tegan. I did what they asked. I waited. I sent Darragh to find her. It didn't work and they came back again…"

"Did you tell dad?"

"I couldn't. I didn't have time... I had to react."

"Why?" Orla asks. Her eyes make her look more like a witch than normal.

I TELL HER EVERYTHING. Orla listens patiently, nodding along and giving no signs that she'll hop out of my car and spill everything to our father. Once I'm done, she adjusts her feet on my dashboard, getting more mud and dirt from the bottom of her shoes everywhere.

"Can you stop spreading dirt everywhere?" I grunt.

"Fuck off," she says. "I'm processing this. I'm processing. Holy fuck, you have a woman trapped as a sex slave in that house and nobody knows?"

"She's not a slave."

"She sounds like a slave. Where did she come from, Romania? Ukraine? Serbia? Bosnia? Macedonia?"

RIGHT. I told her the entire story, but I didn't tell her that part. Just that the woman has a background our father wouldn't approve of.

"Fuck, can you stop guessing? She's... black."

"Ha!" she laughs, her eyes bugging out. "Hilarious."

"It's not a fucking joke, Orla."

She laughs harder. My sister sounds like a donkey crossed with a drunk Red Sox fan when she laughs. It's *very* annoying.

"It's not?" she says. "You're racist, Aiden. I don't know if you forgot. I've pulled your ass out of jail for beating up on Mexicans, Vietnamese, fucking Puerto Ricans... There's no way in hell you have a black woman in your house and you're risking everything to keep her safe. I'll believe it when I see it."

"If I'm so racist, Orla, why would I lie about this? Why would I risk talking to you about this of all people?"

"Good point. But you fucked up already Aiden, and you know it. What do you have? Who are these people and how the hell did they get their hands on Tegan?"

Aiden

"I'm no closer to discovering that than I was before."

"All you've done is make a few weird sex tapes and do something that could get you killed by your own father. Congratulations."

BEFORE I CAN CALL Orla seventeen different insulting names which all rest on the tip of my tongue, we both hear my father's engine. We recognize the sound. He's had a thing for the same car for years. 911 Carrera Porsche.

"Shit. I'm out of here."

"We're not done talking."

"You have to tell him," she says. "Let's hope you hid your pet well. Because he'll kill her, just like he killed Rian's girl."

She means Tegan's mother. We don't technically have proof he did it, but where is she?

Orla presses me, "Do you really think she just disappeared? It's been months. We thought Tegan could have been with her, but what if they couldn't get a hold of her?"

"I don't think she's disappeared at all," I respond calmly. "She shows up intermittently whenever she needs money or wants something. That could have happened now."

"Or dad had her killed finally."

"Thank you, Orla," I respond through gritted teeth, which Orla notices, because she won't wipe the smug look off her face.

"No problem, Aiden."

She leans over and kisses my cheek. Orla's the only person I know capable of a sarcastic kiss. My sister gets out of my car and hops back into hers, disappearing before my father can maneuver his significantly larger body out of the front seat of his car and into the driveway. There really isn't any avoiding this, is there?

"PA? WE NEED TO TALK."

Chapter Eight
Valentina

Aiden leaves me alone in his house often. I'm never completely alone with Roscoe Jr., which is nice. I've never lived with an animal like this. Pulsifer hated dogs and he often bragged about his high school exploits of kidnapping and torturing neighborhood cats. Aiden has carved out a place in his life perfect for Roscoe Jr., apparently the second Rottweiler he's owned.

When he's not sleeping near his food bowl, eagerly hoping for some treats, he curls up on the couch or follows me around the house. Roscoe Jr. has his similarities to Aiden. First, he enjoys listening to the piano almost as much as his master. I won't have forever with the piano, so I love playing it every chance I get.

I slide my butt over the bench and touch the keys. Roscoe Jr. sits at my feet. Warming up takes a few minutes, but I slip into some of my old favorites. Claire De Lune. Moonlight Sonata. Minuet in F. Ecossaise in G. The last one is the most upbeat, but it's my favorite challenge to play.

I play until my fingers hurt. It's hard not knowing what will happen to Aiden. He's given me instructions for what happens if he doesn't show up tonight, but he didn't tell me how to survive all the hours in between. He didn't tell me how to survive worrying about him.

Under all the despicable things about him, there's a man thoughtful enough to hold me after we did what we had to do and to promise me that he wouldn't let anything happen to me. Is it strange that I believe him?

Out of all the men I've known, none have been as kind as the racist, Aiden Murray.

He confuses me. When I still can't get Aiden out of my mind, I walk to his library to find a book to entertain me. Losing myself in a fictional world is probably my only hope of getting that tall, annoying blond man out of my mind. He'll be fine on his own. He's made it to forty in his twisted world and judging by his house, he's not just survived, but done pretty well for himself too. This place is beautiful and it's large enough to raise a family, but seems oversized for just a man and his dog.

AIDEN HAS A LOT OF BOOKS, but I've never seen him read any of them. He doesn't strike me as someone who sits in one place long enough to read an entire book. Someone else must have put Aiden's collection together, and they had good taste, even if all the books on the shelves are written by old white men.

Aiden at least bought me *Their Eyes Were Watching God*, my old favorite, which is the only diversity on his bookshelf. I reach for the book and then a second one, the only well-worn book on Aiden's shelf. *The Sun Also Rises*. I never cared for Ernest Hemingway, but the book reminds me of Aiden.

I read until I fall asleep, and don't wake up until the sun is high in the sky. Just as I uncurl from my cuddle with Roscoe Jr., a loud cracking noise resounds in the library. I look over my shoulder to see a large crack spreading through the glass window, centered around a tiny hole.

Was that a gunshot?

. . .

Chapter Eight

I DON'T HAVE to ask the question twice.

TWO MORE BULLETS whizz by my head and I drop to the ground. I don't know where I find the instinct, since I've never heard a gunshot before. My heart thuds in my chest. The window shatters and glass sprays all over the room. Roscoe growls and runs towards the window, barking.

I'm frozen and crouched on the floor, but I know I have to move. This is bad and most importantly, this shouldn't be happening. I try to call Roscoe's name, but he's barking too loudly at the window. I crawl across the room so I'm away from all the visible windows and then run to the stairs so I can get to the top floor.

I race to my bedroom and consider hiding in the house. No. Whoever came here might know I'm here and they won't stop until they find me. I can't leave Roscoe Jr. either. I don't want to… but I shut the door behind me and lock it. Aiden didn't leave me with any weapons and even if he did, I've never held a gun or loaded one. Reading about guns in books doesn't have the same effect.

Searching around my bedroom for a weapon, the closest thing I come up with is a large gold candlestick above the mantle in my bedroom. All the bedrooms in this place have large fireplaces with mantels that I keep dusted on a daily basis.

I can hear my breathing as I approach the door, and I can hear Roscoe still barking, but so far, I can't hear anyone in the house. Maybe whoever shot through the window assumes I'm dead. I can't risk that and relax. I can't go to the police… and I can't leave Roscoe Jr. behind.

Once I push my bedroom door open, I listen closely and finally hear what I expected – footsteps. I stop moving and hold my breath, listening for the weight of the footfall and attempting to count the number of people entering the house. Damn this big ass house. I'm so far away that I can only guess.

Two. There are two men. I hear Roscoe Jr. continuing to bark. He mustn't know them which means these people aren't Aiden's family. I rethink my strategy. Maybe I can come back for Roscoe Jr. later. There's no way I'm getting past two armed men with a candlestick, and I can't help Roscoe Jr. if I'm dead.

I re-enter my bedroom and shut the door again. I've considered scaling the bricks and jumping out this window a few times. I knew Aiden would spend all night searching the streets of Boston if I did and there would be no point taking my chances out there with the homeless when I at least had a roof over my head with him.

But scaling the brick is possible and if I do it now... I can escape. I don't even think. I toss the candlestick to the floor, throw the window open, and throw all caution to the wind as I climb down the wall and drop to the ground. Aiden's backyard connects with the backyard of a smaller blue house, the two properties separated by a short wooden fence. I take off towards the fence in my sweatpants with bare feet.

I've spent most of my life confined to a rich man's compound, so I won't claim to have any athletic ability. I don't look around, I don't look at the street. I run all the way to the fence before I glance over my shoulder and glimpse the car parked in front of Aiden's house. It's a black Lincoln – nothing special, but I take note of it anyway.

I run towards the blue house and then dart around to the front near the street. I don't know my way around here and the disorientation makes all the long, straight streets more like a labyrinth than a map to safety. *Pick a direction and run, Valentina. Just run.*

I pause for just another beat to listen to traffic and run towards the sound and towards potential witnesses as fast as I can go. I have to worry about my life before I worry about my identity or the police or anyone else. At least the police (probably) won't shoot me where I stand and at least I have clothes on, even if I'm barefoot.

Roscoe Jr.'s barking fades into the distance as I take a right and continue sprinting towards the sound of the largest main road I can hear. A sedan honks loudly behind me and I glance over my shoulder to see a red, black and white Mini-Cooper speeding up behind me.

"HEY!" a woman calls out of the car. "HEY STOP RUNNING! STOP RUNNING AND GET IN THE CAR!"

Okay… that's not suspicious at all. I slowed down for a second, but the woman's yelling forces me to take off again.

"Fuck's sake! I'm Aiden's sister!"

I stop running again and glance over my shoulder. This revelation doesn't exactly make me trust her entirely, but she slows the Mini-Cooper to a stop and gets out of it without turning off the car. The wavy-haired blonde woman stands at about 5'1" and she's a little chubby for her height, which makes her seem warm rather than threatening. I can't lie, I appreciate the second to catch my breath, even if she might be a maniac and I'll have to take off running again.

"I don't know you and I'm busy," I say forcefully.

The woman laughs.

"Okay. I'm Orla and I just watched two men climb through my brother's living room window. I got his stupid dog too."

I glance in the back of her car and see Roscoe Jr.'s pink tongue. I can't make out the rest of him, but he isn't barking anymore, so I assume he knows Orla. *Strange name.*

"I-I… Where's Aiden?"

"Probably dead. That idiot's going to tell our father about you and when he finds out, he's going to kill you. If you want to live, come with me."

I DON'T EXACTLY HAVE a lot of options. I sprint to the passenger door, which opens easily. I slide inside and Orla joins me in the driver's seat. She glances over at me and smirks. Up close I can tell that her eyes are exactly like Aiden's. Seeing him in her gives me chills.

"I'm Valentina," I choke out, still struggling to catch my breath completely.

"Nice to meet you, Valentina," Orla says, her hand curving around the steering wheel, revealing manicured french tips. "Boy, do we have a lot to discuss."

She peels into the street faster than I expect and I grip the door to keep myself from spilling out of the seat. The drive out of the city is just as nauseating as Orla weaves through traffic with a flagrant disregard for the law. She accelerates her Mini-Cooper everywhere it fits and I can't hold on to all the details of the trip. 93 North, then 495 West. We exit in a town called Lowell before I have to close my eyes to stop from throwing up.

She's saving my life... I don't want to get sick all over her nice car.

WHEN ORLA finally stops the car, I can't wait to get out. This thing feels like a death trap. I don't know how this woman is so calm. I stumble out of the car, appreciative for the fresh air filling my lungs. I inhale and exhale twice while Orla grunts her way out of the car, filling the fresh air with ten to twenty different cuss words.

"I need a fucking cigarette," she croaks out before pulling a box out of her pocket and lighting one up. "Fuck, that tastes good. I would offer you one but... you don't look like you smoke."

"I don't."

I don't mean to sound terse, but there are too many thoughts flooding my head and I don't know what to do or say about Aiden and what happened at his house. Orla lets Roscoe Jr. out of the car and commands him to heel. He eventually listens to her command after a minute of excited licking and jumping. He acts like he hasn't seen her in a while.

"You get along with him?" Orla asks, gesturing towards Roscoe Jr., finally sitting next to her quietly.

"Yeah."

I glance around at the parking lot. We're at a motel. Or a little inn or something.

"My sister owns this place," Orla says. "But she doesn't know we're coming. Man, her husband will spit when he sees you. It won't be worse than facing my dad though. Don't worry."

Ha. I haven't even had a split second to worry.
"Okay."

"Her husband's a fucking racist like my brother, but if we're lucky, we'll get you out of here before he gets home. Are your people really from Idaho?"

She talked to Aiden.

"I don't have any people."

He must have painted a much softer picture of my past, which I feel oddly appreciative of. Orla won't stop staring at me between drags from her cigarette. She seems like the type not to care if I notice, so I let her stare. She must be curious, I suppose. She knows her brother's beliefs. It occurs to me that she might even share them.

She's helping me and that will have to be enough.

"Are you sure you don't at least want something to drink? You look like you've been through hell."

"I'll be fine."

Roscoe Jr. makes a quiet whining noise and I imagine that he's offering his support.

"Okay then," Orla says. "Welcome to my crazy fucking family..."

Orla's cigarette smells strongly, but I stand close to her as she knocks on the front door before aggressively slamming her thumb into the doorbell. She leans back and slides her hands into her pockets.

"Evie's going to lose her shit."

Before I can ask her anything else, the woman who must be Evie swings the door open. She's tall. Six feet tall and significantly taller than Orla. They look alike, but Evie has short, brown hair cut into a well-coiffed bob and unlike Orla, she's dressed up like she's about to leave for work.

"I already told dad I'm not hiring Rian's maid. He can pawn her off on Callum if he wants to keep her on staff so bad," Evie prattles off to Orla. Heat rushes to my cheeks. I want to pipe up and say that I'm not a maid, but Orla beats me to the punch.

"She's not a fucking maid, you asshole. She's Aiden's girlfriend."

Evie's brows jump several inches up her face and she gives me a proper first look. *She looks like Aiden. She's either his age or slightly younger than him. I can't really tell. She's had plastic surgery too — not too much, but enough for me to notice as she scrutinizes me.*

"Shut the heck up," Evie blurts out, her accent just as thick as Orla's when she swears.

"I rescued her and now I need a place to keep her."

"Does dad know?"

Orla smirks. "If dad knew, she would be dead."

Evie grabs my wrist tightly and uncomfortably drags me into the house. Orla follows us both inside, snickering. I yank my arm away from her. I don't know if I like this woman. Evie glances furtively in my direction and turns her attention to Orla.

"So you brought her to the house where my children live?"

"I thought your baby daddy dragged them off to Newport for the weekend."

"He's not my *baby daddy*, Orla," Evie hisses. "He's my *husband* and it doesn't matter. You're putting us both at risk for..."

Evie glares at me and chooses not to finish her sentence to Orla. "Where did my brother meet you?"

"This is the part you won't believe," Orla says. "But I'm only telling you if you let me smoke inside."

"Over my dead body," Evie hisses, grabbing the cigarette out of Orla's mouth before she can light it. Orla smirks and shrugs.

"You're taking this better than I thought."

Evie glares at her and turns to me again. "Listen, I need you to answer me properly. Where did you meet my brother and did he tell you what happened to the last *four* colored women to mess around with our family?"

"Geez, Evie, why the fuck would he tell her that? I told you it was a crazy story."

"Then tell me!" Evie shrieks.

. . .

I LEAVE the storytelling to Orla, who takes her time to introduce me before launching into my tale of woe. She doesn't mince words, which makes listening to my story from her perspective a little painful. Orla pauses a couple times to ask Evie if she's *sure* that Orla can't smoke.

It's difficult enough standing beneath Evie's disapproving stare as Orla spills everything she knows, but their periodic arguments drawing out the story even longer make it worse. *How can either of these women help me?* Evie seems competent, but not exactly criminal. I don't know what to make of Orla and I suspect she likes it that way.

"Aiden told me not to tell you," Orla says once she finishes her version of the story, which sticks to the most important details. "But if it weren't for me, whoever the fuck these idiots pissed off would have killed her dead."

"You brought the dog too," Evie sighs, giving Roscoe attention for the first time. He wags his tail, but Evie only rolls her eyes with disinterest and says, "I have Duke's old crate in the basement he can use."

Orla walks down into the basement to get the crate. Evie folds her arms once we're alone and bites down on her lower lip as she stares at me.

"Did my brother rape you?" She asks.

The blunt question feels like a slap.

"N-no," I stammer out unconvincingly. I didn't expect the question, but I don't want to lie.

"Where's Tegan?"

"I don't know."

"What do these people have on you?"

It's my turn to feel uncomfortable.

"My identity."

"Huh? Like your passport?"

"Passport, birth certificate... I've never known who I was, really. I always belonged to someone."

"You talk really well for a... you know... for someone who went through what you did."

"Thank you."

I don't know how she wants me to respond, but thanking her for the compliment feels like the right thing to do.

"You can't stay here long. It's not a race thing though," Evie says quickly. "I mean… I'm no angel, but I'm not as bad as my brothers or my husband. He'll be back tomorrow night. Sorry I keep staring."

Orla calls Roscoe down into Evie's basement, and returns upstairs with her hair in a wilder mess than before.

"Did you get him to listen?"

"I tricked him. Fuck, Aiden's an asshole."

"Agreed," Evie says. "A useless dummy who could get our niece killed. No one told me Tegan was missing and that our only clues were pieces of paper and a sex trafficking victim."

Victim. Her words make my stomach lurch, even if I suppose that's exactly what I am. I don't always feel like a victim, but right as Evie says it, I do. My entire life I've existed in service of one man or another. I've always viewed my compliance as the reason I've survived but… what if this is what's keeping me trapped?

"Are you okay, hon?" Orla asks after I've been quiet for too long. They've been talking about what to do with me, but I haven't been listening.

Why do I always let other people decide what happens to me? I have no identity. No proof of my existence. So what… I can figure something out. I'm not *useless*.

"I'm fine," I whisper. "Sorry."

"She probably needs rest," Evie says. "You can stay in the guest bedroom tonight, but after that, you're both out of here. I'll keep Roscoe Jr. until Aiden gets his ridiculous problems sorted out."

"Thanks," I whisper. My heart pounds. *Guest bedroom.* This is my chance to take my life into my own hands for the first time. There won't be bars on the windows or threats of blackmail.

I HAVE my first real chance at escape.

Chapter Nine
Aiden

"We need to talk and we shouldn't talk here," I tell him. "It's serious."

He sees right through me.

My father's familiar blue eyes snap to mine. I've been told my entire life that I'm like him and it scares the crap out of me when I can see myself in the way he stands or the way he sticks his tongue into his cheek when he's pissed off.

He knows I have bad news. Padraig Murray reaches into the inner pocket of his black pea coat for a silver flask with his initials engraved on it right above an ornate Celtic knot.

This time, he's got gin. I'm at a disadvantage. Shame courses through me as I look into my father's eyes and think about everything he fought for. When I was just a boy, there were gang wars in the city. Blacks and Puerto Ricans came into our neighborhoods and slaughtered dozens of our people. I lost an uncle I never knew. A Puerto Rican man raped my father's cousin before they took care of him. I've heard all the stories of what our people suffered to stay here... a place we were promised would be ours.

And now I have to tell him that I've broken his one rule.

He allows us to rule this city as we wish — to drive fast cars, buy tall buildings, have families. All he asks is that we keep our bloodline *Irish*. He explained it logically too. He's not a senseless, murderous racist, despite what Valentina might believe.

When you dilute blood and heritage, you dilute loyalty. I've done worse than betrayed him. I've betrayed generations of Irish men who have chosen family over everything by even laying hands on that woman.

I'm so ashamed of what I've done, but I'm more ashamed by the direction this impossible woman has dragged my heart. I care about her more than I've ever cared about another woman. She isn't Irish, she's not even fucking close — and I love her.

"It must be bad," my father says, putting his hand on my back. "Spit it out. If you've come all the way here, it must be eating you up."

"Darragh and Callum are here," I tell him, hoping meaningless words can prolong what will surely be the lowest point in our relationship. I know what's coming, but he doesn't. I have to accept that this will be the last time he looks at me like this — like he loves me.

Worse, I know what will happen to Valentina for telling him. If I don't let her go tonight... she won't survive my father's wrath and I will have lost both of them in one fell swoop.

THIS IS FOR TEGAN. Valentina wants this.

"YOU KNOW I love you and our family," I begin awkwardly. *Great, he'll see right through me.*

"Christ, are the Pats losing already?"

"I've done something wrong and I've broken your only rule. I know the penalty for what I've done is death and I'm willing to accept that if you throw everything you have into finding Tegan."

"I thought Darragh was searching for her," he says, raising an eyebrow suspiciously.

Chapter Nine

He senses just how nervous I am and my father, the born predator, changes himself in the presence of prey. He sips slowly from his flask before sliding it into his coat.

"What have you done?" He presses before continuing his thought about Darragh. I don't know what my brother told him, but he must've kept this a secret. That much I'm grateful for.

I have to keep the full truth from my father.

"I received a questionable gift. A bit of blackmail. Instructions."

"I see. When?"

I bite my lower lip. I'm not ready to tell him just how long I've been sitting on this, foolishly allowing myself to fall for a woman I should have never touched in the first place. The weight of what I've done finally knots my stomach the way it should have in the first place. Killing her would have been more merciful than sleeping with her and drawing her close to me only to sentence her to death.

"It doesn't matter. I thought obedience would lead to a faster result for both parties involved so… I fucked the girl they sent me."

My father smirks. "I know you're no virgin. I *caught* you the first time, remember?"

He chuckles, but it wasn't a funny story then and it isn't funny now.

"She's black."

Silence.

Too much silence.

My father stares at me expressionless, just blank blue eyes. He's working. Behind those blue eyes, he's choosing his words or his actions carefully. Or so I thought.

"Bastard," he grunts before he surprises me with a forceful punch to the gut. He knocks the air out of me. My father might be old, but he's strong for his age and with the element of surprise on his side, it's easy for him to hit just the right place and cause me to double over. He's not just a fighter, he's killed more men than I have. He has the tattoos to prove it underneath his fashionable fucking pea coat.

"Fucking bastard," he says again, hitting me before I can catch my breath. Tears pierce my eyes as I gasp and choke for breath. There's no point in begging for mercy.

"Dad..."

He pulls his pistol out of his jacket and hits me on the back of the head with it, hard enough that I fall onto the front lawn face first.

"PADRAIG! PADRAIG WHAT ARE YOU DOING!" I hear my mother's voice calling, but my father just hits and hits me until I black out.

That went well, I remember thinking before the world disappeared. *I'm not dead.*

MY MOUTH IS SO dry when I wake up, that I convince myself for a second that maybe he did kill me and the afterlife is meant to hurt just at the base of your skull where your own father pistol-whipped you.

I'm still outside and it's still daylight, which means my dry mouth must be a symptom of something else and I've only been out a few seconds. I hear my mother wailing and crying, Callum saying something comforting to her, and then Darragh's low voice speaking to my father.

"He doesn't know what he's saying," Darragh says. "Dad, please... I'll handle him."

I groan and raise my weight onto my elbows. I'm a man. I can stand and face my father. I'm not afraid of him. I'm standing strong in my confession and the consequences of my actions, no matter what those may be.

"Darragh stop. I know exactly what I'm saying. I thought I could do something to help Tegan and that's more than any of you. Yes, I did the wrong thing… but I'll get rid of the woman if that's what you want."

"I never asked you to kill her," my father says quickly. "That would be a recipe for both of you getting the fuck out of here. That's not what I want."

He's red in the face with pure outrage, but he doesn't move another step towards me as I rise to my feet. Darragh's presence probably helps. He stands between us two and Callum stands between my mother and the rest of us.

"Mom, go back inside," I say to her. "I can handle dad and I can handle my brothers. If we need to have it out, then let's have it out."

"You *hurt him,*" my mother wails at my father. "Padraig, I can't leave you out here to hurt him. He's made a mistake, but he's your son and he's spent his entire life serving this family."

"There's no point to his life if he's going to spill his seed into spics or niggers," he spits at me, the absolute loathing I feared my entire life turning his blue eyes into coals. He swallows slowly, his hatred for me forming a visible lump in his throat that takes its time to settle along with his angry, heaving chest.

"You have failed me," he growls. "You have failed me completely and you are an embarrassment."

He's always had a talent for finding the words that cut deepest.

"I think he would be a bigger embarrassment if he actually got her pregnant," Darragh offers. "And she's not pregnant, right?"

"She's not."

"Perfect."

"The right answer would be to tell me that she's dead and there's no chance word of your indiscretion could spread," my father says, not bothering to look at me as he speaks.

"Well, he couldn't exactly dispose of her body in Cambridge," Darragh says, attempting to reason with him. "Listen, he's been stupid, but there has to be a way out of this for both of you."

"Yeah, there's a way out," my father says. "I want all you stupid motherfuckers to get the fuck off my property before I put a bullet in each of you in front of your mother."

"Padraig, NO!" My mother sobs, although my father made the same threat when we got into a fight after Rian's senior prom. *He probably won't kill us this time.* I limp forward a step, but before I take another, my father levels his pistol at me. My mother loses her shit and Darragh jumps between me and the gun thoughtlessly.

"Darragh, get the fuck out of the way!" I yell at him. "Are you out of your fucking mind?"

"You can't kill him in front of the house," Darragh says. "Not in front of mom."

That's his biggest issue with dad pointing a gun at me? I suddenly wish I had a weapon, but I don't, though that doesn't make me comfortable with using my younger brother as a human shield.

"Get out of the fucking way, Darragh," my father commands him. "Or I'll shoot you too and there won't be anyone to bury his fucking body."

My mother's wailing becomes a blubber of background noise and choice phrases from Callum as he fails to calm her down sufficiently.

"I won't let you kill him, not until we discuss this like adults."

"Adults obey the rules," my father says coldly. "Adults don't risk our family for selfish reasons. Once you become that selfish, there's no fixing you."

He loads a bullet into the chamber, but Darragh doesn't budge. *Fuck, you stubborn asshole, you're going to get yourself shot.*

"Darragh, move!" I yell.

"Let him die," Callum says. "If it's all over with, maybe that will calm her down."

This, in fact, does nothing to calm my mother, who leaps away from Callum and wraps her body purposefully around Darragh's.

"You can't kill our sons," she wails. "Darragh, Callum, Aiden... talk some sense into him. Listen to what he says. Do whatever he asks!"

She has a limited understanding of the situation, but I can't blame her for suggesting appeasement. That normally works with our father, but it won't work this time.

I've already betrayed him.

"Where is the whore?" He asks, daring me to correct him.

"My place."

"And Tegan?"

Darragh exchanges a quick glance with me that's far too risky for my taste, but goes undetected. We're lucky our father doesn't notice. He doesn't address me when he speaks next. Darragh straightens his back and stares our father down as if daring him to shoot me. *It's risky. He could kill all of us and have our spot filled with more thuggish cousins in an instant.*

"You have 48 hours to find Rian's brat. I think Rian's suffered long enough. He uses all his prison minutes to call and talk about her and where she is and why the fuck we haven't found her."

"Don't you care about your own niece?" Callum accuses, his face darkening with moral outrage. Where the fuck has he been the past two weeks?

My mother emits another sob as I rub the back of my head and struggle to keep composure. The back of my head hurts and it's been far too long since I've seen Valentina.

"Based on what you described, you don't have long before those people retaliate," my father says. "If you don't have your nigger girl out of the city and Tegan back in 48 hours, I want you gone for the next year."

It's not a request.

"Yes. Thank you."

This is as much mercy as I can expect from him.

"I'll go with him," Darragh says. "Make sure he does what you ask."

"Callum, you still have that girl down at the post office?"

"Yes," Callum says. "But they don't do package tracing or that sorta thing. Federal crime."

"Right," Darragh says. "And we're totally above that."

"Totally," Callum mutters. "Totally."

"Get the fuck off my property," my father interjects. "I don't want to see you shit stains until this mess is over."

Darragh gets into the front seat of my car and demands the key. I hand it over because dad's watching and it's in my best interests to appear contrite. Callum takes Darragh's car, presumably down to the post office to ask about large pink envelopes and deliveries to Cambridge.

"I would've gone to him in the first place but you know Callum," Darragh says. "He's more racist than dad. I swear."

He got arrested for beating the pulp out of a black guy up in Lawrence last year after he lost a bet on a Pats game. Cops called it a hate crime and he had to spend 8 months in a minimum security jail. That must've been the year he lost the post office girl...

"He just likes fighting. He's young. Red-blooded."

Darragh scoffs. "I can't tell if this lady of yours has changed you, Aiden. If you still think this family isn't as racist as–

"Enough, Darragh. I just want to get back to Valentina and get her to safety."

My father's threat rings clearly in my head. I'll have to send her away without identity papers, somewhere my father doesn't know about, somewhere I can see her on the weekends. *But she can't be a bird in a cage for long.*

"Fuck," Darragh says as we pull onto my street. "You left your front door open. Or the girl ran off."

"She didn't run off and my front door isn't–

My front door is indeed wide open. Shit. I jump out of the car before Darragh pulls to a complete stop and I run towards my house screaming for Valentina and Roscoe Jr. My entire body aches, but I don't care because everything in my body is telling me something fucked up happened.

There's blood on the front step in a pool that spreads past the foyer and drips into the house.

"ROSCOE!" I call to him. "ROSCOE!"

He's either not here or he's dead. *Oh fuck.* Darragh catches up to me.

"You fucking idiot, you don't even have a gun."

"There's no one here."

Darragh glances around at all the blood. There might not be anyone here, but there's a hell of a lot of blood. Something happened, and there have to be bodies, right?

"Split up," Darragh says. "Get a fucking gun."

"They're upstairs."

Darragh glowers at me. "Get a fucking kitchen knife then."

I pull out the longest and sharpest knife out of the wooden block. My house is far too quiet for there to be other people here. There are two shattered windows in the living room, and two bullet holes through the library windows, with some of the glass blown out. There are books everywhere and furniture strewn about, but no signs of Valentina.

Fuck. The blood smells terribly, but there's no other scent of rot, and very little out of place aside from the wash of blood everywhere and a few items knocked over in some struggle, or hopefully in Valentina's efforts to escape.

Darragh wanders away from me and I move swiftly towards the stairs to the bedroom, clearing every room along the way. No bodies. No Roscoe Jr. and no Valentina. I ought to be relieved, but I can't relax unless I'm certain they escaped and they weren't kidnapped.

There's no one upstairs, but my bedroom isn't how I left it. *Valentina?*

I push the door to her bedroom open. Her linens and the wallpaper still smell like her. The room vibrates with her essence, even in her absence. My precious Valentina. Her room is so cold… I follow the source of the draft to an open window and glance out of it as if she would be there, curled up against the red brick, just waiting for me to rescue her. *Hmph.*

She's not the type. There's a small disturbance in the grass, but it could just have easily been the intruders. More easily. Valentina wouldn't have scaled the brick. Would she? I peer out the window and estimate the drop. She could have survived, but she wouldn't have made it far on foot. I hope she's close.

"I THINK I FOUND SOMETHING!" Darragh calls from downstairs.

SOMETHING. Not someone. Valentina's still out there… and she's in trouble if I can't get her safe in the next 48 hours. If I can't track her, my father can – and then she's dead. It doesn't matter what she thinks of me, if she doesn't believe that I can have true feelings for her because of her color or because of my bigotry. I would lose myself entirely if anything happened to her.

I couldn't stand the thought of it. I may not have the words to express it, but I'll do whatever it takes to keep her safe.

I meet Darragh downstairs with a loaded gun and my clue from upstairs that points to Valentina's escape.

"What did you find?"

"Our first fucking clue. I think whoever did this must be family."

"Family? What the fuck are you talking about?"

DARRAGH HOLDS up a wrinkled piece of white paper that I would have missed. He uncrumples it and hands it to me.

"I dunno if the bastards meant to leave this behind."

"It's a family tree."

"Yup. recognize the names?"

"No. I don't. But these are Italians and…"

"Yup," Darragh says. "That's our father's name."

"Bullshit," I grunt. "Dad never fucked with any Italians. We would have known that. Mom would have gotten wine drunk and told us about it the way she told us about the girl from Ballybrazil or the whore from Clondoo."

Darragh shrugs. "This person wants to get our attention. Well, they've got it. What the fuck are we supposed to do with this?"

"I don't know, but this puts us closer to Tegan."

Darragh's phone rings and to my annoyance, he answers it.

"ORLA?" he says. "Orla, calm down…"

GREAT. What now?

Chapter Ten
Valentina

I never thought I would know what to do with freedom if I had it. I lived so long in the confinement of various cages that I never dared to fantasize too deeply about freedom. Even my dreams had a twinge of despair to them. Now that I can go *anywhere* in the entire country within the budget of everything I saved working for Aiden – which was everything – the world is at my fingertips.

Without identification, I'll have to be creative, but I've read books about hitchhikers who made it clear across America. *I could do that. Nothing could be more dangerous than staying amongst racists and slavers. There has to be some place in America where a woman like me can be truly free.*

I choose Washington DC as my final destination. I'll probably need to stop somewhere else for a night, but it's close enough that I can get there in a couple of days.

It's easy to get there from Boston by my estimate and won't be too expensive. I'll find a place and try to blend in. There's a lot I don't know, but if I didn't read about it in a book, I'm sure I can ask someone for help. A woman. Not a man. I don't plan on speaking with or relying on any more men. Aiden was the last one for me.

I wish I got to say goodbye.

I know it wouldn't mean anything to him. He's probably been with more women than I can count and he doesn't exactly view me as a woman *like them* either. As cruel as he could be, he was the first man to ever give me an orgasm. He touched me, held me and whispered to me with tenderness that I could have easily mistaken for love. I know what to look for now when I do finally settle down and try to find someone – I'll look for someone who makes love to me like Aiden, but who has room in their heart for me to stay.

HITCHHIKING to New York City doesn't take as long as I expect. It seems like the most logical place to stop before trying to get to Washington, DC.

I get there by the end of the day and nobody who picks me up asks me any questions except this one white woman who convinces herself that I'm a victim of a "government conspiracy". I'm too tired to properly understand her, but she just seems satisfied with someone to talk to.

The woman who drives me into New York City insists I spend the night with her and her family. She won't hear a word about where I've been and keeps saying that as a Christian, it doesn't matter to her. I won't argue with that. She lets me stay the night, but she's prompt about kicking me out in the morning. I try to leave her money for breakfast and the bed but again, she refuses.

She explains how I can use the train and go to DC without showing identification.

"Is that legal?" I ask her.

"Listen, do you want legal or do you want help?"

BY THE TIME I get to Washington, DC, I can't remember the woman's name. I feel absolutely terrible for forgetting, but my mind is so foggy with the novelty of being outdoors around so many people and having to think through so many details that the woman's name just leaves me.

Thank you, kind Christian woman.

Chapter Ten

. . .

I NEARLY LOSE fifty dollars to a scammer at Union Station in Washington, DC, but I keep my wits and keep moving until the man loses interest in me. If I were a little bigger, perhaps I wouldn't be such an easy target. I have nothing on my person except some money I grabbed before running, so I find a food truck and spend twenty-dollars stuffing my face with food.

I can eat whatever I want and go wherever I want… It's incredible. At least it's incredible until my stomach hurts so badly I can barely walk. I wanted to try everything at that food truck, and I regret eating so much food. I don't know where I'm going and I'm sick from all the delicious food, but I'm giddy with excitement.

I have to find a place to sleep before nightfall, but I still have all my cash in hand, so I hope it's not too difficult. I go to one of the libraries to ask for help, because if books don't have all the answers, librarians probably do. I used to envy their job when I read about librarians in books growing up. The librarian is *beyond* helpful.

She helps get me into the world's tiniest apartment – but it's mine. There's no furniture in it and I have to part with $1,600 right away, but I have a place before nightfall and she doesn't ask any questions about where I'm from, or who I am.

"Sometimes a woman needs her secrets," she says. "You sound country as hell though, so you'd better wise up quick before this city eats you alive."

I didn't know I sounded like anything, but I don't mind sounding a little country. I have to buy a couple of things, so I go to the cheapest place I can find and a small duffel bag, some toiletries and a couple cheap t-shirts. I find a fabric store and buy some I can use to make a couple new dresses. I spread out some of my clothes on the floor, using a thin fleece blanket the librarian left me to pull over myself.

Curling up alone to fall asleep, I imagine a big warm bicep curling up around me. I don't mean for the image in my fantasy to be colored with black ink. Or the image of Aiden's Celtic knot wrapping around me as he presses his nose into my neck and whispers, "You're mine."

"Stop it, Val," I whisper to myself. "There's no going back there. You lost. You lost who you were and you just need to start from scratch. You can handle it. You can."

I feel stupid talking to myself out loud, but it works long enough for me to drift off to sleep.

IN THE MORNING, I return to the library and learn the librarian's name again. Leilani Morgan stands a few inches taller than me with a full-figure and an eye for color. She wears a lot of makeup and wears her hair in waist-length braids. I've become her personal project, so she doesn't rest until she's taken me grocery shopping, found me a great deal on a mattress and bedframe, and helped me to find a job.

I'll be the nanny for a rich couple staying in DC for a few months. Mickey Ford is apparently some famous rock star and his wife, Rain, needs help with their kids. Leilani arranges a meeting with Rain in the afternoon and it surprises me that she's a few shades darker than I am. I've never met a woman who looks like me with that much money, and I don't feel envious just... *ashamed.*

I lived my life as less than dirt. How can this woman want someone like me looking after her kids?

Rain dispels my insecurities after a few minutes. She has an easy Southern drawl that sounds like something out of a movie and when she talks about her kids, she sounds so happy and excited that I can't wait to meet them. She explains that the kids are at violin lessons, so meeting them will have to wait.

By the end of the meeting, I have the job. Rain loves that I can play the piano. It feels good to know that my love for the instrument has some value outside of my various prisons. By the time Leilani takes me home, I almost have the hang of the subway and I have enough furniture that my home doesn't feel clinical.

Leilani hugs me goodbye and makes me promise to give her a call after my first day at the Ford house.

They live on a much nicer side of town than I could never afford, so it takes a while to get there. I'll have to get up early to make it on time. I'm surprised people that rich don't do a background check on me. If this were one of the thrillers on Pulsifer's bookshelves, a background check would have been their first order of business.

I spend my first day busy from the second I step through the door until Rain wrangles all her kids to school. I don't know how a woman that young could have ever managed so many children on her own. She has a system, so I work with it. Jimi and Janis Ford, the eldest pair of twins, help with the younger sets. I wonder if there's a secret to having three sets of twins in a row, but I don't ask.

Once they're at school, Rain needs my help cleaning up after them and getting ready for their afternoon activities. We don't have time to talk about my first few nights in the city, much less anything about my past. By the time I'm done with my first day, I barely have time to call Leilani. I make the effort because Rain pays me in cash and I can't believe how much it is.

"A thousand dollars a day?!" I screech. "Leilani, why don't *you* have this job?"

Leilani laughs. "Because rich people are crazy, girl. Enjoy it while you can and save up to move out of that tiny ass place. You're a smart girl. You can make it out here. Just don't let any of the DC bums drag you down, okay?"

"Okay," I whisper.

SHE DOESN'T HAVE to worry about me and men. I'm absolutely done with men. Forever.

Chapter Eleven
Aiden

"You don't have time to skip town and find her," Darragh says, trying to stop me from driving over to Orla's and shaking my idiot sister until what's left of her brains falls out.

"Like fuck I do."

"Tegan is what's important right now!" Darragh yells. "These fuckers have a little girl who they've probably been raping!"

"Christ, Darragh. She's your fucking niece. Watch your language."

I can't bear to think of what might be happening to Tegan. This must be tearing Rian up too. It ought to be ripping all of us to shreds. Everyone in our family is too sick in the fucking head to process their emotions properly.

"It's the truth. We have to do something. Don't you think I've been trying? It's been an absolute bitch to keep this from dad. If I knew you were going to tell him anyway, I would have softened the blow. Stop being a cunt. We have what we need. We can sort this out."

"Let's go to Evie's," I grunt. "Knowing Orla she probably took her there. Whoever came here obviously has eyes on the place. Which I should have known."

Aiden

I expected eyes here, I just didn't expect them to act. And what the fuck did they want anyway? To hurt Valentina...

If there's someone out there who still wants to hurt her, she isn't safe. There's a part of me that wants to take this chance I've been given to let her go. But I won't be able to sleep at night knowing that I let something happen to her. If she's still out there, once I save my niece... I'll find her and make sure she's safe.

I HOPE she can stay out of trouble until then.

EVIE REFUSES to let us in. She stands in the doorway with more wrinkles than the last time I saw her. Red lipstick glues her thin lips together and she has one foot between the door and the frame to stop us from stepping over.

Darragh doesn't appear ruffled by Evie's I'm-gonna-fucking-kill-you-both glare.

"We're your brothers," Darragh pleads, failing to come off as sympathetic. "Please. If you don't let us in... I'll have to shoot you. I don't want to do that."

"Can you show up to my house without threatening to kill me for once? My kids are home. I don't have time for either of you or your bullshit," Evie says, unperturbed by the threat on her life. "If dad finds out I helped you idiots, I won't hear the end of it from him."

"Is Orla here at least?" I venture. If Evie won't talk to us, maybe my meddling younger sister can provide some insight about Valentina, whoever broke into the house and the piece of paper in Darragh's pocket.

"I kicked her unruly behind out too. I have a family. I'm not like you losers. I *care* about people and I don't want to get involved."

"If you care about people, you care about Tegan," I say before my sister gets started tearing into us again. "We have a clue. And I do care about someone else."

Evie scoffs. "If you cared about that dark girl, you wouldn't have slept with her. Wherever she went, you'd better hope she went far away, because dad will kill her."

She's matter-of-fact, but doesn't contain her disgust.

"I'm honestly surprised you didn't kill her," Evie snipes.

"Will you let us in or not? I'm tired of standing out here."

"Unload your guns. Then come in."

WE SURRENDER our bullets to Evie and do the obligatory uncle thing with the twins until Evie ushers them off to the basement to watch a movie guaranteed to drown out our conversation upstairs. Darragh spreads the piece of paper with the family tree on the kitchen counter. Evie lights up with recognition once she sees it.

"Are you fucking kidding me? Where did you get this? Is this real?"

Evie rarely swears.

I don't know what she sees on this useless bit of paper. It's like the tree is written backwards. The name at the top is Italian and Evie's finger points to the woman's name.

"Don't you remember she stopped by our house once?" she says to me with frustration, as if it were my responsibility to keep every detail of my childhood balanced in my head at once.

"No."

"Dad took us to the Red Sox game after he got into this *huge* fight with mom. I can't believe you don't remember," Evie says. "That woman was there. I remember her name. I remember thinking it was funny that dad knew someone who looked... you know... so dark."

My parents fought so much when we were kids, I don't know how Evie can remember one fight from another. As soon as I was old enough to get out of the fucking house, I did.

"Aren't the Aurelio people related to the Zagarellas?"

I bristle uncomfortably. Yes. I just got into business with Sammy, the eldest of the Zagarella boys. I met him a few times before we got to working together. I trust him just enough to do business with him and a bunch of lawyers, but I don't know the details of the man's family tree.

"How the fuck should I know?"

"They could be," Evie says. "That woman knows our father."

"Are you saying this motherfucker could be our brother? Dad would have never allowed any affair to get that far. It's been years and he's never brought another kid home to our mother."

"Wouldn't that piss off anyone?" Evie says. "It's dad's way. He pisses people off and he leaves the entire family to deal with it."

"Be respectful," Darragh chides her. "You can't talk about him like that. He's done everything for us and if it weren't for him, you wouldn't have such a big house to put your kids in. It's certainly not your useless fucking husband paying for this shit."

"I want to slap you every time you open your mouth," Evie spits at him, color rising to her cheeks. They don't get along. Then again, it's hard for anyone to get along with Evie. She's always been the perfect eldest daughter. Orla only manages her because Orla's the problem.

"Great," I interrupt the two of them before they can start up again. "We know this woman, but what about this alleged brother of ours? If he's her son, that ought to be pretty fucking easy to find out. If he lives in Boston and he runs in our circles, surely one of us would have heard of him by now."

Owen Aurelio.

"It could be an alias," Darragh says.

"Or you haven't put any effort into tracking him yet. Call that Italian you're working with and get out of my house."

"Damn, Evie. You won't even make us a cup of coffee first?"

"Go to Dunkin'," Evie responds unsympathetically. Before I let my sister usher us out to find the asshole on the crumpled piece of paper, I need everything I can get out of her about where Valentina could have gone. Evie shows me the room where Valentina stayed the night, sure to mention her kindness and hospitality with all the humility you can expect from Evie.

"I even let her use my good pillows," Evie says. "I'm a good Catholic. I think what this family needs is a whole lot more church."

Chapter Eleven

Darragh grunts. "I completely agree."

I raise my eyebrows. Darragh caught the church on fire during his First Holy Communion. He hasn't been back since except for funerals and weddings. *He wants something from Evie.*

My sister, never fooled by any of us, narrows her eyes. "What do you want, Darragh?"

"Nothing. Nothing at all. I'm just building up good will in case I need it."

This does little to assuage Evie's suspicions, but she carries on telling me her suspicions about where Valentina might have gone.

"I BET she went back to the first man that had her," Evie says. "She's never known a day of freedom in her life. How could she possibly survive on her own?"

"You don't know Val," I grunt.

Once I find Tegan, I'll come for you, Valentina. I'll give you everything you need to be truly free – I promise.

I JUST HAVE to find her and Tegan before my father does. It's time to call Sammy.

Chapter Twelve
Valentina

I have the day off today. Rain and Mickey took the kids on a spontaneous trip down to Florida since Janis excelled at her latest piano recital. Rain won't stop gushing about how my teaching pushed Janis to advance even more than she expected.

Her compliments make me a little uncomfortable, but the extra pay causes me to splurge on something special for my house – a little keyboard. It's not the grand piano I dreamed of, but I bought it from a little music store in South East DC and carried it all the way home despite the stares and a few rude comments from men.

It's not much, but it's a start. The music helps me deal with having no one to talk to. Leilani works today, and I haven't the faintest idea how to make friends. I never really had friends before Leilani and now that I have her, I feel like I'm just the smallest part of her life and she's everything to me.

I didn't mind talking to Aiden, but he wasn't exactly a friend, so I can't look to our relationship for any clues that may apply to making friends. I play for an hour before I get too numb to continue. When I'm not working with the kids, I just feel incredibly alone.

It's been two weeks since I left Evie's house and some twisted part of me almost believed that Aiden would show up. I don't know what I even want from Aiden anymore. I've given up on my identity and the strange way we ended up in bed together could hardly be called making love – even if his touch set every inch of my skin on fire.

I text Leilani, even if I know she's at work, and she sends me a link to a deli downtown.

Leilani: Hot guys. Go meet one.

I SMIRK at the text message. She doesn't know about my past at all, but meeting men hasn't ever been one of my priorities. I want love, I don't want to be picked up along with a hoagie and Diet Coke. But I have nothing better to do.

I don't know what to wear to a deli, but I know I'll feel most comfortable in one of my handmade dresses instead of the outfits Leilani and Rain keep donating to me. I slide into a dress made out of orange cotton, tie my hair up in a wrap after getting it nice and clean, and I walk outside with my metro card and a hundred dollars in my pocket.

I save almost everything I make from working for Rain, so I don't feel too guilty about leaving my house with a hundred dollars. Getting to the deli doesn't take too much work and there isn't a huge crowd when I enter. A nice woman with almond-colored skin takes my order and recommends a few of her favorites off the menu to try.

I order over forty dollars worth of food. I'll take most of it home, but I can't resist all the delicious cooking I can have all the time now. I've tried almost every type of food available in DC. Cajun food has won me over the most, but this sandwich smells good as I unwrap it from its brown paper bag and absorb the scent of salty meat and onions. *Yum.*

Just as I press my nose to the sandwich to inhale, barely avoiding spreading mayo on my nose, a man clears his throat.

"Excuse me, may I join you?"

I glance up. He sounded so much like Aiden for a second, that I nearly thought it was him. Of course it isn't Aiden. If he hasn't come in two weeks, he won't be coming. I shouldn't be thinking about him anyway.

"Y-yes. Sure," I answer quickly, mostly because not-Aiden is handsome. *Incredibly* handsome.

"What have you got there?" he asks, grinning and unwrapping his own sandwich. He has a nice, easygoing smile, much different from Aiden's perpetually irritated scowl.

"I think it's salami."

I glance around and catch myself indulging in my worst, paranoid fears. Just because I've seen the worst humanity has to offer doesn't mean I have to worry about a perfectly nice gentleman in a deli having an ulterior motive. The man nods.

"I love salami. Did something different today and got turkey. I don't know what I was thinking."

He chuckles and I get the impression I'm supposed to laugh, so I try.

"Hey, sorry for being such a dick. What's your name? I saw you sitting alone and had to come over. You're stunning."

"Val."

He beams. "Val. Pretty name."

I glance up at him. His eyes are a darker shade of blue than Aiden's, but they pop out against his tanned skin. He smells like expensive cologne and wears three rings – none of them on his wedding finger. The ring on his left index finger has an inscription but the cursive is either indecipherable, or it's in another language.

"Thanks," I mutter, glancing down at his large hands wrapped around his sandwich. They look worn, but his nails are clean and short. Clean nails aren't the only sign this handsome stranger takes care of himself. He dabs a spot of mayo off the side of his chin politely.

"Do you live in DC or do you just commute for work?" he asks.

He has an accent of some kind, but I can't immediately place it.

"I live here."

"No shit," he says, grinning more broadly. It's easy to like his tranquil demeanor, his nice smile, and straight teeth, plus the way he seems to spit out everything on his mind. I can't imagine having no qualms about talking to strangers like he does. *Maybe I've already said too much.*

I don't want to spill every detail of my life to this stranger, but DC is a big place so it's not like my confession will make it easy for him to find me. He doesn't seem concerned that I've said too much so I relax and take another bite out of my sandwich.

"I live in Bethesda," he says. "So I commute. I'm sorry, Val. I just... I can't stop staring at you. I can't believe my luck meeting a woman who looks like you on a Tuesday morning."

He would put me entirely at ease if it weren't for the compliments. None of the men I've ever met have gushed about my beauty. Aiden certainly didn't.

"You don't need to lay it on so thick," I say a little more sharply than I intend to. This doesn't bother the man who still hasn't bothered to introduce himself. His neutral, calm response sets me at ease again.

"Sorry," he says. "I don't meet women like you too often."

"But you do run around local delis meeting women?" I ask him, hoping my sharp tone pushes him away again.

It doesn't work.

"Not normally," he says. "But I don't see any women in delis as beautiful as you."

"Okay, stranger. You're officially coming on too strong."

"Would it help if I told you my name?" he asks, relaxing in his chair with no intentions of moving.

"Probably not."

"Fine, then. Will you go out with me?"

He's a hot guy. Leilani sent me out here to meet a hot guy... Maybe she knows something about picking up men that I don't. She doesn't have a boyfriend or a husband, but who would bother if strangers like this sidle up to you on a whim every time you order a salami sandwich?

Chapter Twelve

The blue-eyed stranger might be hot, but he's still a stranger and I don't imagine going out with him is a particularly good idea.

"I don't think so. I'm not available."

"You seem available to me, having a sandwich all by yourself."

I roll my eyes.

"Okay," he says. "Don't go out with me. Just a walk. I'll walk you to your bus stop and then I'll leave you alone forever. I promise."

"Promise?"

"Yes," he says. "I promise. And if you like me… maybe you'll come back to this deli and we'll run into each other again."

Well wouldn't that be a fairy tale? I bite my lip, fighting back images of Aiden popping into my head. No love story starts with a man unwrapping a woman he received as a slave. This is how love stories begin – in delis.

A man this handsome could never hurt anyone. He's clean shaven. No tattoos. Polite. He doesn't have a hint of thuggishness about him. If I can submit to Aiden, I can let this gentleman walk me to the bus stop.

"Fine," I tell him. "But I need to finish my sandwich first."

"Take your time, beautiful."

I do take my time. He talks to me about the weather, his favorite museums in the city and more recommendations for great delis. It's a relief that I don't have to do much of the talking, but I can't for the life of me decide why he came up to me. There were other women eating sandwiches and most of them wearing clothes that weren't handmade.

I GUESS I have a lot to get used to when it comes to normal life.

Once I finish my sandwich, I'm eager to get home so I can play the keyboard. Going to the deli and talking to a nice man was enjoyable enough, but I have just enough energy to head back inside for alone time. He jumps to his feet and clears away my crumpled brown paper bag, half-eaten dish of french fries and all the sauce cups I demolished without even asking. His politeness strikes me as utterly different to any of the piggish men I encountered in my past.

He holds the door to the deli open for me as we leave.

"I'm Owen," he says. "Since you're going for a walk with me, you might as well know."

"Well, you already know my name."

We walk a few steps out of the deli.

"Yes, Valentina," Owen says. "I do."

A strange twist of panic settles in my stomach. I told him my name was Val, not Valentina. I turn to face Owen and he still has that broad grin on his face. He doesn't look so genuine out here in the daylight.

He grabs my arm, drags me against his chest and I feel a sharp pinch at the top of my hip. I cry out and slump over into Owen's arms.

Chapter Thirteen
Aiden

I haven't seen my father since we brought Tegan home. Getting her out of that place was brutal. I don't think I've ever seen such filth in my life. And there she was, the tiny little thing, amongst all the garbage and the dirt and the rotten food. Her brown hair was stuck to her neck and her wide eyes gazed at us as if she'd lost hope long ago.

My heart breaks to think of what happened to her. I don't want to fathom what sort of cruelty could provoke someone to hold a little girl like a rodent in a cage. She had dirt all over her face, she looked hungry and she looked like she had the humanity whipped out of her. I'll kill whoever did this to her – I swear it to myself when I first pick her up and hold her.

She breaks my heart when she thinks I'm her father, Rian, but I don't let her go when I take her out of the filth and into the safety of her family – the family that should have never let this happen to her.

Sammy Zagarella's contacts led us to our suspect and more importantly, the only place where Sammy's suspect could have held Tegan.

Owen isn't there when we arrive, but Tegan's there – alone. I break down the door to her holding cell first. Darragh and Callum are with me, making sure the house stays clear.

Aiden

We're four hours north of Boston, in some shitty underdeveloped New Hampshire town with too many trailers scattered amongst thick, dense northern woods. Tegan's in the back bedroom of the double wide and when I open the door, my niece screams.

"DADDY!"

I look nothing like Rian, but Tegan looks nothing like Tegan. Her wild brown hair matts over her head in thick dreadlocks that will probably need to be shaved. She's filthy, smells like piss, and she's wearing the same clothes she was wearing the last day my brother saw his daughter – the day of his arrest.

I run towards her, even if she doesn't seem to know who I am, and I scoop her in my arms. Tegan wraps her skinny arms around my neck and I hold her tightly, careful not to squeeze too tightly. She feels fragile and she lets out a deep, hacking cough once I hold her against my chest.

"The bad man is coming," she whispers and her tiny, shaking voice pummels me with emotion. I withhold tears for the sake of being the strong man Tegan needs me to be.

"You're safe, Tegan. I promise, you're safe."

BACK HOME, I insist Tegan stays at my place with me. I don't want to keep my eyes off her until we find the man who took her. Valentina doesn't have just my father to worry about now. I just need her to stay out of sight a bit longer. Until Tegan's properly safe.

My niece shows clear effects from her captivity and it scares me how much she reminds me of Valentina. She's skittish the way Valentina was, glancing over her shoulder with a furtive look whenever she thought I wasn't paying attention. It hurts to see Tegan like this. She's not the girl I remember, even though it's only been 4 weeks since she went missing. Still, there's something missing from Tegan's eyes...

Those wide blue Murray eyes tell me more than any words possibly could. The girl needs her father and if my father won't help get Rian

138

out, that won't happen anytime soon and what will happen to Tegan then? I can't take her in and I don't know if I trust anyone else in my family to look after the girl.

I bring Tegan's clothes and items from Rian's house into Valentina's bedroom, but she shows little interest in her toys or coloring books, even her favorites. Orla thinks I ought to take her to a child psychologist, like I don't have enough on my plate. Tegan doesn't sleep through the night, which means I don't sleep through the night. Every spare minute I have outside of work, I talk to people who might've seen something – anyone who might know where Val is or how much pressure dad's applying to find her. We haven't spoken since the blow up outside my parents' house, but it's only a matter of time before he summons me to his office.

Another reason I can't sleep. Men like my father don't forgive betrayal. It doesn't matter if what I'm about to uncover would be an even bigger betrayal. He doesn't see it that way. He has his reasons, right? And none of ours matter. He makes me question everything about our world. *Not just him – her. You miss her and you hate how much it hurts to be away from her.*

Evie thinks it's most important for Tegan to get back into school, but I don't have time for that either. I need to work harder at finding the man on the note. Owen Aurelio – Sammy's cousin. His mother was an Italian from Florence who lived in Brooklyn with Alfonso Vicari for three years while studying at Barnard College twenty-one years ago as part of an exchange program.

If we can trust this slip of paper discarded on the floor of my house, we have a brother out there, a brother we didn't know about who might have it in his head that we are sworn enemies.

Maybe we are, then. Maybe my father was right and his foolish mistake only serves to prove the point he's made our entire lives, that mixing our blood with others only leads to our ruin. I don't want to believe that about Valentina but.... His mistake clearly had consequences. Tegan's broken. Valentina's gone. And I'm still healing from the punch he threw into my stomach.

Aiden

This is the first time in years I've questioned my loyalty to my father and my family and I don't enjoy the position he's put me in.

AFTER FIVE DAYS, Tegan appears more chipper. I'm not a natural parent, but taking care of a kid is kind of like taking care of yourself. If I need help, I call Evie for advice, which normally helps even if she spends every phone call chastising me for not possessing innate parenting knowledge.

Tegan wanders into the kitchen dragging a buffalo plaid fleece blanket behind her and the music box I gave her in the other hand.

"I want bacon."

It's the first time she's requested breakfast instead of waiting for me to run through the options.

"Good morning Tegan. Bacon, coming right up. How many strips do you want? Two strips or three?"

"Hmmm," she says, tilting her head to the side. We had to cut most of her hair off, so it falls in a sharp angled bob along the side of her face. She cried when it happened, but now she can't stop running her fingers through the soft, short crop of hair. She's been through so much and she's still so strong.

"Four strips," she says. "I'm starving."

She climbs onto the bar stool and waits for me to get the bacon out before muttering, "Thank you, Uncle Aiden."

"No problem, darling. How did you sleep?"

"I didn't."

She barely sleeps. I know, because I can't. Every night, I load my gun and pass most of my hours alone, pacing my new bedroom – I have to pick one with functional windows until the contractors come and fix everything.I double check the window reinforcements all over the house, even the nails on the boards over the broken windows. I stay up almost all fucking night every night hoping foolishly and against all reason that Valentina will return.

"I didn't either."

"Then you'd better have four strips of bacon too," Tegan says before yawning. She still has dark circles under her eyes and outside of necessary conversations, she doesn't talk much. Still, it's been my task to bring my niece back to life. Everyone else has their orders and I have mine. No rushing off to find Val.

"You know Tegan, your grandfather worried about you when you were gone."

"I wasn't gone," she says. "A man took me. He says he's my uncle."

This isn't the first time she's said this and what she says confirms the family tree we found on the slip of paper, but Owen's delusions aren't necessarily the truth.

"Family doesn't do that to family," I tell her. "You're safe now. I promise. But I understand. I can't sleep either."

"Where's my dad?" Tegan says. "I thought… I thought if I got back, he'd get out of prison and he'd be here."

If only life were that simple. If I could wish my brother out of prison, I would. But I have to do the right thing, even if it costs me Valentina. She wouldn't want me to abandon Tegan to chase after her. No, she'd probably call me a sociopath if I did something like that. *Hmph.*

"Your father wants to be with you. He just can't. Not until he fights this case."

Tegan rolls her eyes. "He's spent my entire life in prison. If he cared about me, maybe he'd stop breaking the law."

She's a bit too clever for her age and far too young to understand that her father doesn't have a choice. He took an oath just like I did. We knew what we were doing, just like Evie and Orla did when they put our family business behind them and took as much distance as our father would allow.

"Listen, Tegan. What would help your father… what would help all of us, is if you talked about what happened."

Her fierce Murray eyes meet mine and her brows harden in a way that unnervingly reminds me of my brother. Her mother might be a Puerto Rican, but the girl is pure Murray with a cobalt gaze and a wild mop of hair that the best efforts couldn't tame.

"I don't want to talk about the bad man."

She sounds more annoyed than scared. Annoyed I can work with. She's a feisty child, a fighter like none of Evie's kids ever were, and if I can bring that anger to the front of her mind… we can help each other. This is the most important thing I will have done.

"You must. There are people who he could hurt."

Her next words nearly cause me to drop my spatula into the bubbling bacon grease.

"You mean like Valentina?"

What does she know about Valentina?

"What did you say?"

"Owen told me about Valentina."

My heart quickens. I shouldn't allow myself to read too much into this. She's a little girl and this is the first she's mentioned Valentina since she's been here. Maybe she snuck around the house and read something with her name on it or heard Darragh say the name or something like that.

"What did he tell you?" I ask her, giving Tegan a curious look. I need honesty from her right now and more importantly, I need all the details of where Valentina could possibly be.

"A lot of things."

"What do you know about Valentina?"

"He said he was gonna do to her what he did to me."

My throat tightens. When I find this motherfucker, I'll take immense pleasure in killing him. He deserves no sympathy, no explanation, all he deserves in a bullet to the fucking intestines — something slow and painful that will cause him a bloody and grotesque descent into the afterlife.

"Tegan…"

"He didn't touch me down there," she says. "But he hit a lot."

She falls silent. I dab the grease off Tegan's bacon before sliding the plate over to her. I add some toast and butter, which is normally her favorite, but she reaches for the bacon first. She crunches on a piece of bacon.

"I'm sorry you went through that."

I try not to choke on my words when I talk to her about what happened. I don't want to stop her talking. I don't want my niece to feel like she isn't protected.

"He said our family was filled with bad people."

"Every family has their share of bad people. Doesn't mean you can go around hurting children."

"Who's Valentina? Is she your mistress?"

My cheeks turn pink.

"Where did you learn that word?"

I suppose she's old enough to know it, but it doesn't exactly make me comfortable that Tegan would associate me or anyone in the family with mistresses. She's right about her father. If he hadn't spent almost all of his daughter's entire life behind bars, she wouldn't have been around us assholes long enough to know about mistresses and God knows what else. At least she hasn't started saying the f-word. Maybe Evie ought to bring her to church…

"Does it matter?" Tegan fires back. "Who is she? The man talked about Valentina a lot. He said it wasn't her real name and he was the only one who knew who she really was and that you would pay a lot for that information."

That part surely was a misunderstanding because as far as I know, my blackmailer never requested money. This was never about money, always about blood and family and the things that have driven human beings to kill from the beginning of time.

"She's a friend."

"Did he kill her yet?"

I don't like the way she says yet.

"I hope not."

"I figured out where he's keeping her secrets," Tegan says. "I wasn't totally useless."

"Useless?" I growl. "You ought to be useless. You're a child. And don't you for a second think I expected more from you than survival,

Tegan. I'm proud of you for staying strong and I promise, I will never let this person hurt you again."

"You didn't go to the police," she says.

"That's not how our family handles things," I tell her. "When you're older, you'll understand."

"That we're a mob family? I'm not *stupid*, Uncle Aiden."

There's an edge to Tegan's voice that's very new. She's had it since she returned and I want to pretend the changes will go away and that they don't represent something that will forevermore be absent in Rian's little girl.

"I never said you were," I respond. "It would be foolish to think a Murray girl stupid."

Tegan cracks half a smile at that, which brings me the tiniest bit of comfort.

"He's keeping the stuff you want in the poke nose."

"The what?"

"The poke nose."

Fuck. Just when I thought I had something, was dangerously close to a necessary detail, she hits me with this.

"I see."

Tegan shrugs, perhaps sensing my disappointment, but not terribly perturbed by it.

"That's what he said. He put everything at his place in the poke nose."

THEN IT HITS ME. Tegan isn't talking nonsense at all. She's a child and she was undergoing some of the most extreme trauma a child could go through. Through all that, she managed to get me something — something I can use.

"TEGAN, SWEETHEART," I ask her gently. "Do you mean the Poconos?"

Her eyes darken with familiar Murray frustration. "Isn't that what I just said?"

It's not perfect, but that narrows down where we have to look — by a lot.

"Thanks, Tegan."

A phone call interrupts my next order of congratulations.

"What do you want, Darragh?"

"Two things," he says. "I found your girl before dad did."

"Excellent!"

"I haven't given you the bad news yet," Darragh says. "Her place is empty, a bit ransacked. Looks like someone found her before me or dad even could."

"Fuck," I hiss, glancing over at Tegan, who doesn't seem bothered by swearing, not like she would be growing up around a bunch of animals like us. "Is there blood, signs of a struggle? Where the fuck are you?"

"Not too far from you," Darragh says. "DC."

"As in Washington, DC?"

That significantly limits how much time I have. If I can get down there in six hours, a motivated Padraig Murray can get whoever he wants down there in three or four hours. I have to move quickly, and make sure Darragh doesn't do anything stupid that could get us all killed. *For all I know, Valentina might be dead.*

"The one and only. How fast can you get down here?"

"I have Tegan," I murmur into the phone. "I can't just leave."

My niece stares up at me with wide blue eyes, slowly chewing a piece of toast and butter. She doesn't have to say anything.

"Well you can't bring her," Darragh says, stating the obvious.

"Thank you, Darragh."

Aiden

"You're welcome," he says, without the slightest hint that he's absorbing my frustration with him.

I WANT to strangle my brother nearly every time I talk to him. At least he's less frustrating than Rian.

"I'll see you soon," I respond tersely. "Don't leave the city and don't talk to anyone until I get there."

I hang up and Tegan won't look up from her plate.

"You're leaving me," she says.

"I don't want to."

Tegan rolls her eyes. "You sound like my dad."

It would kill Rian to know how much his daughter's voice drips with disdain when she refers to him. There may be healing for them yet, but it won't come soon and leaving Tegan behind will only make it worse.

"You know my friend, Valentina? She's in trouble."

"Why can't Uncle Darry help her?"

Tegan and Darragh have special nicknames for each other. He just isn't responsible enough to be around children — at all.

"Because he needs my help to protect Val."

"Who's going to protect *me*?"

"Aunt Evie. It'll only be for two days."

Tegan raises a skeptical eyebrow. How many times has she heard this before? I can't blame her for not trusting me. Men in my family have been lying to Tegan since she was a little girl and if I'm not back in two days, I'll just add to another list of liars in her life.

We do all this for family, right? That's what all the deceit, lies, and killing I've done my entire life should have been about. But what about Tegan? What about Rian? What about everyone else not covered by Padraig Murray's good graces? If we don't please him exactly the way he likes, look what happens. There's nothing but pure chaos.

I take Tegan's hand, finally getting her to look me in the eye.

"Listen, kid," I tell her with all the seriousness I can muster. "I'll be back for you, okay? I swear. Two days. That's all I need."

"Does the bad man have Valentina?"

"He might," I tell her honestly. "And it's not just him we have to worry about. Your grandfather isn't very happy with her."

Tegan snorts. "He's *never* happy."

She's met him only a handful of times. On account of her parentage, Rian thought it might be best to keep her away from our father unless absolutely necessary. He doesn't have any qualms about hiding his disinterest, so it's no wonder Tegan shows little love for the old man.

Even so, she might be right about her grandfather.

"That may be so," I answer neutrally. "But he's your grandfather and he's terribly important to the family."

"The bad man says he's a killer."

I don't want to deny the truth, but how dare the man who kidnapped a little girl criticize anyone in our family. My father might be cruel, he might be sour and he's definitely racist, but he would never harm a child the way Owen hurt Tegan.

"Listen, Tegan. I just need you to trust me and promise that you'll be good to Aunt Evie. I'll be back soon and once I'm back, everything will be okay."

Tegan's wide blue eyes brim with doubt and then shimmer with tears.

"I don't want you to go."

My heart shatters as I look at her. I want to look away, but I know I have to be the brave one in this situation. I have to be strong, calm and intelligent so my niece has someone to look up to.

"I'll be back, Tegan Murray. I promise."

I kiss her hand, sealing my promise to the little girl that nothing will ever happen to her again. I hope I can keep that promise.

"Promise you won't get yourself killed or thrown in jail," she adds for emphasis, showing perhaps too much understanding of our way of life.

"I promise that, too."

"Good," she says. "Are you gonna kill the bad man?"

"No," I tell her. "We'll let the law decide what happens to him."

I'm lying, of course, but there's no way in hell I'm going to tell a child my burgeoning murder plot. I have a fantasy in my head of how it will play out, a vision of how *Owen*, this alleged brother of mine, will meet his end.

I TAKE Tegan to Evie's house shortly after breakfast with very little explanation. Tegan doesn't talk the entire way over and she screams bloody murder when she has to let go of me and allow me to drive away.

I still have the wet patch from her tears on my shirt and I break down myself once I'm an hour out of Boston, allowing a few tears to fall before pulling myself together. I love my niece and I'll miss her. If I'm not there to protect her, I worry about what will happen. I was the first person she held after her rescue. She clings to me because I remind her of Rian and I have to remind myself that's who she really wants – her father.

The first place we need to go is the house in the Poconos. After sifting through everything in the place we found Tegan, Darragh deduces this blackmailer of ours keeps his documents in an isolated safehouse in the Pocono mountains. He refuses to leave the city, but he gives me an address with no guarantee.

I want to go to Val's place first, but I can't deny the potentially compelling evidence we might find if we go to the safehouse in the Poconos. I want Darragh to give me more than suspicions and circum-stantial evidence dragged out of the rubble, but he asks me to trust Saint Patrick, and that's the end of that.

I ask him to come with me one more time at the end of our phone call, but he tells me to take Callum. My younger brother Callum isn't a bad companion for road trips, but he doesn't keep me as light-hearted as Darragh does. I don't have much of a choice. We prepare ourselves for the trip and keep researching potential houses in the mountains until we narrow down the most likely address. Darragh turns up details about the owner. It's an LLC with the initials O.A. That's enough evidence for me.

THE HOUSE SITS at the end of a long private drive. I don't know what we will find here, but the house appears well-kept from the outside.

Darragh refuses to leave the city, so I take Callum down to Pennsylvania. Odhran is the only brother I have younger than Callum. He's a bit of a fuck, but he loads the car with weapons and doesn't bitch when I play Lynyrd Skynyrd the entire ride down to Pennsylvania. Callum loads his pistol as he looks at the house.

"Rich fuck, isn't he?"

"Yeah."

"I didn't tell dad I went with you. In case you were wondering."

"I wasn't."

Callum sighs. "I love you, Aiden, but why are you doing all this for a strange woman?"

"She's not strange to me."

"Because you made a sex tape?"

"It's more than that, Callum. Now shut up."

Callum talks too much, but at least he can follow orders. Every young Murray boy can follow orders.

There are no cars, no signs that the house is occupied, but there could still be an alarm system. Callum checks the house as I load my weapon and help him search. There's nothing we can find from the outside, so we try the front door. It doesn't budge.

"Are you going to shoot it open?" Callum asks.

"That would be the most efficient way."

"I can pick locks, dick," Callum says. "Move out of the way."

I have my doubts about Callum's lock picking skills, but I move out of the way. He presses his ear to the lock and removes a small black leather kit from his jacket breast pocket. My younger brother defeats my skepticism and pushes the door open.

I hear a loud whooshing noise and push Callum out of the way. I feel a nick on the side of my shoulder and feel a sharp sting as I get him out of the way and we both watch the crossbow embed itself in the ground in front of the bastard's house.

"Holy fucking Christ!" Callum swears. "Fuck! What the fuck!"

"Booby trap, Callum. Relax."

"Relax?!"

I'm the one bleeding, but Callum rakes his fingers through his hair and paces as he turns bright red.

"Fuck, Aiden! Look at your shoulder!" Callum yells. Bright red blood soaks through my shirt. It hurts, but I can't worry about a little blood now. We have to go in and hope this bastard doesn't have any more little traps like this one. The crossbow was a nice touch, but that means he knows we're onto him, or he wants us to chase him… or something.

"I'm fine. We have to go in there," I growl.

Callum ought to have a stronger stomach. He's red as a tomato and then he walks over to the arrow and pulls the broad head arrow out of the ground. *Fuck.* If that thing had pierced either one of us completely, we would be dead or at least significantly slowed down.

"What if there are more traps?" Callum asks. "We should call someone."

My brother's an idiot. What's the point of a secret trip to the Poconos if we get more Murrays or more people potentially loyal to my father involved. He'll find out about this eventually, but I'll worry about that part later.

"And wait four hours for someone we barely trust to show up here? No thanks," I growl. "Pull yourself together, Callum. We need to search this place."

"What happens if I get hit by an arrow, huh? What happens if I bleed out and die?"

"Fucking hell, Callum. Calm down. This is important."

"To you," Callum says.

"If you don't want to be here, why didn't you run to dad?"

Callum rolls his eyes. "Fuck, Aiden. Don't be so sensitive. I'll help. I swear."

Chapter Thirteen

"Why?"

"Because we're brothers. And we both know dad's a cunt."

I grunt. There's nothing I can say to that because it's the truth. Dad's a cunt, but it's not Callum's place to say that. It's not his place to disobey.

"You aren't going to disagree?" Callum says. "The golden child finally turns away from the light."

"Shut up, Callum. We all know dad might have his flaws but... he loves his sons. He loves our family."

"He loves you, but he doesn't love that woman you want to save. We both know he'll kill her."

"Not if I have anything to do with it."

Callum snickers. "You are such a fucking square, Aiden. If it were me, I would take the woman on the back of my bike and fuck off to Florida."

Florida sounds nice. Lots of sunshine. Great food. But I have responsibilities here.

"I'm forty-years-old, Callum. I can't fuck off to Florida. And anyway, dad would find us and he'd kill us both. Now let's get this shit over with."

Callum is young, filled with foolish ideas and youthful notions. I can't let him influence me. Taking Val to Florida would be just as dangerous as leaving her here. It's in my best interests to get her what she needs and send her off to England, Canada, or somewhere very fucking far away from here.

IT ONLY TAKES me thirty minutes to find the documents. But there's another problem. In the back bedroom of Owen's home, there's a safe screwed into a walk-in closet and no signs of a key. I call Callum in and he grins.

"Light work, Aiden. Light work."

All I can hope is that it isn't another trap. Callum gets to work on the safe and just when I'm ready to give up hope, after twenty minutes of sticking his tools into the tiny keyhole, he finally cracks it open. *Fuck yes.* Callum might be more useful than I thought.

Once the safe opens, there are no more traps, just brown envelopes that spill onto the floor.

"Fuck's sake. What's all this shit?" Callum says."How the fuck would I know, Callum?" I growl. "Bloody idiot."

"We have to go through all this shit. Put your gun down, brother. We've got work to do."

Chapter Fourteen
Valentina

I wake up in complete darkness. I'm not in a box again, but that doesn't make me feel any better. I'm not tied up, but I can't see anything and my head feels uncomfortably foggy. Not again. This can't be happening again. It hits me that Aiden isn't coming. He won't be coming and I can't let that stop me from trying to survive.

He might not be here, but he would want me to survive. Aiden was nothing if not a fighter and he would want me to fight.

My eyes finally adjust to the darkness and I make out what I think is the vague outline of a door. I crawl towards it and press my hand against it. It's metal. I run my hands up the length of the door and then I find it — a handle.

It's locked, Valentina. Obviously.

I try the handle and it's locked. But there still has to be a way out. I knock on the door, hoping that Owen will respond. There's nothing.

"HELP!" I scream. "Is there anyone out there?"

There's nothing, obviously. But I'm not ready to give up.

The room is big enough for me to scramble around in, a 10 x 9 prison cell by my estimation with a small cot in the corner. There's nowhere for me to go to the bathroom.

I keep touching up the wall and then the door. The door might be metal, but the walls feel hollow when I tap them. I don't know a lot about housing materials, but I wonder if I could put a hole through that wall. I'm in a house somewhere and even if it's crazy… I wonder if I can break through the walls. I slam my body into the wall and make a small dent. I'm not the strongest woman, but if I keep working at it… maybe.

After half an hour, I can feel my shoulder throbbing. My shoulder and the entire right half of my body hurts like hell from slamming my elbow and as much of my body as possible into the wall.

There's a tiny hole in the wall, but it's not exactly *Shawshank Redemption*. (That was, ironically, Pulsifer's favorite movie.) Using my less dominant arm, I poke my finger through the hole in the drywall and try pulling more of it apart.

But I'm tired… I'm so tired and even if I've been trying to push it out of my mind, I'm hungry.

Do you want to escape or not, Valentina?

I REACH my hand into the hole and feel something smooth and cold, like a pipe or something. I don't know what to do about that, but I know I have to keep pushing this hole open before Owen comes back, wherever the hell he is. He must've had me in here for hours, maybe even days, although I can't really tell.

It doesn't matter how long he's held me here. What matters is that I have to get out of here. I push my arm through the hole and find the other side of the drywall. I have to make another hole. *Please help me, God.*

My arms hurt too much to push and create another hole, but I have to try. It's dark, I'm in pain, but I've tasted freedom and I'll never give it up. It takes me another few hours. My clothes are dripping in sweat and sticking to my body. There's only a small hole to the other side but through that little hole… *there's light.*

. . .

I HEAR FOOTSTEPS OVERHEAD. I haven't exactly been quiet, but if Owen has been home (or wherever this place is) the entire time, he would have come down earlier. I take my shirt off and plug the hole so there's no light filtering in and then I'm so quiet that I can hear my own breathing. The footsteps sound heavy.

I push my back against the wall of my prison. The footsteps are getting closer. I don't want to be afraid, but my hands are sweaty and I can't stop my heart from racing. The footsteps sound only feet away from the door. My throat tightens and I'm too terrified to scream.

You're close, Val. Maybe he won't open the door.

I'M NOT THAT LUCKY. There are a lot of loud noises, thumping sounds and then metal crunching. The wheezing metal sound hurts my ears. The door opens and the light that pours through blinds me. Tears fill my eyes and I can't see the figure in the door. I throw my hands over my eyes to block out the light because I've been in darkness too long.

"Tyesha Valentina Baker. By God, woman… I've tracked you to the ends of the fucking earth."

It's not Owen.

IT'S AIDEN. He's here and I'm too blind to see him, too tired to move. Despite my blindness and tears from the light streaming down my face. I stumble forward, nearly losing my balance as my knees collapse from exhaustion. I push myself to my feet once more.

Once I'm on my feet, I realize how weak and tired I am. My knees buckle and I fall forward, only to fall into Aiden Murray's chest.

He grunts and then his arms wrap around me instantly.

I gasp for breath as he squeezes me so tightly that I can't get any air in. He tightens his hold on me and then kisses the top of my head.

"You're alive. Damn it, woman. You're really alive."

"Why did you call me that? Tyesha?"

Aiden kisses my forehead again. I still have my eyes squeezed shut, but I slowly wipe the tears away on his shirt and try to open my eyes. The first thing I see once my eyes flutter open are Aiden's blue eyes gazing at me and his dark brows completely furrowed, but his eyes brimming with emotions that I've never seen from Aiden before. Aiden's covered in blood. I want to ask questions and I definitely want to know if he's hurt, but he starts talking before I can say anything.

"I'll explain," he murmurs. "I need to get you out of here."

I throw my arms around Aiden and he loosens his grip on me, only to put his finger under my chin and draw my face to his. I'm slick with sweat, absolutely disgusting, and horrified by the thought of Aiden touching me in this condition, but he doesn't seem to care.

He kisses me like we've never kissed before. His lips taste salty, deliciously like Aiden and this is the most romantic kiss I've ever had in my entire life. His lips seal against mine. I kiss him back and then Aiden's tongue slips into my mouth and I can taste the metal from his piercing. I press my hands against his chest. He's really here and I almost can't believe it.

Aiden pulls away and sighs. "Fuck, woman. It feels so good to kiss you again. Now let's get out of here. My brother's waiting outside with my car. Can you walk?"

"Yes."

"Good," he says, sliding his hand into mine. "I could stand here and kiss you all day. But we need to move."

My body hurts, but I find enough strength to follow Aiden upstairs. My eyes are still adjusting to the light, but I hold onto Aiden, stick close to him and walk through a maze of metal doors to a staircase.

"How did you find me?"

"Don't worry about it," Aiden says. "We don't have much time. But I promise you, Val... I will find the man who took you and Tegan, and I'm going to kill him."

The severity of his tone sends a chill through me. I know exactly who Aiden is, but hearing him talk so calmly about murder still isn't easy for me. *I know he's no angel, but I don't want him to become a monster for me.*

"Did you find Tegan?" I ask him. My voice is raspy again and weak, but I'm slowly finding strength. I don't know what that man could have done with that little girl, but I saw no signs of her during my captivity.

"She's safe. She's with family," Aiden says, running his thumb along the inside of my palm. Good. Maybe everything will be okay.

I MEET AIDEN'S BROTHER, a quiet man closer to my age than Aiden's with half as many tattoos as his brother and fierce scowl. He doesn't say more than a couple words to me, which I don't mind. I fall asleep in the back of the car, holding onto my sore arm.

I don't know where we are when the car stops. Aiden's brother gets out of the car and walks ahead to the door of a small house with a blue roof. Aiden drives off, leaving him behind. I don't ask any more questions until we stop again.

This time, I definitely know where we are. Partially. *Holiday Inn Express.*

"We'll stay here for tonight," Aiden says. "Tomorrow, I'm taking you to Canada."

"What?"

Now I'm wide awake, but Aiden doesn't answer my question. He exits the car and then holds the door open for me.

"I don't want to go to Canada," I say firmly, standing outside Aiden's car and folding my arms. My lower lids are puffed up, making it difficult to give him a fierce look, but Aiden's lip just purses into a thin line in response.

"I don't care."

"I have a life in Washington, DC. An apartment. I have *rent* and a job."

Aiden scowls. "Fuck, Valentina. I don't want to discuss this right now. Let's go to the hotel room and then we'll talk."

"I'm not leaving until you promise you'll listen."

Aiden rolls his eyes in obvious and visible frustration. "Yes. I promise."

He doesn't sound convincing, but I take his word for it and follow him into the hotel. Aiden brings me to the room and it's luxurious, with a large king bed. My throat tightens. It's been weeks since we've been together and now we're going to share a bed. I can't stop looking at the bed, but Aiden obviously has other things on his mind. He has a small duffel bag unpacked with items strewn everywhere including firearms, to my dismay.

He strides over to the small hotel table and grabs a brown envelope, walking over to me and setting it in my hand.

"Here," he says. "This is everything you need. And that name I called you... it's yours."

"Everything I need?"

"This is who you are, Val. Tyesha Valentina Baker. Born to a woman named Kesha Baker and a father, Tychon Baker, in New Orleans. When you were six years old, Governor Ezekiel Pulsifer legally adopted you and then... there are more documents in there. I shouldn't tell you everything. It's yours to know. Your history. Your family. Your past."

Aiden doesn't take his eyes off me as I slide my finger under the opening of the envelope. I thought I could handle this. I thought when I finally got the thing I've always wanted that it would be easy for me to look at it, to absorb it and to learn about the life I once had. The person I was before the Governor.

"He abused you for your whole life," Aiden whispers, his eyes still fixed on me. "I'm so sorry for what you've gone through Valentina."

My eyes flutter to his and Aiden runs his tongue nervously over his lips.

"I know," I tell him.

"I wish you were safe with me."

"I am."

"Bullshit," Aiden snaps, the tenor of his voice changing immediately. "If you were truly safe with me, none of this would have happened. And that *bastard* hurt two people I love."

"You didn't make him do that. And you rescued Tegan. You rescued me... Not like I needed it."

Aiden scowls. "You didn't need it? I found you in a basement and you're thinner and… fuck, Valentina… Do you know how much I worried about you?"

I don't get the envelope all the way open before Aiden shows me how much he misses me. He grabs my cheeks and draws me against his chest. He's so warm that I don't want to leave Aiden's firm embrace. I thought about him during my work weeks, and hated myself for wanting him when he clearly wanted nothing to do with me. But now… he's here with me, his large, masculine hands perfectly rough against my face.

He narrows his gaze and runs his tongue slowly over his lips, a flash of gold popping out of his mouth behind perfect, ivory teeth. I want to kiss him again, but I'm afraid of lunging for him, afraid of showing him just how badly I want to touch and hold him.

"I don't know," I whisper and he draws me in again, kissing me deeply. I run my tongue over the golden knob in Aiden's mouth, tasting his lips, his tongue, the tinge of metal from the gold. His chest heaves as I kiss him back. I enjoy touching his chest, tasting his lips and there's absolutely no part of me that wants to break away from the kiss.

I need to breathe, so I move away from Aiden and he moves his hands to my hips.

"I love you," he murmurs. "I love you more than I've ever loved another person and that makes this very fucking dangerous."

I don't care. I kiss him again and Aiden lets me. His hands curl around my dress and he draws my hips against his, so I don't just feel the warmth of his chest, but his hardness growing in his trousers. Heat from his hips and mine send a shudder of desire through me. I've never *wanted* sex before Aiden, but now I crave it and I desperately feel my lack of him from the past few weeks as he holds me.

He bends his lips to kiss my neck and a needy whimper escapes my lips. Aiden chuckles.

"I love you, Valentina," he murmurs. "But before I show you just how much, you need to look in that envelope. It's your past. Your future. Not mine."

"I don't want this to stop," I whisper back, my eyes fluttering closed with a dart of shame surging through me as I cling needily to Aiden's bloodied white t-shirt. He doesn't appear to mind how my fingers sink into his t-shirt like I'm a capuchin holding a treasured piece of fruit.

"Neither do I," he says back. "But it's time I do the right thing with you."

I don't appreciate the insinuation that what we did before was wrong. We were both desperate, craving answers, safety, freedom and in Aiden's case, there was a little girl involved.

"You never hurt me, Aiden," I tell him.

"But that still won't make you love me," he says softly, pushing some of my hair out of my face, but not before twirling one of my black coils around his index finger. The gentle tug on my hair sends another shiver of excitement through me. How could he say that?

"Of course I love you," I whisper. "But... I've never said those words before. I've never said them to another person and I've certainly never said them to a man."

His grasp on me tightens and I sense him standing between two choices, wanting me and wanting to let me go so I can see what's in the envelope. His hands unclench slowly and he drops his gaze.

"Look," he says. "You deserve to know the truth."

I take the envelope again and open it, desperate to know the details of who I really am, where I came from and who I was meant to be.

AIDEN TRIES to explain the documents once I've looked through everything. I have my birth certificate now, which prints my true name. I can't imagine anyone calling me anything other than Valentina, but Tyesha's a very pretty name. I was originally born in New Orleans, there aren't many details about what happened after that, but I can fill in the rest. I disappeared into the home of a dangerous man who had no intentions of "adopting me" but every intention of using me for his own sick purposes.

I keep flipping through the documents until I reach another signifi-cant conclusion...

My parents are still alive.

That's the hardest part of the sheets of paper to truly contend with. Two people walking around with beating hearts who either gave me up or lost me all those years ago. As I flip through the adoption papers, Aiden moves to my position on the bed and sits next to me, throwing his bulky arm around my shoulder. I lean into him, indulging in Aiden's warmth.

"What are you thinking?" He murmurs, planting a kiss on my shoulder.

There are too many thoughts and ideas swirling around my head for me to think of much. I just want to lean into Aiden's shoulders and cry. I'm not one for crying, but hot tears stream down my cheeks and Aiden wraps his arms around me. The tears just come. I'm a person. I'm not an object. I'm not a possession. I'm not a toy for men to pass around.

I'm Tyesha Valentina Baker and somewhere out there, I have a family. A real family.

Aiden holds me until I stop crying and shaking. I cling to his shirt, a pang of guilt passing through me as I see how wet I've made his t-shirt.

"I'm sorry," he whispers. "I'm so so sorry."

He doesn't say what he's apologizing for, but I don't care. I hold onto him and then gaze up into Aiden's eyes, which aren't just fiercely blue, but blue in general.

"I can't take you to bed when you're like this," he murmurs, pressing his thumb under my eye and wiping away tears.

"I'm fine," I whisper. "And you're warm…"

"So are you," Aiden says. "I want to help you, Valentina. But I need you to trust me."

"Of course I trust you."

Aiden has given me the greatest gift any person could.

"I love you," he repeats. "No matter what happens, never forget that I love you."

"I won't."

"Good," he says, tilting my chin towards his and giving me a rare

Aiden smile. I love his smile. It lightens up his face and makes him look more boyish with his cropped blond hair and those eyes... I can't stop staring into those eyes once he fixes them on me.

"Can I kiss you properly?" He murmurs. "Or have I fucked everything up between us?"

"You haven't."

"Good," Aiden says, and then he kisses me again. I've spent ages craving his lips and this time, I don't want to be shy. I want him. I love him. Aiden has given me hope that I won't spend the rest of my life as a man's prisoner. I press my fingers to his chest and push him backwards onto the bed.

He lets out a satisfied grunt and a grin spreads across his face. I straddle him and lean forward, letting my hair cascade wildly over him as I grab his cheeks and kiss him. His hands move eagerly to my hips and then he cups my ass as he draws me against him. He grunts as I shift my hips and place my heat right over the hardness straining through his trousers.

"I love you," he says, sliding his hands up my spine and pulling me close for another kiss. We kiss until my lips feel red and swollen. Aiden doesn't push me for more. I'm the one who reaches between his legs and grab his cock through his cobalt jeans. He grunts as I wrap my fingers around the thickness straining to get free.

We need no words as we strip each other's clothes off. We're messy and clumsy as we get naked, but I push Aiden onto his back once we're both unclothed and run my fingernails gently over the spread of tattoos on his broad chest. Aiden chuckles.

"I love how your hands feel, Val," he says, a happy little smile on his face. "I spent so long dreaming of this."

"Then hush," I whisper. "Let me kiss you..."

Aiden grunts and lets me spread kisses all over his body. I don't know what any of the black ink on his chest means, except for the Celtic knot, but I allow myself to touch his tattoos. I kiss every inch of Aiden's skin that I can. He turns pink as I touch him and his cock stiffens as my lips draw closer to the thatch of hair surrounding his impressive staff.

He grunts as I grab hold of the base of his staff and tighten my grasp around his delicious dusky rose cock. I kiss around the base, letting soft patches of light brown fur tickle my lips as I kiss him. Aiden grunts and thrusts his hips upward, eager for me to do more than kiss him.

Patience, you ruffian…

I kiss him until the head of his cock darkens to a scarlet shade and clear gooey fluid oozes from the tip. He's ready…

My tongue juts out of my mouth and I gently slide it over the oozing tip of his cock.

"Fuck," he grunts, his eyes slamming shut as I take the head of his perfect cock between my lips. I tighten my lips around his cock, easing his girth into my mouth. Aiden has a ridiculously thick cock and my mouth has to stretch awkwardly to accommodate him at first. He soothingly strokes my head.

"Gentle," he whispers. "You're always so gentle."

His softness encourages me to take him deeper into my mouth. I brace myself for the intrusion of Aiden's thick member. Veins bulge from the sides as I take him deeper. He grunts as I take half his length into my mouth. *More. I want more of him.* I hold on tightly to the base of his dick as I take him into my mouth. Aiden thrusts his hips up again and I work up a rhythm of tight suction around his shaft.

His skin exudes every possible shade of pink as I ease him into my mouth, teasing him with my tongue sliding along his shaft. I might not have all the perfect, pretty words to tell Aiden Murray how I feel, but I can indulge in this physical expression of my pleasure with ease.

He groans as I take him deeper. After a few minutes of pleasuring his cock with my lips and tongue, I feel the powerful invading muscle stiffen with his desire. I don't want him to finish in my mouth. I want to feel him between my legs. Making love to him has always been different and this time, I tell myself that it will be special.

What we have *is* special. It's love, right? And there's nothing more powerful, more divine than love. That's the theme of my favorite book, the emotional state that makes life worth living. Love is something I never thought I would have in the governor's mansion, or when my buyers twisted my body into an uncomfortable knot and shipped me in a box across the country.

I quickly withdraw my lips from Aiden's member and watch the red flush fade from his face. His hand darts out and quickly wraps around my wrist.

"You aren't going anywhere," he growls in his gruff, Bostonian accent. His voice makes my heart skip a beat and my pussy throbs. My nipples harden, stiff from my own arousal. Heat and moisture pool between my thighs as my desire dampens my thick mound of black, coiled pubic hair.

I had no plans of leaving Aiden or myself unsatisfied, but he sits up, continuing to grip my palms as he pulls me against his chest for a deep kiss.

"I love feeling your mouth on my cock," he murmurs, burying his nose into my neck after kissing me. "I know it's wrong to want someone of your color. At least... it's what I was taught. But I can't help thinking you have the most beautiful lips I've ever seen."

The slickness between my thighs turns into a pool. Aiden might've just said he loves me, but to refer to me as *beautiful* was beyond my expectations. He grew up in a world where women like me weren't just taboo, but considered filthy and beneath him, but there's no misinterpreting the expression on his face. Not just lust, but pure, unadulterated love and desire.

I touch his face with my free hand. Aiden grins and kisses me.

"You're very pretty," he says. "And... I don't know how the fuck I let you get into my head."

He guides me to a position over him again, allowing me to straddle him and feel the warmth from our body hair grazing each other. He's so warm to the touch that I feel like I'm melting into him. He guides my hips so I'm hovering over his cock and he slides the tip down the length of my slit, teasing my clit and then finding my opening as he reaches my entrance. My elastic entrance widens as Aiden's cock attempts to push through.

I bite down hard on my lower lip, remembering how hard it has always been to get his massive cock between my legs. I can't tell if it's his size or mine that's the problem. I don't care. Balancing with my palms on his muscular chest, I allow him to guide the head of his cock to my opening again. His first thrust pushes the dusky rose head past my entrance. A strangled moan escapes. Aiden grunts and pushes deeper, unwilling to have more patience than he's demonstrated so far. My nails sink into his chest as my entrance stretches to accommodate Aiden's shaft.

He pushes his hips up and I sink onto his cock, ignoring the initial burst of pain to focus on the pleasure of Aiden's impressive member stretching me wide. I bite so hard on my lower lip that it nearly bleeds, but once I have Aiden inside me, it's pure bliss.

"Mmm," he groans as our hips nestle together and I have the full length of his cock between my legs.

"I want you," I whisper. "I want you to..."

I can't bring myself to finish my sentence, because the pleasure surging through me makes producing any sensible noises impossible. I rock my hips and move them slowly to allow myself time to adjust to Aiden's invasive dick.

He holds my hips gently, allowing me to control the pace. We don't stop staring into each other's eyes. We move together until pleasure builds in me so greatly that I can't control myself any longer. I lean forward to kiss him as our hips move in unison and a burst of euphoria spreads through me as I cum.

I moan and lean against him, my stiff nipples grazing Aidens bare chest as my first climax of the night shakes me to my core. I tremble and rock my hips against his as I cum and the orgasm just doesn't seem to stop.

Aiden grunts and pulls out of me, easily flipping me over onto all fours so he can enter me from behind. I arch my back, allowing him access to my entrance. Aiden's hands cup my ass as he spreads me apart and finds my entrance again with his dripping cock.

"I want to cum inside you, Val," he grunts. "Even if it's a bad fucking idea."

He doesn't explain, nor does he stop himself from sliding his entire length inside me with one quick thrust. I cry out from the initial pain, but my hips take control as I rock back against him. He grips the smallest part of my waist, grunting as he takes me with quick, urgent thrusts.

"Fuck, you feel good," he grunts. "I love your tight black pussy..."

His racially tinged language sends a gush between my legs. There's a strange and possibly inappropriate sense of satisfaction from my physical appearance being the very thing that provokes Aiden's untamed arousal.

If sex is what it takes for him to see the foolishness of his bigotry... so be it.

He gently wraps my hair around his hands and tilts my head back so he can gain better access to my wetness. We grunt and moan together until I feel Aiden's cock stiffening between my legs and I know exactly what will come next.

"Oh God," he grunts. "I'm gonna cum..."

I can't respond because my own climax surges through me and I feel my tightness clenching around Aiden's dick, which pushes him over the edge. Our bodies tighten together and Aiden releases *deep* between my legs. There's no control to his thrusting or his climax this time, but I don't mind. A gush of cum erupts from Aiden's cock and I feel the heat rising between my legs. Thick pumps of Aiden's cum rush into my tightness and I moan as I feel even more of his seed between my legs.

He withdraws and his cum gushes out of me like a fountain. White liquid spills down my leg and the warmth spreads goosebumps over my body. Aiden's body hulks over mine and he kisses the back of my neck and then my cheek.

"You look fucking great with my cum spilling out of you," he grunts. "It fucking hurts that... Fuck... never mind."

Aiden drags me against him, uncaring that there's cum spilling between my legs. He kisses me and I rest my head against his chest. Our hearts are still beating quickly, still euphoric from the pleasure of joining with someone who you desperately, desperately want.

"Will you remember that I love you?" He murmurs.

"Yes."

"Always," he whispers. "Whenever you have doubts, whenever you want to question me, remember that you have a piece of my heart that no one else has, Valentina. And that will never change."

"Okay."

He kisses my forehead and brings me a glass of water from the hotel sink. We snuggle together after I drink it and I quickly fall asleep in Aiden Murray's arms, utterly content.

Chapter Fifteen
Aiden

"Promise me she'll be safe," I tell Callum, giving him the most threatening gaze I can muster. He glances at Valentina, who's fast asleep on the bed, and purses his lips disapprovingly. It's late at night, but nearly morning. It feels like there are screwdrivers boring into the back of my eyes I'm so fucking tired. I could use some Dunkin' coffee...

"You drugged her?" My brother asks, raising his brows. *Fuck, I don't need his judgment right now.*

"I'm doing the right thing."

"I promise," Callum says. "After this, my debt to you is paid, Aiden."

"I understand."

"I won't tell dad, I won't tell Darragh... Where she is will die with me."

"Good."

I won't even know where she is and it'll hurt like hell not knowing what she's doing everyday. It'll hurt like hell knowing I'll never hear the piano in my home again because I certainly won't play it. It'll hurt like hell seeing Tegan's face and always remembering Valentina... the only woman I will ever love.

Callum glances over at her again. "Are you sure, Aiden? Because once she's gone... she's gone."

"Yes. And you'll tell dad that you followed his orders. Bring him proof. Make it convincing."

Callum nods and thrusts his hands into his pockets. My brother owes me a favor and after ten years, I've finally come to collect. A life for a life. I protected his secret for a decade and now, I need him to protect mine. *She's more than a secret.*

"You'd better get out of here. Evie says Tegan can't stop talking about you."

"Yes. Thanks."

"And dad... he's not ready to see you yet. He's gonna let you finish the project with Sammy but after that..."

"I'm not going to see dad," I lie to him. I don't want him giving dad the head's up or being a guilty party to my actions. "I'm going to find our half-brother. And then, I'm gonna put a bullet in his fucking head."

BEFORE YOU PUT a bullet in a man's head, you need permission from the boss. My father hasn't spoken to me since our fight outside the house, but he's at Mulligan's since it's the last Red Sox game before the playoffs. But I have a plan. Better than a plan, I have what was used on me — blackmail.

I'm not enough of a dumb fuck to blackmail my father outright. But I can use this information to make him an offer: I clean up your mess and you let me go.

I don't know where the fuck I'm going to go, but it's better if I get the fuck outta Boston, stay the fuck away from Valentina and just... *move on.*

I tried my hand at love and I nearly lost her because of my selfishness. Because I just had to have her.

Before I visit dad, I pick up Tegan from Evie's before taking her to my mother's house. She's a very Catholic grandmother and Tegan doesn't exactly enjoy all the prayers and talk about Mary from Mrs.

Murray, but I give her a stern warning to behave herself before drop-ping her off in a cute white tartan skirt with her hair in little pigtails that none of my siblings will believe I did myself.

I can't leave Tegan. I don't want to leave Tegan. She'll never forgive me if I do, but my home and my life isn't for her. I'll never be a father. I'll never be a lover. I have to accept that. I chose my life when I chose my tattoos. I've killed seventeen times. I've sworn a vow to keep my bloodline pure and I've broken it.

Getting older should have made making the right choices easier, but I've fucked it all up with selfishness and now I have to pay with blood. That's our way. Saving Valentina was my last act against my father's wishes. I can't risk anyone else getting hurt.

I CAN SEE my father sitting at the bar illuminated by the warm light spilling through the small window of the pub. He appears alone, but a quick scan of the room as I push the door open proves nothing could be further from the truth. Two of my cousins sit in a booth and my brother Odhran, despite being well below the drinking age, plays pool with our Uncle Tommy in the back of the bar, an illegal pistol in a holster on his hip.

Illegal. Half the fucking Boston Police Department is in Padraig's back pocket. I slide into the bar next to him and he barely looks up at me, acknowledging me with a grunt.

"Guinness," I call out to Finnegan, who nods and proceeds to pour me a pint on tap.

"What do you want, Aiden?" My father mutters, glancing back up at the Sox game. His lip curls as the black man in the State Farm ad plops onto a couch and my father reluctantly turns his gaze to me. I have his eyes, I've always known, and I have his coldness, I've been told. We've always been close, but this will rip us apart. This could rip our family apart.

"To talk."

"Then talk. I don't have anything to say to you."

He finishes his beer and snaps his fingers. My pint arrives along with his and he guzzles half of his as I watch condensation drip down the side of my drink. Alcohol could make this easier, but if I start drinking, I'll be a wreck by the end of the night and that'll end even worse than I could possibly think.

"Fine. Then don't say anything. I don't have anything to say to you either. You can just–

"I know what Callum did."

My heart pounds as I do my best to sound detached.

"Don't expect sympathy from me," he says, as if I would suffer any illusions that he could have an ounce of sympathy in him after everything. No father, I know exactly what sort of man you are. I don't even expect him to ask after Tegan.

"I don't need sympathy. I need permission to work again."

He snorts and drinks more beer. "On what? You already have a job. Putting up buildings, giving me 15%. We don't have a relationship anymore, Aiden."

"You will always be my father, even if you hate me. Even if you have me killed."

If he were going to have me killed, he would've.

"You're a man, Aiden. I understand we have our indiscretions, but you betrayed the purpose of our family. Our purity. Our goodness."

Purity. Goodness. I've heard those words a thousand fucking times and I wonder if they mean anything. It doesn't matter. Meanings don't matter. I just need to punish the man who hurt Valentina, and then disappear.

"I understand," I tell him. "I have my indiscretions and you have yours."

"Hmph."

"An Italian woman," I mutter in a low voice. "Nina Aurelio. She had a son, you know. *My brother.*"

He stiffens, but he tries not to react, because he doesn't want to confirm what I already know. Not all of his mistresses were sweet little blonde girls with a hope of siring a Murray bastard and having enough money to swim in for the rest of their lives. This Sicilian woman ought to have been lower than dirt to him. The Sicilians are the worst of the Italians — vicious, brutal, with no concern for anything except money, prostitutes and the thrill of murder.

"What do you want, Aiden? Because I'm growing tired of you of all people pushing up against my rules," he mutters, tilting his hand and tapping his large gold Celtic knot ring against the bar.

"I want to solve both of our problems and make things right."

"Kill the bastard?"

"Yes."

My father smirks. I hate how much I see my face in his right then. I've never loathed him before, but I can't help it. It's his fault Val's gone. It's his fault I'm in this fucking position and everything that happened to Tegan happened because of him.

I can't imagine hurting my blood, but I want to be very fucking far away from him now.

"Okay," he says. "Where is he? Not Boston?"

"I don't know where the fuck he is. I'll head out after him and... when it's done, I won't come back."

"What about the business?"

"I'll handle it," I reply, although I don't know if it's the truth. "I'll come back and if you need work done... I'll be there." *This could be a lie, but it feels right to say. I want him to think I'm loyal, even if I don't know the point of it any more.*

He chuckles. "I don't know if I believe you've learned your lesson. You're just as stubborn as I am."

"There's no trick, Pa. I want to be done with this dirty business. It's torn our family apart. Callum won't talk to me. Odhran..."

I glance over at my youngest brother, who hasn't acknowledged me since I walked in. My father's orders most likely. And Odhran was always a little shit of a mama's boy anyway.

"Yes," my father interrupts. "It would be best if you left. Best if you eliminated my problem and even better if you never returned."

"What about ma? What about Tegan?"

What about the fact that I'm the only one who can wrangle my unruly fucking siblings?

"I don't give a fuck," he says. "You take care of this, and you will be forgiven. But I don't want you back until I order you back, Aiden."

"Sure," I mutter. "Sure. I can do that."

I have to make myself believe it. I set down a twenty dollar bill for the drink and leave the bar without saying a word to Odhran. He doesn't look up from the pool game either. If my father wants me to disappear, I will. But I won't leave without saying goodbye to my niece.

TEGAN DOESN'T WANT me to leave. I don't tell her how long I'll be gone and I promise I'll be back, even if I don't have a right to make a promise to her that I can't keep.

My mother pulls me aside into her kitchen after I've spoken with Tegan, who's now sitting in front of the television trying to cover up the sound of her tears with the TV volume.

"You're going away for a long time, aren't you?" She asks, her eyes swimming. Ma's eyes are always brimming with tears. She's been this way since I was a child. The only thing that helps her is wine or Xanax, although I don't know how much help either provide.

"Ma, I'll be back. I swear."

"I'm not a fool," she says. "I know you and your father…"

She whimpers and dabs her eyes with the sleeve of her navy cashmere sweater.

"Take care of Tegan, will you?" I tell her. "I don't want to leave, ma, but I have to make things right for the family."

"I begged your father not to be so angry with you," she says. "I don't want you to leave the city."

"I'll be back."

"When?"

"I can't tell you."

"What about that woman?" She asks, continuing to wipe tears away.

"She's dead," I say quickly. "And I can't stay here where it all happened."

She wraps her arms around me. It's been ages since I've had a proper hug from my mother, and I feel strangely like a child as she holds onto me. I don't want her to stop and I hug her back, kissing the top of her head.

I'm doing this for her too.

"Ma," I whisper. "Will you promise me to look after Tegan until Rian gets out? Make sure she knows I love her and I'm only following orders."

"Where are you going?"

"I can't tell you."

"I'm your mother," she responds, pulling away from me and giving me the sternest look she can muster. "You have to tell me."

"I can't, ma. I'm sorry. But believe me, I'll be back," I whisper, wiping away her tears. "When I'm ready… you can trust I'll be back."

"When will you be ready?"

I kiss the top of my mother's head.

"You'll know…"

Chapter Sixteen
Valentina

Dear Valentina,

When you read this, I'll be gone. I don't know where you are and you don't know where I am and this is the first time I've ever written a fucking letter, so I'm sorry if it's terribly shitty. I love you. I want to say that first, because I mean it with my entire heart. I love you more than I've ever loved another living thing and it scares the crap out of me.

In my family, love and duty are married. There are people who have hurt you walking this earth and your safety is my duty. Wherever you are, you will always be safe. You have your identity and in this envelope, you will find $16,000 in cash, and the deed for a small condo wherever my brother has brought you.

There is documentation for a bank account in your name, a trust which will allow you to live comfortably.

Valentina, I haven't left you because of who you are, but because of who I am — a filthy racist, a murderous killer, a man who has abused your sexuality and bonded with you when I had no right to expose you to the danger of getting involved with a man like me.

By the time you read this, I'll be halfway to Idaho. Owen isn't the only man who has to worry about me. When I write to you that you'll be protected, I mean it. You are safe. You will always be safe.

And you will always be in my heart. No other woman will do what you've done for me, Valentina.

You are better than I will ever be. I hope you find love from a better man than me. I hope you find a man who can make your heart soar, who loves the way you play the piano, who can't help but stare at you when you're sitting in a beam of sunlight with a book spread over your lap.

I hope you find a lover who appreciates your gorgeous dark skin, the scent of your curly hair and the way you love so hard that you can melt even the hardest heart.

I love you. I love you. I love you.

Aiden Murray

I've read Aiden's letter every morning since I woke up here three months ago. It's a nice condo — a penthouse in Nashville — but I can't help but want to sell it. Aiden took my life from me. He told me he loved me and then he drops me here with this letter, with those words, when if he really loved me, he would've never left me behind.

I don't want his money. I don't need this apartment. Aiden knows I don't care about material things, so why would he leave me here with all this money and this letter as if it were the same as having him here? It isn't.

Once I'm out of bed, I get ready for work. Despite all the money in my accounts, I would feel strange sitting around all day with nothing to do. I turn on my television, the biggest I've ever seen, and watch the news. I never watched the news before and I like keeping up with the outside world now that I can.

Holding my cup of coffee, I start towards the couch to watch for a few minutes when I hear the announcer.

"Governor Ezekiel Pulsifer of Idaho found dead in his living room yesterday evening at 5 p.m…"

My mug hits the floor and shatters. A loud ringing in my ear drowns out the rest of the headline as I freeze. My stomach turns and my entire world feels like it's swirling around me as a tornado of emotions whips me into a frenzy. My hands shake as I run back into the kitchen for a towel and meticulously clean up the spilled coffee and the shattered pieces of my mug.

He's dead.

I know Aiden killed him. I don't know how and I don't know if he'll be caught, but I know Aiden killed him. I hear a loud thud against my front door and I make an unwilling squeak. The news has me shaken. *Pull yourself together, Val.*

The thud turns into a knock.

Knock. Knock. Thud.

What the hell? I don't know too many people here in Nashville, and I don't try to get to know anyone. I'm especially suspicious of tall white men with blue eyes or anyone who seems just a bit too friendly towards me. I hate that I have to be this way, but I'm not as easy to trust as I once was, especially not men.

That's why I keep a small handgun under the sink. They're easy to get in Nashville. I keep my ammo in the living room, but I don't know if I need to load the gun yet, I just want to have it nearby. I walk to my door and peek through the peephole.

"I CAN SEE YOU," says the last voice I ever expected to hear again. "I can see your feet and I know it's you..."

He sounds drunk.

"I tried to stay away from you," he continues. "I really did. But you... you have me wrapped around your little finger."

I swing the door open without giving it a second thought and I leap into Aiden Murray's arms.

HIS BICEPS CLOSE around me and as I hold him, I dig my nails into his firm back muscles and whisper with every ounce of meaning I can muster. "I'm going to kill you, Aiden. I swear. I'm going to kill you."

Despite my tough talk, I can't stop myself from holding him, squeezing him like my life depends on it and pulling him against me.

"I couldn't stay away," he murmurs. "I'm sorry."

I don't know what he's apologizing for, but I'll make him pay for it later. Right now, I just want to hold my big blond man and feel him against me.

"You left me," I say to him, trying to hide all my emotions, but completely incapable of controlling my voice's trembling. "You big stupid Irish man... you left me alone and I thought you would never come back."

"Ninety days," he murmurs. "That's the longest I can live without you and even then, it was pure fucking agony."

"Bastard," I whisper back. But before I can say anything else, Aiden stops my lips with a kiss. It's one of the best kisses I've ever had. That's never been a problem with Aiden. Right now, even if a part of me wants to smack him hard across the face, I can't deny how good it feels to be kissed.

His hands go straight for my curls. His fingers sink into my tight coils as he gets his fingers through as much of my hair as possible until his rings tangle in the coils and he has a firm grip on my head.

"I'll burn the fucking world for you, Val," he growls, pulling away for just a moment before his lips return to mine and he thrusts his tongue into my mouth. I tease his tongue ring and Aiden moans pulling me even deeper into him. His chest is warm, firm, and perfectly muscular. He has a chiseled body with rippling muscles over every inch of him. Not an ounce of body fat. Every time I see him, he gets hotter.

Even when I first met him in that horrible position with pain shooting through my knees and my heart quickening like an animal in a trap, I couldn't stop myself noticing his good looks. He drags my lower lip between his teeth as he pulls away.

"We should probably… talk," I muster up, working up the energy to yell at him for abandoning me again, for leaving me nothing but this stupid letter for weeks on end, for leaving me with his far less likable younger brother Callum. As for that one…

"No," Aiden growls. "No words."

He slowly detangles his fingers from my hair and his hands wander from my hips to the small of my back as he draws me closer to him, our hips pressed together and my hands pressing against his chest. The logical part of my mind wills me to shove him away, but that would never have worked with Aiden Murray, would it?

Hearing the word "no" only makes him want me more and pushing against his chest only ignites him to chase me harder.

He kisses me again and my hands slide underneath his plain white t-shirt, seemingly against my will. My pussy throbs with desire for him. He's the only man I've ever truly wanted and I can tell he's the only man I'll ever want. He's *mine*.

"You belong to me," he grunts, as if he can read my mind. "I was fucking foolish to think I could let another man have you."

This time, we stumble backwards as we kiss until my back presses against the first wall in my apartment hallway. I land there with a grunt which prompts Aiden to cup his hands beneath my ass cheeks and lift me off the ground effortlessly. He draws me to him and my thighs wrap around Aiden's waist as my hands remain under his shirt, feeling up his rock hard stomach and chest muscles as he holds me.

It feels good to have a man pressed up against me, especially this one. Aiden's cock shifts in his trousers and I feel his arousal growing against my leg which gets me very wet. I feel the dampness pooling between my thighs beneath my long, flowing dress. Aiden's hands only cup me over my clothes, but it's enough to drive me wild with lust.

I hook my ankles around his waist, taking what control I can. Aiden chuckles.

"I missed this," he says, using his hips to pin me to the wall as his hands reach for mine. He runs his fingers over the length of my arms before taking both of them and pinning them over my head. "I missed taking you. Feeling how wet you get for me. I missed making love to you, Valentina."

He kisses my neck and I respond with a soft moan. What's the point in hiding how I feel for him now? My hands push against his grasp as if testing his strength, but it's effortless for Aiden to hold me in place. I belong to him and he fucking loves it.

He lets go of my hands and I push his shirt up further until I get it off. Shirtless Aiden is even better than I remember. It's not just the muscles on his chest but the tattoos. There's a new one on the side of his rib cage, another Bible verse, and the cursive black letters against his pale skin are raised just enough that I can feel the shift in texture beneath my fingers. I love his tattoos. His pale skin. Unlike Aiden, I've never had a problem with people of different races.

As his lips fix firmly on my neck again, I caress his shoulders, indulging in the firmness of his large muscles and how good it feels to be with a strong man. Perhaps the strongest I've ever been with.

"Mhmm..." I whisper back, touching him like I'll never get the chance to do it again.

"Unzip my pants," he commands, keeping me pinned to the wall with his hips as he releases my hands so I can do his bidding. "I want to feel you."

I want to feel him too, and the urgency causes my hands to rush to his belt buckle. I unfasten his belt and slide his jeans and boxers over his ass as his dick springs forward eagerly. He's muscular everywhere, including his big butt, and I can't help but enjoy touching it. .

Aiden's well-stacked in the back with a butt that perfectly fills out his signature pair of All-American blue jeans. His ass tenses as his cock stiffens and juts forward towards me and my hands tease the curved taut muscle. His deliciously big butt is one of my favorite things about Aiden's lean musculature and he apparently likes when I touch it. My fingers slide across a thin spread of light blond hair on his butt cheeks and I reach for the base of his hardness.

He groans fiercely when I wrap my hands around his dick and his member thwacks against my inner thigh as clear fluid oozes from the tip. Aiden's cock leaves a trail of his arousal across my thigh as he slowly moves closer to me, bringing our hips closer together. Our heavy breathing synchronizes as the tip of Aiden's cock lines up with my entrance. He's so big and even if it's been a while, I remember exactly how much it hurts to take his impressive length and girth between my legs.

Aiden kisses my neck as the tip of his cock slowly works my entrance open.

"I will never leave you again," he growls. "Never…"

He pushes his hips forward and enters me with one quick thrust. There's more pain than I remember, but I don't care. He's here. We're joined at the hips and belonging to Aiden has always included a confusing mixture of pain and pleasure.

I cup his muscular ass to pull him inside me deeper, but Aiden needs no encouragement to begin thrusting into me. He takes me against the wall with urgency I've never experienced from him before. If he was ever in control of himself before, he's lost it now. His skin changes into a brilliant red flush and he grunts with each pleasurable thrust. He's rough and needy, sinking his teeth into my neck and forcing me to moan as he fucks me hard against the wall.

"Tell me no one else has had you," he growls.

Of course not, but a possessive alpha like Aiden needs to hear the words spilling from my lips.

"No one else."

"Good," he growls. "This pussy is mine. Only mine. Forever mine."

I moan as his big cock hits the perfect spot between my legs to deliver pleasure to every inch of my pussy. He grows inside me with each thrust as blood pumps through his engorged staff and veins pulse with arousal along the length of his shaft.

He swivels his hips with an unbelievably pleasurable rhythm as he thrusts into me and within a few minutes, I lose control of my moaning and whimpering. He has me completely under his control and whenever he senses me closing in on a climax, he slows down, extending my pleasure and keeping me away from the edge.

But fuck, I need to cum.

I push my fingers into his blond hair and grip it tightly, hoping that I can drag him over the edge and force an orgasm out of both of us. With each forceful thrust, I can feel him getting closer. I can feel his desire for me growing along with mine. Our bodies slicken with sweat and Aiden slows down his thrusts as he gets closer to climaxing.

"I love you," he grunts, his teeth sinking into my neck again. "I told you to never forget it, Val. I love you..."

He pushes deep inside me one last time, saying the three words that give me hope I never wanted to lose in the first place. The best orgasm I've had with Aiden takes over me as he finishes inside me. He spills his seed inside me and I wrap my thighs around him, making sure he doesn't let go and pull away from me too soon. I couldn't bear it if he pulled away and didn't return.

I couldn't stand not feeling his hardness slowly return to its softer state between my legs. I kiss him until I'm finally ready to let him go. When my thighs ease their tight grip around Aiden, he slowly lowers me to the ground with a self-satisfied look on his handsome face. His eyes twinkle with delight and heat rushes through me as a gush of his cum spills down my thighs.

Aiden pulls me closer, and leans in for another kiss.

"You're not going anywhere," he murmurs. "Promise me."

Where would I go? I think to myself. But I don't say that. Aiden finds me wherever I go, and I like it. A lot.

"Promise."

"You've changed me, Val. I was a real piece of shit when we met and... I suppose I'm still a killer."

"Pulsifer?"

He nods. "And Owen. Both dead. We only have one person to worry about now."

"Who?"

"My father. But... I've chosen you. I've left Boston. I've left everything behind because... I just can't fucking leave you."

"What about Tegan?"

He blushes and looks away from me. *He's ashamed.*

"I abandoned her," he says. "With my family. I tried to do the right thing. I sold my house to pay his legal fees. He'll be out sooner."

"You didn't sell Roscoe, did you?"

Aiden chuckles. "No," he says. "The dog is in the car. I thought we should reunite first without him sniffing around."

I grin. "Let's go get him."

"Your rules, Val. This is your place."

He glances around for the first time, his eyes lingering on the fresh sunflowers in the vase at first before they land on the freshly baked chicken tenders I had covered on the kitchen counter to eat later.

"Let me guess," I tease him, touching his soft blond hair again. "You're hungry?"

Aiden nods eagerly and my heart does a little skip. He's here and maybe we could be a real family. He could be my first real family. Everything is going to be okay.

Owen's death doesn't make the news and I don't ask Aiden the details. I've seen so much cruelty in my life that Aiden's efforts to keep me safe don't fill me with the horror he expects. He has a dark side to him and I have a dark past. We both have secrets. We both *had* secrets. All the secrets are out on the table. My past. His past. None of it matters anymore because we have each other.

The first night Aiden spends in my bed, we don't do much sleeping. My back hurts for three days after. I go to work and Aiden stays in the apartment either cleaning it up, organizing it or keeping my pantry well-stocked. He spends a fair amount of time working out, which I definitely don't mind.

He wakes up before me every morning and when I wake up without him in bed, there's always this jolt of worry that he's gone and run off again, but every morning, he's there in the kitchen whistling Irish ballads or making coffee. He must miss his family. His heritage. The people he grew up around. But he doesn't complain. That's not Aiden. He wraps his emotions up and keeps them in a little box out of view, all except his love for me.

He's very expressive about that and I tell myself this is it — our happily ever after.

But three weeks after Aiden moves in, everything changes.

I DON'T KNOW if we'll be happy anymore.

I DON'T KNOW if *this* will ruin everything.

Chapter Seventeen
Aiden

Val's changed. I can't expect her to stay the same as she was when I met her. That's not realistic, but the change in her this time scares me. She gets up earlier than I do, for once, and she disappears outside for an hour or so before returning quietly, normally wielding very distracting *Krispy Kreme* donuts and creamy coffee.

The woman spent her life as the slave to a man's whims, so it doesn't feel appropriate for me to infringe upon her personal time. She's been through hell, even more hell than I have, and she has a right to process that however she wants.

But the quiet bothers me. Valentina has never quite been shy with her opinions or her emotions, so I find her silence too conspicuous. I don't want it to mean anything, but my mob instincts tingle every morning that she sneaks out of bed and into her white Adidas sneakers for her mysterious adventures.

I have to follow her.

Sure, relationships are built on trust, but they're also built on a man knowing what the fuck is going on under his own roof. Well, technically her roof. But that doesn't mean I'm not curious. I love her...

I don't know if I need a gun, but the next morning, I make sure to get up long before Valentina and load my gun before slipping back into bed and pretending to fall asleep. I just have to hold still and wait for her to slip out of bed. She's soft and gentle when she leaves. She's not trying to be secretive, just quiet so she doesn't wake me. She even kisses my cheek before sliding out of bed.

Fuck, Val. What are you doing?

I don't get out of bed until I hear her shut the front door behind her. She still doesn't have a driver's license or a car — she's never shown any interest in either — so wherever she's going can't be terribly far from here. I race to the window and watch which direction she's headed before I slip into a pair of sneakers and follow her outside with my t-shirt and a pair of Patriots sweatpants. Roscoe doesn't like the idea of me going outside without him, so I throw him a few bacon treats before sneaking out behind Valentina.

It's Nashville, so there's already sweltering fucking heat. I'm sweating the second I step out my door into the swamp.

I jog to the corner where I saw Valentina turn and slow down my pace once I see her in the distance. Maybe I should have disguised myself, but I didn't exactly have a lot of time on my hands. She turns left again, walks for a couple blocks, then turns right. I follow her to a small brick building which looks like a doctor's office.

She's having an affair with a doctor?

It's a stupid, ridiculous, and completely insecure thought, but I already want to strangle the man who put his hands on her. Fuck, what is wrong with me? It's a doctor's office. Maybe she's sick. But if she's sick, why would she keep it from me? If she's sick... I would want to know.

I pace outside the office allowing my thoughts to run wild. She's cheating. She can't possibly be cheating. She's sick. She's dying. Oh fuck... I shove the door to the doctor's office open and demand loudly, "Where is Val?"

A mousy brown-haired receptionist rises nervously to her feet, her hand on the office phone in case I'm a nut job and she has to call the cops. It's not illegal to carry a weapon down here, but it won't exactly make me look good to have my pistol on me.

"Sir!" The receptionist exclaims. "We don't have a patient named Val. Can I help you?"

"She just walked in here. Dark skin, orange dress, sneakers."

"Tyesha?"

Fuck. My cheeks darken with embarrassment. Of course she would use her legal name in the doctor's office.

"Where is she?"

The back office door opens and Val steps out, her face expressing her bewilderment and betrayal in equal measure.

"What are you doing here, Aiden?" She asks, her nose wrinkling and her face twisting into uncharacteristic anger with me.

The doctor — a red-headed woman — puts her hand on Valentina's back.

"Is this him?"

Val turns to her doctor, her voice vibrating with rage that I know she wants to direct towards me. "I'm sorry, Dr. Johnson. I'll handle him."

"Are you sure?"

"Yes," Valentina says. "You. Outside."

Those two words are for me. What the fuck did I do wrong? She's the one sneaking around over here and I'm the one worried sick about what the hell is going on with her.

"I demand answers."

"You shouldn't be here," she snaps. "Outside, Aiden. Now."

I know my cheeks are red, but I can't let my visible emotions stop me from getting to the bottom of this. Once we're outside, Val folds her arms and judging by the look on her face, those folded arms are the only thing stopping her from smacking me clear across the fucking face.

"What is your problem?" She snaps.

"What's yours? You've been sneaking out here for days and I—

"I'm dealing with my own shit, Aiden," she says. "I'm not your property anymore."

"You were *never* my property," I growl at her. Why the fuck is she acting like I'm doing something wrong here?

"You are so damn stubborn," Valentina pushes with outrage I've never heard from her before. "You can't just leave well enough alone and I'm not ready... *Fuck!*"

I've never heard her exclaim like that before and her loud swearing stuns me into silence and seems to surprise her just as much.

"What the hell is going on?"

She glances at my sweatpants.

"Did you follow me with a *gun?*"

"I thought you were in danger."

"God, Aiden. You can't control everything. You can't control *me.*"

"I'm not trying to," I snarl. "I'm trying to love you."

"Ah," she says sarcastically. "True love, following your girlfriend with a gun."

My cheeks are hotter than before and I can feel what my mother would call my "Irish temper" flaring.

"You are *not* my girlfriend," I reply. "You're my... You're my fucking everything."

"Oh yeah?" She yells. "Well guess what, Aiden. I'm *pregnant.* I'm pregnant!"

I nearly stumble backwards.

"What?"

We haven't exactly been careful but... we've been lucky so far and...

"See?" She snaps. "This is exactly why I didn't want to tell you."

Val pushes past me and runs across the street, nearly getting hit by a red Ford Focus. The driver honks on his horn hard, but Val doesn't care. This woman...

I take off after her, narrowly avoiding an accident myself.

"Valentina, get back here!" I yell at her as she continues sprinting down the block. She's faster than I remember, but still not fast enough. I push myself to get closer to her and the second she's within arm's reach, I grab her.

Valentina yowls like a mountain lion and whirls on me with her hands curved into claws. She swipes at my face, giving me the opportunity to grab her other arm.

"Let go of me!"

"No," I say firmly. "I'm not going anywhere. You're pregnant."

She runs her tongue along the inside of her lower lip and narrows her stare like she's getting ready to spit on me. She'd better fucking not...

"Yes," she says. "I'm pregnant. And you're racist, Aiden. I could look the other way over everything else but... I can't have a baby with a racist man. I can't put a child through it. I can't."

I drop her hands. This shouldn't surprise me, but her accusation hits worse than a punch would have. I should have let her spit on me. That would have at least given me the moral high ground.

Valentina continues, which only makes it worse. "I can look the other way about your beliefs when it's just you and me but... I know what it's like to grow up with a parent who hates your skin color."

"Are you seriously comparing me to him?" I reply immediately, barely containing my rage.

I keep my hands away from her. Touching her will only make this worse, because I don't want to be angry with her. I want to kiss her. I want to take her into my arms and promise that I will keep her and our child safe.

"Aiden... It's not that I don't think you have feelings. Or emotions. Some things are too deep to just disappear."

"But it's our child," I tell her, my voice strained and low. "I would do anything for my child. My family."

"You could never see someone like me as your family," she says. "Not completely."

How does she expect me to define the person I've become since meeting her? I've only known one way my whole life. One way of thinking. One way of loving. I've never known tenderness until Valentina. But I want it. I thought I was proving to her that I wanted it.

"I would love my own blood, Valentina," I tell her. "I would learn to be whoever you needed me to be for her. Or him. Or whoever."

Is she really going to leave me? After all of this?

Valentina takes a step closer to me, her eyes brimming with tears. She presses her hand to my heart, which means she can feel how fast it beats for her.

"How can I be sure?" she says. "How can I be sure my child won't end up like Tegan?"

"Tegan is safe now." I know it's a weak response and Valentina knows it too. Her hand drops away.

"But she won't be with your father around."

"We're nowhere near my father," I tell her. "And I don't want to go back, Valentina. I want to be with you. I want a family. My own family. A new family."

"That could all change," she says. "And then what? I will never let what happened to me happen to my own child. Do you understand? I will become a very crazy woman to keep my child safe."

"I have no doubt about that," I tell her, taking her hand and placing it back on my chest. If she's still going to pull away from me, I'm not ready for it to happen yet. My mouth feels dry and my nerves raw. Pregnant. Valentina's pregnant and my child will be...

"You have to think about this carefully, Aiden. If you choose to have a black child, you will have to change. Forever. You can't go back. Because if I see you look at our child with anything resembling loathing or hatred, I'll disappear."

She digs her nails into my chest. She's serious, and a little bit scary, but Valentina's offering me a choice.

"I won't make you raise a black child," she says. "I won't force you to go that far."

My head dips in shame. I don't want to look at her and see how much she pities me for my commitment to hatred. It's worse than pity. There's revulsion too. How can she stand it? How can she stand to lie in bed with a man like me, who has been cruel and hateful when she never deserved it?

I almost want to cry. I've been so terrible that she thinks I would abandon my own child. What would be the point of my life if I did?

· · ·

I just can't. I can't abandon her and I can't abandon our kid. It doesn't matter what I've believed. She's right — I'll have to change.

"I want to raise our child," I tell her. "Black. Brown. Whatever color. I have to let go of my past, Valentina. It's my responsibility. I'll spend every single day of my life being the man you need me to be. But please, let me be with my child. I want to be a better man than my father."

Valentina pushes her finger up to tilt my head up to move my gaze from the ground to her eyes..

"Look at me," she whispers. It's difficult to meet her gaze, but I must. If I want her to see how much I fucking love her, I have to face her and my past and all the hurt I've caused her and other people.

"I've been a monster," I tell her. "The fact that you think I wouldn't want my own kid. Fuck, Val…"

She presses her finger to my lips, silencing me. Her touch feels good. I wouldn't have it any other way than to have her touching me right now. I slow down my breathing. She's not leaving. She can't be.

"Forgiveness takes time," she says. "But I'm only eight weeks along so… we have plenty of time."

"Can I kiss you?" I ask her, my lips and tongue grazing her finger as I speak. Valentina pulls her finger away from me.

"I would like that," she says. "I've wanted to celebrate but…"

"You were lying to me?" I finish.

Valentina stops my next words with a kiss. I let her kiss me right there in the streets. I let her hold me and touch me and I believe in the deepest parts of me that everything will be perfect between us and we'll live happily ever after.

Right?

Chapter Eighteen
Valentina

24 Weeks Pregnant

I wake up before Aiden again. He sleeps like a bear in the winter, I swear. I don't mind the heavy sleeping or the snoring, but I don't like that he keeps his weapon at his bedside. We've been out here for months and we haven't had a hint of his family down here in Nashville. I love it out here and I don't want Aiden's paranoia to push him to move us. This place has it all – country music, hot chicken, some of the friendliest people in America, and way better weather than I'm used to.

I put on my sunflower yellow dress and throw my hair up in an orange wrap before starting breakfast. Aiden loves food and cooking for him keeps him quiet about my safety for at least thirty minutes. Roscoe joins me in the kitchen, hoping for a piece of bacon. Aiden insists on bacon every morning and refuses to believe me when I tell him about all the articles I've read about how unhealthy bacon is.

The man wants his breakfast. The smell of bacon wakes Aiden. He stumbles out of the bedroom shirtless and I stop cooking to get a good look at him. *He's so damn sexy.* I can see all his tattoos with his shirt off.

My favorite is the Celtic knot on his bicep. His thighs and defined leg muscles bulge through his sweatpants.

"Hey, beautiful," he says, a smile twinkling in the corner of his brilliant blue eyes. "Bacon smells good."

"It smells too salty," I tell him. "Are you sure you don't want something healthy, like a spinach smoothie?"

"Yech," Aiden grunts, sitting at the kitchen counter. Roscoe runs over to him for some pets and Aiden chuckles. "Did he get bacon before me?" he asks, scratching Roscoe's ears. The dog barks hearing his name. I shake my head.

"Not this time."

"Good," Aiden says. "I'm the man of the house around here."

"Oh really?" I mutter, flipping the bacon.

"Yes," Aiden says cheekily. "And the man of the house demands coffee. Please."

"Hm," I say, strutting over to the coffee pot. "You are very spoiled this morning."

I pour Aiden his coffee and add enough creamer to fatten up a baby seal to it. He grins as I walk close enough for him to grab the coffee and takes it with a smile.

"Have I told you how good your ass looks in that dress yet?" he asks as he takes the coffee.

"No," I reply. "Because you haven't seen my ass in this dress."

"I'd like to see your ass out of that dress."

"The last time we did that I burned the bacon," I remind him. "And I'm pregnant. *Very* pregnant."

Impossibly pregnant. All those years, I believed that I couldn't get pregnant. I'd experienced enough to make me think I didn't have a chance at that. I never expected or wanted a child particularly. Despite that, my instincts kick in and I can't stop myself from loving the baby growing inside me.

I've become used to being pregnant. It helps that Aiden's all excited. He wakes up every day with this cheeky smile on my face and he asks a million questions about the baby.

"I know," he says. "You look bigger today."

"Thanks," I mutter sarcastically.

"I think that's a good thing," Aiden says, impatiently craning his neck to check the status of the bacon. "I like you bigger. It means you're more pregnant. I think I'll have to get you pregnant every year."

"I'm not a cow, Aiden."

"No," he says with his typical self-assuredness. "You're better than that. You're beautiful when you're pregnant. I like your nose. Your butt. How wet you get…"

I turn off the bacon and slide it off the pan onto a paper towel to get the grease out. I shake my head at Aiden's comment. I have to focus on the bacon right now, not his morning horniness. Serving Aiden a platter of bacon – I can tell he's far too impatient to wait for the eggs – I end up walking too close to avoid his grasp.

I set the plate down and Aiden has his hands on my hips immediately. He pulls me between his legs with a mischievous smile on his face. "You know, I'm hungry for something else this morning…"

My stomach protrudes beneath us and Aiden glances down with his typical excitement at my growing belly.

"Let me guess," I tell him. "More sex?"

"Uh huh."

"I swear, you have more pregnancy hormones than I do. Aren't you hungry?"

Aiden grins and nods. "I thought I already mentioned that."

"For real food."

"For something better than food," He says, leaning forward and kissing my shoulder. "I have to say thank you for the bacon."

I wriggle a little, but I have to admit that Aiden's kiss feels incredible.

"I also bet that you're incredibly wet," he says, kissing my earlobe and tickling me with his tongue. "Because you're always wet in the mornings…"

"Aiden…"

"The bacon can wait," he says, sliding off the kitchen stool and getting to his knees.

"Plus," Aiden continues. "I have to form an opinion on this new dress. You look great in yellow."

He kisses my stomach through the dress and a jolt of excitement surges through me. Maybe he's right. The bacon can wait. Ugh, I'm always weak in Aiden's arms. He seems to enjoy it a little too much. He hikes up my dress as much as he needs in order to get to my thighs.

"Fuck, I love you," he grunts before sinking his teeth into my soft cotton underwear and pulling them off with his teeth. He is ridiculously good at that. I gasp as Aiden's tongue swiftly spreads my lower lips apart. I can't hide from him when he's on his knees between my legs.

"I love you too," I moan as his tongue slides over my clit.

"I was right," Aiden grunts. "You're so fucking wet."

His tongue moves in an easy, slow circle around my clit and within a few short minutes, I can already feel myself losing control. He knows my body so well that he can make me cum within minutes now. I spread my legs to allow him greater access to my wetness. Aiden flattens his tongue and runs it all the way from my clit to my back door. His warm tongue twists in a small circle around my ass before he slides back to nibbling gently at my lower lips.

I moan and slide my fingers into Aiden's hair. I love his hair when he's just had a haircut. It's all blond and neat, and he adds this delicious mousse stuff to it that I absolutely love.

Aiden spreads my pussy open and then wraps his lips around my clit. He sucks gently on my clit while massaging my entrance with two fingers until I cum. As I get closer again, Aiden cups my ass with both hands and drags my body close to his face so his tongue can plunge deeper inside me. He slides a finger inside me, making it easy for me to cum repeatedly.

The waves of orgasmic pleasure feel like they're knocking me into the next dimension. I don't want him to stop, so I keep moaning and pushing my hips forward. Aiden's stamina keeps him going long enough for me to lose track of how many orgasms I've had. He pulls his face from between my legs and kisses the tops of my thighs.

"Bacon," he grunts. "Bacon and then we fuck again."

He rises to his feet, all six-foot-four-inches of him towering over me. I wrap my arms around him and pull the father of my child in for a hug. He hugs me back and kisses the top of my head.

"That good, huh?" he murmurs.

"Yeah," I tell him. "I'll make you more coffee if your mug got cold."

Aiden's hands wander to my ass and I don't know if he'll want more coffee or more sex.

"Hm," He says. "I'd rather have something else right now."

"What might that be?" I murmur, closing my eyes and nuzzling into Aiden's bare chest. I don't know how the hell he's shirtless and manages to be so warm. He's like a furnace and I want to sink into his embrace until I burn right up.

"I'd rather have you as my wife. I want to marry you."

I pull away from Aiden sharply and slap him across the face. Well, I try to slap him. He stops my hand and gives me a bewildered and disapproving look.

"What is wrong with you?"

"Arc you crazy?"

"Am I crazy?" he repeats, as if deeply considering it. "Why yes, it's absolutely *insane* to think that I might want my child to have married parents."

"You can't marry me, Aiden. If your family found out–

"They wouldn't," he insists, as if those two words could disable the enter Irish mafia in Boston. I fold my arms, giving him the look you give the man you love when you would still do anything for him, but you're wondering how on earth he could suggest something so stupid.

"And what if they did? I would become an even bigger threat and so would our child. Your family has millions in assets they want to protect."

"Exactly," Aiden interrupts. "I have to protect my child by giving them legal rights. It's more than that. I have to protect you."

"Aiden, we've discussed this before," I say to him.

"I love you," he insists. "When a man loves a woman, this is what he does. He gives her the family. He gives her the big fucking ring and the expensive wedding. I love you, Valentina. I can't imagine going through life only calling you my girlfriend."

"Then call me your baby mama."

"You are not just a *baby mama*," Aiden says, taking a piece of bacon off the plate and angrily crunching on it, even if it's a little too cold.

"Who cares about these stupid labels?"

"I care," he says. "I promised you I would be a better man. How the hell can I be a better man if I knock you up and treat you like a whore?"

"You are not treating me like a whore. You're respecting my wishes. At least I thought you were respecting my wishes."

"Woman," he growls. "Why are you so damned stubborn? I want to marry you. Why are you acting like it's the same thing as wanting to keep you prisoner?"

"Isn't it?"

Aiden gives me an annoying and sarcastic smirk. "You're carrying my child, Val. There's no escape after that. You have my kid, you're mine forever."

"I'm not getting married to you, Aiden. I won't have the wrath of your family descending onto us because we have to give some judge a marriage license or however the hell it works."

Great. I've done the worst thing you can do in an argument with a man – get too emotional and stop making sense. I have very rational reasons for wanting to stay away from marriage, but naturally Aiden is making them all seem very silly, which makes me want to give him a good slap.

"Let's get one thing straight," Aiden says. "I would *never* marry you in a courthouse. I want the whole thing. The big church wedding. The priest. The white dress. Taking off the white dress. Fucking you in a hotel…"

"Aiden…"

His cheeks darken. "I'm marrying you and that's final."

"The proposal of a true gentleman," I grumble, giving him a fierce glare.

Aiden doesn't stop frowning. "What's the sense in giving you a gentleman's proposal if you're not going to take it? I'm marrying you, Val."

"You're not going to marry a woman who came to you in a box," I say to him sharply, sounding more shrill than I intend to.

"Is that what this is about?" Aiden says with frustration as if the circumstances of our first encounter were something small. Everything is about that, isn't it? My identity. What pushed us together. His distance from his family.

His face continues changing into various shades of red, all out of Aiden's control.

"Val, answer me," he says. "You don't shut down on me. Not after all this. I've given you everything. I will continue to give you everything. If you stop trusting me–

"This is *not* about trusting you," I say to him. "Not everything is about you. It's about me. You're proud of your heritage, your history, your family, but I don't have a clue who I am except for what I learned in the governor's mansion and with you. I don't have a life."

I expect his expression to soften, but it doesn't.

"You're too smart to think that," Aiden says.

"Thanks, Aiden. What a completely emotionally intelligent response."

"I mean it," Aiden says. "You didn't choose your past any more than I chose mine. You have a family too. It's not your fault you were ripped away."

"What am I supposed to do with that, Aiden? They haven't known me for almost two decades. They can't possibly care. They might not even be alive."

"You saw the documents. They're most likely alive. Most likely at the same address. We could go."

"No! Are you out of your mind?"

I want to get away from him, but Aiden is too fast and he grabs my wrists, holding them securely so I can't hit him.

"I am out of my mind in love with you Valentina, and I will go to the ends of the earth with you if it means that you give my proposal consideration."

"You're hurting my wrists, Aiden," I reply through gritted teeth. I don't want to talk about this stupid proposal anymore and my wrists really do hurt. Aiden's body never hides his passion. He doesn't bother dropping his frown even for a second.

"We're going to New Orleans to meet your family," he says. "Then we're getting married. That's final."

"Do you want to know what grade I give your proposal?"

"No," Aiden commands. "Because you're coming home with me, getting your things packed and I'm hiring a private jet to take us to New Orleans."

"Aiden, that's ridiculous."

Aiden commands me to pack my things and disappears into our bedroom. I storm inside after him, my hands on my hips. "Can you stop acting like a freaking caveman for five minutes"

"I'm not letting you get away with this," he grumbles. "You're carrying *my* child."

"This is exactly why I didn't tell you when I first found out."

"Why? You were afraid I would act like a father?"

"You're packing a suitcase and dragging me off to some strange part of America like a maniac."

Aiden huffs and points to an empty teal suitcase at the end of the bed. I suppose he means for this one to be mine. He has seven white t-shirts and three pairs of jeans already packed in his black Adidas duffel bag. He's out of his mind. I fold my arms and glare at him.

"This is ridiculous," I tell him, fully intending not to budge.

"You're scared," he says. "I understand that you're scared but I've had to face a lot of shit to be here with you. We're facing your shit now. Together."

"These people don't want me," I tell him, panic rising in my voice. Aiden remains unbothered by my inaction and he flings my side of the closet open, dragging out his favorite dresses from my collection. Two made out of white linen, a red cotton dress with puffy sleeves, an emerald green dress, and then a royal blue wrap dress that fits me like a kaftan.

"They'll want you after I talk to them," he says threateningly.

"You can't wave your gun at absolute strangers and force them to accept me," I tell Aiden. "It's the past. It's best I move on from it."

"Clearly, you can't," he says. "And maybe it will be good for me to see your world."

His eyes flicker to mine and I finally see a hint of the softer side of Aiden that I fell so hard for. He's not all rough edges, vicious scowls and more tattoos than necessary.

"I want you, Valentina. We can't choose how we met but... you aren't my property."

He sounds frustrated again as he continues, "That's why I want you to be my wife. I want it to be absolutely fucking clear to everyone where I stand with you. I want you to be Mrs. Murray."

It's not that I don't understand his feelings. I share Aiden's love. I feel it when our bodies join together. I feel how much he loves me when we're curled up in bed on Sunday afternoon watching football games. I feel how much he loves me when he brings me green tea in bed or rubs my feet after I've had a long day. Love isn't the problem here, but with Aiden's family, we have more practical concerns.

No one gets a perfect love story with a perfect happy ending. It's enough of a miracle that I'm pregnant, this might just be the price that we pay for our happiness. We can't have marriage though. Aiden doesn't understand the word "no". He's too stubborn to comprehend it.

"I can't be your wife, Aiden. You knew that the moment we met. You've always known that there would be a wall between us and I've known the same thing. I've never asked you for marriage. I've never asked for something I know you can't give. You might change your beliefs, but you've still made promises that you can't break."

"Promises my father breaks all the time," he says.

"You're nothing like that man. You're decent. You've treated me like a princess even when you didn't have to."

Aiden's scowl returns. "A decent man would do anything for his own children. You *will* become my wife, Val. There's simply no way around it. Now… how much underwear do you need?"

A I D E N   R E S P O N D S to all my attempts at conversation with impatient grunting so I stop trying until we get to New Orleans. It's not my first time on a private jet, but it's the first time I haven't had to be sedated heavily to withstand it. Aiden doesn't share my appreciation for the different rooms until I walk down the wide aisles with my arms spread and push open the door to… a bedroom.

"How often do you charter private jets?" I ask suspiciously.

"Rarely," Aiden growls. "It's *very* expensive. I'm *very* motivated to drag you down the aisle."

"There's an entire bed back here. I can't imagine what you've been up to in those…"

That has his attention. He glances back at me and seeing the smile on my face, he tenses right up again. *Sigh.*

"As much as I'd love to take you to bed, I'd much rather marry you first."

"Are you forcing me to be celibate until you get your way?"

Aiden is reacting in the pettiest manner over this and he thinks grunting like a caveman will make him get his way faster. He is the most frustrating man alive. *But I love him. I love him so much it hurts.*

Chapter Nineteen
Aiden

I ought to drag Valentina into that bedroom, swing her over my lap and spank her senseless. She's the one forcing me into celibacy with her complete unwillingness to listen to reason and do exactly what I ask her to do.

"We will both be celibate until you marry me."

"Aiden…" she says, perfectly aware of the effect her voice has on me. I can hear her sneaking up behind me and I relax *just* a little when she puts her hands on my shoulders. Val gives a killer massage and there's something enjoyable about making her work for my affection.

I want her to want me as a life partner, not just in sex. It hurts to think that she might find my presence as a father to our child irrelevant. She's seen the worst sides of me and I have to know she wants the whole mess of me the way I want all of her. I just want Val to want me as much as I want her.

I want to know our love is real. I want to know that I don't have to search anymore – that I've found the one. She's my one and only but I want to be hers.

She presses her fingers into the knots in my shoulder and I groan with pleasure. She's unraveling my anger with her hands. Making me want her. My cock stiffens as she rolls out the tightest knot in the back of my head. That woman has magical fucking hands.

"Fuck..." I grunt. "That feels good."

She leans forward, the scent of her shea butters and perfume invading my nostrils and affecting their mind control on me. My cock is very fucking hard. She smells delicious and I want to bury my nose in that scent while pressing her gorgeous pregnant body into the bed back there and making love to her until she begs me to marry her. Ha. Like that would ever happen. She'll hardly admit that she loves me.

"It does, doesn't it?" Valentina whispers, her hair falling over my shoulders, tickling my forearms. Hm... I want to wrap my hands around that hair and tilt her head back while I'm making love to her from behind. That would release some of my anger with her. Definitely. She kisses my neck and I lean back, enjoying her hands teasing my shoulders.

"I've always wanted my cock sucked on a private jet," I say to her, giving her a mischievous smirk and waiting for her reaction.

Valentina rolls her eyes. "I suppose that would make you very forgiving?"

Her thumbs work deep knots in my deltoids and a groan of pleasure escapes my lips.

"Very forgiving," I answer, grunting as Valentina works her magic on my tense muscles. She is so fucking good at melting me in her hands. It's not fair. What right does she have to be a fucking goddess like this? She's so goddamned perfect.

"Okay," she whispers, running her tongue along my earlobe. "I'll suck your cock, and you quit acting like a pig for at least an hour."

"Deal."

I spread my legs to accommodate Valentina on her knees. I lean back as she frees my dick from my pants. Holy fuck, this is a dream come true. I'm tempted to give her everything she wants right there. Fuck the wedding, just give me head on a private jet every day until the fucking world ends.

Her tongue juts out and runs over the head of my dick in a slow, smooth circle. I groan and as I let the explosions of pleasure surge down my shaft, Valentina takes my entire length in her mouth and it's nearly impossible not to cum instantly. She won't let me though. This little reward turns into a game of torturous teasing until I can't take it anymore.

She pulls her mouth away from my cock right as I'm about to burst.

"Get to that bedroom," I command her. "You win. This time."

Valentina saunters to the back bedroom and I don't hesitate to climb into that bed with her and join the mile-high club somewhere between the Mississippi-Alabama border and Baton Rouge. Making love to her makes it easy to forget how easily she gets under my skin.

She's mine in that bedroom and I can feel it with every stroke of my cock between her perfect brown thighs. Making love to her while she's pregnant only makes me want to keep her in that state for as long as possible.

When we're both covered in sweat and spent, we dress quickly and seat ourselves for an easy landing at a private airstrip just outside the city. Sex calms Valentina only temporarily and once we step off the plane, she's quiet and contemplative. I know I'm pushing her, but I can't help but feel this is the right thing.

Who we are matters and if she becomes a Murray, she ought to know what it meant to be Tyesha Valentina Baker. At least she doesn't have to do this alone. A private town car drives us to an old plantation-style villa a few miles outside the city and I insist we take the evening to enjoy New Orleans and formulate a plan.

"You're in control here," Val mutters bitterly. Her little complaints don't affect me. I *am* in control of at least one family.

"I am. And you're going to enjoy yourself tonight."

I'm correct about one thing. Valentina enjoys her first night in New Orleans. In case things go poorly, I want her to have the memories of a perfect night in the city. We have dinner at a family owned cajun restaurant and wander around the city together. Valentina loves the

French Quarter, especially the beignets at Cafe du Monde where I take her for dessert and decaf.

I promise her we can come back to get more delicious beignets to do some shopping … once she takes care of her family business.

"What do you want me to do?" she asks in the taxi back to our villa. "I can't take those addresses and just show up unannounced. "

"You can and you will. Listen, this isn't the best way, but it's the only choice you have. Whatever happened, those people brought you into this world and they don't get to throw you away."

"Right," she says. "That'll be easy."

"I'll be there with you, Val. I promise."

"What do you think is going to happen, Aiden?"

"I don't know," he says. "But I know it's important to you. I know it would make you feel better to know that you come from some-where. You're not just a woman in a box."

"They could shoot me," she says. "That could happen."

"But… it's very unlikely. Stop worrying, Val. I've got you. I promise."

I'M surprised that she hasn't run away by morning. She refuses to eat breakfast and only pokes at the bacon and eggs I cook for her. I ask her if she would rather go out and get breakfast, but she shakes her head.

"I'll be there with you," I say to her. "And if they aren't there, we'll keep looking."

"Do you know how big this country is? If they aren't there, we can't keep tracking them down. I'm pregnant."

"We're going to get lucky," I tell her. "We have the luck of the Irish on our side."

This doesn't seem to move her.

"This is your plan," she says. "Not mine. My plan is to curl up into a ball and pretend I love someone who is far less stubborn."

"Get up," I grunt. "We're doing this. 2543 Wagner Street. Let's go."

I rent a car instead of hiring someone. I don't want to inadvertently expose Valentina's family to any harm. This information belongs to us – specifically to her. She doesn't speak at all in the front seat, but this is the day I've decided that she's the most beautiful she's ever looked. Pregnancy suits her well and her baby bump protrudes from her pretty royal blue wrap dress.

Her hair refuses to cooperate with the humidity of New Orleans, so she doesn't bother pinning it back. Valentina's wild mane spreads over her shoulders and bounces with each movement from the car. I like the rented Mercedes, but I prefer trucks. I miss my truck more than I miss anyone in my family.

Valentina's breath hitches as we approach the last known address of the people who signed her adoption papers. I stand next to her as we approach the house. There's a mid-2000s white Volvo parked out front and a slightly newer lime green Prius parked behind it. If her parents still live here, they might be home.

"I shouldn't do this," Valentina says. "We should turn around before I embarrass myself."

"Luck of the Irish, Val," I say, putting my hand on the small of her back. "We have that on our side today."

Chapter Twenty
Valentina

There's one of those fancy modern doorbells with a camera. I can't stop staring at the house, hoping to activate memories of some kind. It's made of red brick with a royal blue door with gold fixtures.

The windows have white shutters but I don't remember this place. I hear footsteps on the other side of the door and I glance over at Aiden, not so much looking to him for support but looking for a way I can back out of this and escape. He shakes his head, so I ring the doorbell. *This is my life – I have to uncover it.*

The door swings open and I'm out of luck. A girl opens the door. She's several shades lighter than I am with caramel skin and green eyes.

"Hello?"

"Hi," I say slowly. "Do Kesha and Tychon Baker live here?"

"Um… who are you?" the girl says, her eyes darting from me to Aiden. He must look terrifying to her.

"My name is Valentina and…"

"Najwa!" I hear a voice from within the house. "Who you talking to out there?"

The green-eyed girl named Najwa doesn't take her eyes off Aiden as she yells her answer back into the house. "Some black lady with a big white man. He looks scary, I'll be honest."

Najwa seems like she's about sixteen-years-old. Maybe it's best if I talk to her mother. *This can't be my mother's place. How would my mother have a biracial child?*

The woman calling from inside of the house approaches the door. I hear the sound of her footfall clearly, but that doesn't jog any memories. When the woman materializes in the doorway, there isn't any doubt in my mind. She's my mother. She looks… exactly like me. She doesn't even look that much older than me.

Her expression changes when she sees me.

"It's not possible."

Her dark brown eyes roll to the back of her head so only the whites are visible. Her knees wobble and she faints. Aiden catches her before she hits the ground. Her daughter screams and Aiden grunts as he supports her weight.

"I'll take her inside," he says. "Show me where."

The girl eyes both of us with suspicion, but she has no choice but to trust Aiden to drag my mother into the house. *Our* mother? This girl might be my sibling. There's a knot in my stomach considering it. I think she's considering it too. Once Aiden gets the woman on a pretty yellow floral couch, I introduce myself to her daughter. "My name is Valentina."

"Hi," she says. "Najwa."

"That's a pretty name."

"Thanks."

"Is your mom named Kesha Baker?"

"Uh huh," she says. "Does she know you from somewhere? She acted like she knew you."

"Hey kid," Aiden interjects, "Mind getting her a glass of water? And do you have any ammonia in the house?"

"She keeps the ammonia in the bathroom," Najwa says. "The kitchen's that way for water. I'll get the ammonia."

I get the glass of water. Walking around the house does nothing to jog more memories. I don't know why I expect it to, but I wish there was something to hold onto. My emotions here feel numb and if she hadn't fainted, I might have already left this place behind. What's the point of the past?

Najwa and Aiden kneel in front of my mother with the ammonia.

"This might shock her," Aiden says. "Stand back in case any arms swing."

Najwa already seems to trust him. He slowly wafts the fumes from an open bottle of ammonia in front of my mother's face and she coughs as she regains consciousness. Aiden swiftly moves the bottle away and Najwa waves her hands in her mother's face.

"Mom, you fainted. Can you hear me? Can you count to three?"

She coughs again and once her eyes open, her gaze snaps sharply to me. "How can you be here, Tyesha? Who sent you here?"

She knows my real name. It's hard for me to swallow and harder for me to speak. If this woman knows my real name, then everything in the documents must be true. I've found my past. I try not to let the moment overwhelm me, but it does.

"Nobody sent me," I say, a prickle of frustration at her line of questioning. "I found you. I came because you're—

"I'm your mother," she says. "I know who you are. But you *died*. The organization helping pay for your treatments had us sign these documents... You *died*."

"I don't feel dead," I reply, although I'm not so sure. There was nothing in the documents Aiden stole from Owen that showed I died. No death certificate.

"You don't look dead either," she says. It's creepy staring at her face. We look exactly alike and both Aiden and Najwa notice.

"Mom," Najwa says, a mixture of panic and realization in her voice. "What's going on?"

Her life is about to change forever. Aiden and I didn't consider that before coming here. I could ruin another family in pursuit of people who gave me up.

"Najwa," my mother says gently. "This is the daughter I had with my first husband. Before your father. Her name is Tyesha Valentina Baker and when she was a girl, she was very sick..."

She stops her story and scrutinizes me. She has more important things on her mind than her side of the story. We both want answers.

"But how could you be alive?" She says. "They told us the only way to get the treatment was to sign the adoption papers, but then... you were dead."

"I don't remember ever being sick."

"You were," my mother says. "Acute bronchitis. Pneumonia. We couldn't afford the treatments and there was this organization in our church that..."

She trails off again and then her voice hardens. "They must have lied to us."

"I grew up in Idaho. A man named Ezekiel Pulsifer adopted me and he was my guardian until... recently."

There's enough going on and with Najwa in the room, I don't see the sense of getting into the details.

"We never saw a body. I always told Tychon it was suspicious," she says. "Come here. Sit next to me. I want this to be real..."

I want to ask what happened to Tychon, but she's stammering in different directions and staring at me with such intense curiosity that I can't help but listen to her instructions first.

As I sit next to her, Aiden asks the question burning the tip of my tongue.

"Where's Tychon?"

My mother glances up at Aiden, taking him in for the first time. I sense her body language change when she properly notices how gigantic he is. Aiden has that effect on people. He's a tall hunk of blond muscle covered in tattoos and his constant scowl only makes him more intimidating.

"He's dead. He died four years before I met Najwa's father. Heart attack. I'm sorry."

It's so much information at once that I'm numb. I don't know what to say so I offer my condolences.

"My daddy's in the army," Najwa offers, sensing the awkwardness and trying to do something to step in. My mother reaches over to me and takes my hand. When our hands touch, I *finally* feel that thing I was waiting for. The connection. It's a spark of energy as our hands touch, nothing as tangible as memories, but something real and powerful all the same.

She feels like family. Her fingers tighten around mine.

"Losing you tore me apart," she says, her eyes tightening shut. "I want this to be real, but I haven't had a lucky life, girl. So I hope you've had the opposite of my luck."

Aiden clears his throat. "Maybe I should get some tea or coffee going? You two can talk."

My mother agrees and Aiden beckons Najwa to the kitchen to help him. He's handling this perfectly. Hell, he's handling this better than I am. Once I'm alone with my mother, I'm even more clueless about what to say.

"Is he your husband?" She asks me when Aiden leaves the room. My throat tightens. I don't know how to answer that question. She can obviously tell I'm pregnant. But how to explain Aiden Murray…

I DON'T EVEN KNOW if I have him figured out.

Chapter Twenty-One
Aiden

We don't leave the house until hours after midnight. Valentina doesn't cry as she says goodbye to them, but she cries in the car. Maybe I pushed her too far. I don't know. She's quiet until we get to the plantation villa. Once she steps out of the car, she turns to me before I can walk towards the door.

"Aiden, wait."

"She speaks," I mumble.

I don't mind quiet car rides, but they suck when you don't know if you're gonna get your balls stepped on for screwing up somehow.

"Thank you for encouraging me to do this. It feels weird and overwhelming but for the first time in my life I feel like... I *belonged* to people. They wanted me."

"If I pushed you too hard..."

"You didn't," she insists. "You were everything I needed. My mother asked if you were my husband, you know that?"

"Did she now?"

"She said you looked at me like I was the love of your life."

My cheeks are definitely turning red. I close the distance between us and put my hands on her hips. Words aren't my thing, but I can touch her and show her exactly how I feel about her, right?

"Is that so?"

Valentina presses her lips to my chest. "Yes. But you aren't my husband."

"Right…"

"Not yet," she whispers. "I think… for the first time ever… you might be right."

"The first time ever?"

"I'm saying yes to your proposal. If you still want to marry me."

"If?" I snort. "I already threatened to drag you to the altar if necessary. That still stands."

"That won't be necessary, caveman," she says, "I'll go with you willingly."

"Wearing nothing but a sexy white thong…" I murmur, kissing the top of Valentina's head. She pulls away with a scowl on her face.

"I can't get married wearing nothing but a thong," she scolds. "Nice try."

I can't let this moment pass without kissing her. I squeeze her hips and pull her close, nearly lifting her off the ground so I can touch her lips. It's our first kiss all day and she tastes better than that first sip of Guinness. Her scent is in everything and now it's on my lips. I yearn for more of her taste and I definitely want to tangle my fingers in her thick hair as I hold her body against mine.

It's impossible to think clean thoughts around Val, especially with the baby on the way.

"Can I get you in bed upstairs wearing nothing but a thong?" I tease her, cupping her ass through her dress and wishing I could drop to my knees and take her panties off with my teeth right here in the villa driveway.

"We'll see," she says coyly. "We've both had a long day."

I give her another peck on the lips which turns into several minutes of kissing, seemingly against both of our wills. When we reluctantly pull away from each other, Valentina has a pretty, uninhibited smile on her face. I did the right thing. That feels good. Better than killing people.

What I don't appreciate is Val's hesitation about the bedroom. I want her. I've wanted her since she slipped into that sexy dress this morning. She looks incredible in that dress and even better pregnant.

"Hm," I grunt. "We'll see indeed…"

Valentina's dress billows around her like flower petals as we hold hands and tease each other all the way to the bedroom in our villa. It's a perfectly warm New Orleans night and so humid that we're both covered in a thin layer of sweat standing still.

Valentina is fucking gorgeous tonight and there's no chance of me letting her slip away from me tonight. Fuck. No.

"Can I help twist your hair up?" I ask once we're in the bedroom, hoping not to rouse her suspicions too soon that I'm trying to get her into bed.

She undoes the wrap keeping her curls off her neck and nods. There's a nice old-fashioned vanity in the bedroom, so Valentina sits in front of the mirror. The lights cast a warm glow on her gorgeous dark skin as her mass of unruly curls and coils falls down her back. They're usually tangled after a long day like this.

"I feel *so* pregnant," Valentina says, spreading her legs slightly to accommodate her baby bump. I grab Valentina's little spray bottle and get to work on her hair. She removes the tangles from the curls on one side of her head with water and a little jojoba oil and I work on the other side, giving her a little scalp massage as I separate the curls and prepare to twist them up for the night.

"Hmmm," she moans as I massage the tenderest spot on her head. "You know exactly what you're doing, don't you?"

"You're going to be my wife. This is my husbandly duty."

"To give me an orgasmic head massage?"

"Followed by real orgasms…"

SHE'S SO MUCH MORE patient than I am. Valentina twists her hair into four large twists and I help tuck them out of her face with a soft, silk hair tie. My hands are covered in oil which I desperately want to rub into her smooth, dark skin. I just want to touch her so fucking badly.

Once she rests her arms, I peel the strap of her dress away from her shoulder gently and plant a deep kiss on her shoulder.

"Mm," she whispers. "That feels nice."

"There's a lot more where that came from Mrs. Murray."

She sighs and I try to kiss the sighs away by planting several more kisses on Valentina's shoulders, tearing away her sleeve to bare her collar bone and more flesh on her neck. As she tilts her head to the side, I nibble on her earlobes and cup both of her shoulders in my palms.

She said yes. She's going to be mine and my body wants desperately to consummate that 'yes'. I move over to Valentina's other shoulder, my plan so far remarkably successful. She's agreed to be my wife and yes, that may cause some problems with the Murrays, but she's carrying my child, she's the love of my life and...

"I'm not so good with words, Val," I murmur, kissing her other shoulder as I remove the strap. "But you know I love you, right?"

"Uh huh..."

I run my finger over her bare shoulder.

"You're the mother of my child. My forever. In my family, routine and ritual are everything."

"Will I ever be a part of your family?"

I move her twists away from her shoulder. She shudders as I cup her shoulder again and kiss her neck. I glance at her in the mirror.

"Yes. You're already part of my family."

"I mean the racist part of your family."

I don't want to ruin our day by thinking of my family. I've been banished from Boston. There's nothing that could bring me back.

"That doesn't matter."

"You're covered in tattoos that say otherwise."

"My tattoos say a lot of things," I say. "But they're a part of my history. My family history. I want to write a new history. I'm tired of pretending to be perfect when no one else gives a fuck."

"That won't make me stop worrying about our safety."

I push more of her hair out of the way and give her what I hope will be a more reassuring kiss.

"I will die before I let anything happen to you."

"What happens when you die?" She says, a little too coldly.

I grab her shoulders again and kiss her on each of them. "Don't be silly. I'm immortal. Now... take that dress off all the way... let me prove it to you."

"This has to be your cheapest pick up line yet."

"Yup," I whisper. "I feel very cheap for you tonight. Now take that dress off."

I have plans for what I'm gonna do to Valentina once she removes her dress. My cock stands at attention the second my lips touch hers. There's nothing sensible about how I feel for her. I just want to touch her body, feel her hips moving against mine and her baby bump pressing against me.

I want everything.

She rises, getting ready to drop the dress, but I'm too impatient to wait for her. I move my hands to the elastic that keeps it around her waist and easily slide Valentina's homemade dress over her tummy and hips.

"That feels nice," she whispers, leaning her weight back into my body so I can kiss her shoulders. My hands wander immediately to her breasts. They've grown rapidly throughout her pregnancy and they're even bigger and softer than before.

I hold her against me by cupping her breasts. She wriggles her hips to nestle into my grasp and her ass grazes my dick, making my raging hard on even more impossible to control.

"I love your breasts," I whisper, rubbing my thumbs over her nipples. Since her pregnancy, Valentina's nipples are easy to get hard and she's become infinitely more sensitive. I fucking love it.

"I can feel that," she says, barely concealing a moan. I run my tongue over the length of her neck as I tease her breasts.

"Take those panties off," I command her. She moves her hips away from me so she can grip the waistband of her panties. She peels the soft, damp cotton away from her mound and slides the underwear to the ground.

It takes me seconds to get out of my pants and press my cock against Valentina's entrance. She's soft and so fucking wet that it takes everything not to slide into her at once without warning. I wrap my hands around her hips and ease against her entrance again, teasing her clit with the tip of my cock.

She's fucking perfect and I want to feel her. Val grips the edge of the vanity as she feels the large head of my dick rubbing against her entrance. She rests her baby bump against the vanity and I clutch her body close as I press the tip of my cock against her soaked pussy.

Val moans as I push the first few inches inside her. I groan with pleasure as her pussy grips my cock tight. Pushing past the tightness and holding back from emptying every ounce of my seed between her legs is impossible. She's just so tight that it's hard not to cum. As I hold her hips, I ease more of her onto my cock, pulling Val backwards and allowing her ass to settle as I fill her completely.

She tries and fails to wriggle away when I slide another few inches between her legs. Her juices drip from her pussy as I bury my full length inside her. Val leans forward and braces herself against the vanity to adjust to my size. Her tight, textured walls make my dick feel incredible.

"I want to cum inside you every night," I murmur. "Look at yourself, Val. Look how beautiful you look getting fucked by my big white dick."

She moans as I drive my hips forward, driving the point home by sliding every thick inch inside her.

"Yes," she gasps, tilting her neck back and moving her hips to meet my thrusts. Her neck cranes forward and she nervously glances at herself in the mirror. I hope she sees the dark-skinned vision that I see. Her smooth, moisturized skin is addictive to touch. I plunge my hips forward and she squeezes her thighs together as I thrust into her, creating an incredible sensation around my dick.

I'm inside her, gripping her and I just want to move. My body curves forward around Val as our bodies move together.

"Easy, babe," I say, kissing her neck and shoulders as I move my dick between her legs. With each stroke, she moans louder and I swear, she keeps getting tighter. Her pussy feels impossibly tight around my dick. "Fuck, you're so tight."

She moans and arches her hips back as I encourage her. Valentina's body is so warm and soft that pushing into her brings me nothing but pure bliss. I have to have her. I have to finish inside her. I move my hands around to the front of her mound and glide my fingers through her pubic hair. I spread her lower lips as I press one of my fingers against her clit and rub slowly as I thrust into Val from behind.

A squirt of her juices gushes from her as I tease her clit to arousal while making love to her. Val gasps desperately for breath between each moan as her pleasure heightens. She's getting close to an orgasm and watching her gorgeous body approach the point of no return is such a fucking turn on.

I keep rubbing her clit as I fuck her harder.

"Look at how pretty you are with my cock inside you," I say to her, rubbing her gently and spreading open her lower lips so she can watch me fucking her with my cock and teasing her with my finger.

"Yes..." she gasps.

"No," I command her. "Look properly. Look at your pretty hair. Look at your gorgeous skin..."

I take some of her skin between my teeth and nibble on her neck possessively.

"You're mine forever," I say to her. "Mine..."

Val shudders one last time before she explodes. The gush of warmth sends me into a state of bliss, but her pussy clenching around my dick pushes me over the edge. As Valentina cums, I empty my seed inside her. Releasing feels so fucking good. My soaked hands travel from my clit to her baby bump and I hold her gently against me as we both finish. Thick spurts of my seed coat her walls and we both struggle for breath while watching each other in the mirror.

I can't take my eyes off her. She's everything. Her stomach looks so cute in my hands and the sharp contrast of our skin tones... What would have once filled me with a profound mixture of revulsion and guilt now just makes me feel guilty and hopeful. Guilty for my past, but hopeful that I can change it.

"You look so hot with my cock inside you," I tease her. "Second round in the bed."

"Can I catch my breath first?" she says, nuzzling her hips back against me. I don't think she wants to catch her breath as much as she wants to stay joined. I don't blame her. She's squishy and soft like this. Cozy. I slowly withdraw and turn Val around to face me.

Her twisted hair drapes down her back and it's taking everything not to undo the twists so I can lose myself in the delicious scent of her curly hair. I love touching that hair.

"You're my everything."

As Val wraps her arms around me, I feel a swell of pride in my chest reminds me that I can impregnate her whenever I want. As soon as she's had this child, we'll have another and another and forget all the fucking rules I grew up with.

Where did those rules get me? I followed them my whole life. I carried out orders. I still ended up here – cast out for rules half the fucking family has broken. Our vows meant something to me. Now, the only person who makes any sense at all is standing right in front of me, perfectly untouched by hatred.

I touch her face, letting my hands wipe away a thin layer of sweat from the edges of her hair. My thumb slides carefully to her lower lip and I touch the soft flesh of her full lips, my cock already rising to attention again.

"I like your lips," I say. "Have I ever said that?"

"No. You haven't."

"They're big. More to kiss." I lean forward and take her full, lower lip between my teeth. I tug gently before sucking on it and pulling Valentina in for a deep kiss. She braces herself against my chest and her hands against me is more than enough for my dick to be completely ready for her again.

"Bed," I growl. "Get in my bed, woman."

I move away from my position pinning her to the vanity, but as I slide out of the way, my phone rings. I want to ignore it as it buzzes on the vanity and plays the most annoying wind chime noise.

"You should answer it," Valentina says as she moves aside, but doesn't move towards the bed yet. I'd rather have her in bed than talk over this stupid phone.

Is she fucking kidding me? Leave a naked woman behind to answer a phone?

"I don't fucking think so."

She glances at it. "It's Callum."

"I don't care."

"He hasn't called you since we moved to Nashville. Don't you think it could be important?"

The phone goes silent only temporarily before the incessant buzzing and ringing begin again and sure enough, Callum's name flashes.

"I'm gonna fucking kill him."

Val hands me the phone and walks over to the bed, her ass and her protruding stomach doing absolutely unkind things to me. I answer the phone with fantasies of strangling Callum at the forefront of my mind.

"What the fuck do you want?"

"Good morning, Aiden. I wouldn't be calling you if it weren't important. So chill."

He doesn't sound very chill, which isn't normal for Callum. And he has a good point.

"What's wrong?"

"Dad's in the hospital."

"What do you expect me to do about that? Do you know how much we risk every time we talk? Let's hope you're using the encryption crap that–

"Shut up, Aiden. For once, can you shut up," Callum interrupts.

I grunt in response. Callum sighs and then takes a couple deep breaths. Does my younger brother have to be so fucking dramatic? Dad's in the hospital. So what? He's not dead.

"He had a heart attack last night and it's fucking chaos down here, okay? The Feds stopped by the strip club, not Harrison Ave, the other one, and took everything and I'm talking everything. Filing cabinets. ATM machines. There ain't a fucking picture left on the walls."

"Fuck."

"Luckily, he signed Harrison Ave over to Darragh," Callum says.

There's an instinctive part of me that wants to give a fuck that the Feds are crawling all over our family property. Threatening our families. Threatening what we've built.

I can't be that person anymore.

This isn't my problem. I'm here. I chose my happily ever after. It's Valentina and our baby. I can't bring her or my family into the belly of the beast again. It doesn't matter if my father were in the hospital or nailed to a cross. He might be the biggest danger to Val, but he isn't the only one.

"What happened to the accountant?"

"He's fucking gone, Aiden."

"Dead?"

"I fucking wish."

"Do you think he ratted on us?"

"I don't know," Callum says. "It's a shit show. Three robberies in the old neighborhood. Mom's scared out of her fucking mind and there's something else."

"What?"

"That man you killed, Owen Aurelio. You saw the body?"

I glance nervously at Valentina. There are still some things about my life she doesn't need to know. I walk into the bathroom and shut the door so she can't hear me. I can still hear her though. She sighs and flops back into the bed. I should be with her right now.

My family's pull on me shouldn't be this strong. I should be stronger right now because I chose her.

"Yes," I say to Callum, running the water in the tub to quiet our phone call. "I killed him and I cut him up into several pieces and... I still have his teeth."

"Oh thank God."

That's not the response I expected.

"What the fuck, Callum?"

"Do you know if he had a brother?" he says. "Do you think that sick fuck had a brother?"

"I don't know. I don't have any evidence of that. Slow down, Callum."

"I'm fucking trying," Callum says. "It doesn't help that you have the patience of a fucking teenager, okay? Dad's not the only one in the hospital. Darragh… someone broke into his gym and broke his wrist, knocked him out clean, left some of their blood and a note. I have a hunch it's related to your thing."

It's not impossible. I thought I turned everything over with the half-brother situation. Naturally, I couldn't have expected my father to confess to multiple affairs. I should have guessed. He was too calm in how he handled things and too quick to send me away instead of killing me. In his own odd way, he wanted to distract me. If he couldn't save one brother, he'd save another.

"I need more than a blackmail note and an attack," he says. "Darragh's a boxer and dad's been running bets on his fights since we were teenagers."

Darragh in the hospital explains why he isn't handling this right now instead of Callum. It's not like he can go to Evie or Orla.

I hate the sense of duty I feel to them, even after they've cast me out, but I can feel myself getting drawn in. Callum helped me when I needed him. So did Darragh. They kept their beliefs to themselves and now, I could make things right with them and help undo the position I've put them in.

Dad's in the hospital. Darragh's out of the picture. And what about Tegan? Her idiot father still has about a year in jail, even with good behavior. They need me.

Callum explains further about the note. He describes the details and everything clicks into place. There must be a brother. Or a cousin. Or someone who still has a vendetta against our family.

"I want to help you, Callum, but I can't come back to Boston."

I have my orders and despite my brothers and family tugging on my heartstrings, I can't violate these orders and run off to Boston. Dad's word is final. If there's one thing that's still true, it's that. Callum doesn't back down. Of course he doesn't, he's a Murray. That doesn't make it any less frustrating.

Aiden

"You don't understand, Aiden. We need you to run the family. Dad's in the hospital but... he's not gonna make it. We don't know how long he's got, but this place is falling the fuck apart."

"You've hung in there so far, you can make it a few more days."

"It's been two weeks, Aiden. I wanted to call you earlier but... you deserve your freedom from this bullshit. You really do. I just don't have the power that you do and neither does Darragh."

"Power to do what, exactly? I'm in exile, Callum. I have other people to worry about now."

"You mean Val."

"Yes, I mean Val."

"We won't hurt her," he says. "Aiden, our father is the only person who lives by those old rules aside from..."

"Yes?" I want to know all possible threats to Val's life before I even give this the slightest consideration. Because it's not just our father. It's our cousins. It's the people who watch our family's every move searching for weakness. My brothers only know peace time, but I was born towards the end of the wars.

I can't let this become my problem.

"I mean you," Callum says. "You're the eldest. You've always cared more."

"I'm not that person anymore."

"Forgive us if that's not so easy for us to believe because you're in lust with–

"It's not lust," I interrupt Callum impatiently. "I'm marrying her."

He's quiet for a few beats too long. I nearly hang up on him, but he replies just before my finger hovers over the button. Fucker.

"Are you fucking messing around?"

"No, you idiot. I'm trying to end this conversation because I have a life now and that doesn't involve dragging my black wife to Boston so when dad wakes up he can have her skewered. He told me to stay away. He was generous. I have to respect his wishes."

"He's going to die, Aiden," Callum says. "And when he dies, who will lead our family? We'll lose everything. There will be another war."

"What's wrong with Darragh?"

Chapter Twenty-One

"He's been balls deep in a bottle of Wild Turkey for the past five years. What the fuck do you think he was doing when they broke into the gym? He's out of his fucking mind and there's nobody else. You have to come back."

It's not just about Val now, but also our child. I don't want to talk about my child to Callum. It's not that I don't trust him. It's just that the information is better kept. The fewer people who know about Valentina's pregnancy, the better. We're supposed to go back to Nashville and back to safety tomorrow, but if my brothers get it in their head to find me and drag me home, maybe we'd better move.

"You can lead our family for all I care."

"What about Tegan? She misses you."

"Don't stoop so low. I can't disobey our father because a child misses me and you know that."

"Are you really going to make me beg?" Callum asks. "Darragh tried to warn me you'd do this. He was on enough tramadol to knock out a horse, but I thought he was exaggerating."

"He is. No amount of begging will bring me back to Boston. I can't save our family, Callum. I just can't anymore. It's not who I am."

"You will always be a Murray," Callum says. "You can also change what it means."

I hang up on him without saying goodbye.

Chapter Twenty-Two
Valentina

Aiden emerges from the bathroom in all his naked glory. Black ink swirls over his pale skin. Tiny blond hairs stick up all over his forearms, making him glow like a lion. He's grown his hair out a bit and it always looks so wild. His brows pinch together in a furious scowl, even deeper than the one normally marking his face.

"He wants you to move back to Boston, doesn't he?"

Aiden's scowl deepens and his cheeks turn his familiar frustrated purplish color. I know I'm right, which is what annoys him. I don't care if he's annoyed or if he gets all prickly and stubborn. I want to know the truth.

"Were you listening in?"

"I'm a good detective. Come."

I pat a seat on the bed next to me. We're both naked. We can't hide from each other now. I know Aiden keeps his emotions to himself. The thought of exposing certain parts of his inner world fills him with a cruel mixture of terror and dread.

He joins me on the bed, his large thighs touching mine as his soft blond hair grazes my leg. His closeness gets me immediately aroused. *I love him so much. I'd do anything for him.*

"You don't have to worry," he says. "I told them I wasn't coming. It's too dangerous and I have orders to stay away."

"Why do they need you back?"

"My dad's dying. Or so they claim. As far as I know, it could be a trap."

"That doesn't sound like Callum."

Aiden makes a frustrated grunting sound. *No, you impossible giant. I'm not letting you pull away from me anymore.* I take his hand and set it on my lap. He's not alone in this decision and I need him to know that.

"It's my job to protect you and our child. It's also my job to obey my father's orders. If I run back to Boston because my brothers can't handle their own shit… what the fuck is gonna happen to you?"

"Your father is in the hospital. He's the biggest threat to my life. Who else could come after us?"

"Whoever came after Darragh, maybe?" he says. His eyes are insanely blue. His lashes form a thick line around his eyes, further highlighting how pale they are. They're so light that they're almost clear. Aiden's eyes have always made me weak and I can tell that I'm frustrating him.

"I can protect you more easily when you're away from that den of vipers."

"You're talking about your family. You love them and you care about them, despite everything that's happened."

His eyes don't soften. "This could be a trap."

"Do you really think your brothers would do that to you, just to get to me? You said yourself that Tegan has a Hispanic mother. You've hinted at other so-called indiscretions in your family. Maybe everything is changing."

"Mob families don't change," Aiden growls. "But come here."

I'm just as weak to Aiden's commands as I am to his eyes. He holds me close to him on the bed. Our soft mattress already feels more like home than anywhere else. I hate the thought of anything dragging us apart, but now especially, we have to be open and real and honest with each other. We're creating a family together. That's special.

"I appreciate you loving me enough to risk your life," he says. "But I can't risk my child."

"Isn't it important that your child know about their heritage?" I ask him. "I'm still learning about mine and I hoped that was a journey we could all take together."

I don't know how Aiden will respond to something so... *sensitive.* It's not exactly his forte. His gaze narrows with frustration.

"My family would not accept our child," he says forcefully.

"They accepted Tegan. Your brothers know we're together and they still want you back. I took a chance on you, Aiden. Can't you take a chance on them?"

He scowls. "You are fucking impossible, you know that?"

"Yes. That's always been part of the deal."

"You would really leave your life down here behind?" he says, his fingers curving into my bare skin. He's the first man who ever touched me and made me enjoy it. I feel bonded to him in a way that's both special and sacred, despite the adrenaline rush of our first meeting.

Aiden always does this when he wants me. He silently clings to me and draws my body to his like I'm fragile and like I belong to him. I love how possessive he gets. Little by little, he's made me certain that he would never let another person hurt me.

For once, I feel safe. "My life is wherever we can be a family. I didn't know men could be decent before you."

Aiden chuckles. "Decent? I'm a monster, Val. You know all the monstrous things I've done."

"I also know that you've fought hard to keep me safe and you've given up your life and your duty to your family. They need you now and I think we'll be safe."

"What happens if you aren't? What happens if I screw up and something happens to you?"

"You won't do that. You just won't."

"I love you," he says. "I love you and I don't want anyone to hurt you because of your skin color. Or our child."

"Then protect us. Do what you've always done. Boston is your home, Aiden. We can make it our home together."

"You're a dreamer," he grunts. "I want to tell you that going back is a completely ridiculous idea and there's no part of me that wants to go."

"You took vows that existed before I did."

"I've done lots of things before you. Lots of things I regret. I can't be that person anymore."

"Then don't be that person. Be a different Aiden Murray. Lead your family in the way they need to be led."

"You're impossible," He murmurs, leaning forward and kissing me. I don't know if he's agreeing to return to Boston or not, but I know he wants kisses and probably a much longer distraction, knowing Aiden. He can't stand feeling tense and he always has one idea to relieve that tension – sex.

I push my hand out against his chest. He stops kissing me and gives me the slightest smile. I've caught him.

"I need an answer," I tell him. "I want to know."

"I'm taking you to bed tonight," he says. "And tomorrow, we'll discuss my family and my father's health and our place in all of that."

"You are so unbelievably stubborn," I protest as he strokes my cheek, his ring grazing along my skin. Aiden's gorgeous blue eyes illuminate with lust."Yes," Aiden says, "I'm very stubborn and I'm demanding that you let me touch you so I can remind you how I feel about you."

"I need to get rid of the dress for you to do that?"

"Yes," Aiden says commandingly. "I have every intention of feeling your thighs wrap around me and getting deep inside you. Now lose the dress."

"You have *never* become less of a caveman."

"You like cavemen, Val. Don't lie."

He kisses my neck as I wriggle beneath him. Our mutual nakedness makes him so much harder to say no to. Aiden has the perfect body. I can't resist his rippling muscles or his broad back. I yearn to touch more and more of him once I start. I run my fingers over the ink on his pale skin and push my hips up against him.

Maybe he's right – I like cavemen.

My breasts spill forward and feel so heavy until Aiden cups them and runs his thumbs over my nipples. They're so ridiculously sensitive that I gush all over my thighs as he runs his thumbs all over my nipples, teasing them awake.

"They're so dark and hard," he says. "I fucking love your breasts."

Aiden flicks his tongue out and sucks on my nipples while running his tongue piercing over the tips until I moan. He cups the small of my back and drags me toward him until my baby bump presses into Aiden's chest. He kisses my breasts until I can't stop moaning with arousal and he slips his hand into the front of my underwear.

Aiden finds me soft and gooey with anticipation as he slides his fingers between my lower lips. I push my hips against him and he rubs my clit slowly. I spread my legs to give Aiden greater access between my thighs. He sucks on my lower lip, kissing me deeply as he massages my entrance. Aiden thrusts a finger inside me once he finds my center and massages my clit until I moan.

He uses his finger to fuck me to an intense orgasm. I clutch his shirt as Aiden cups my hips against him to finish the job. He takes his soaked finger out of my pussy and wipes it on his jeans without a care in the world.

"Put your mouth on my cock," Aiden says. "I want to feel you."

He knows exactly how to get me wet. He knows how to make me want him. *He awakens something in me that I never expected.*

"Fuck," He growls. "I want to feel your mouth."

Aiden's dick feels thick and heavy in my palm. I wanted to wrap my mouth around him even if he hadn't asked for it. I slide down to my knees. The pain in my knees from kneeling stopped a while back, but I still flinch every time my knees touch the ground. My pride swells in my chest as I take the tip of Aiden's dick between my lips. He moans the second I take him into my mouth, but he waits for me to take more of his shaft down my throat.

I grip Aiden's buttocks and slide as much of his dick as possible down my throat. He groans again as I run my tongue along the length of his shaft. I tighten my lips' grip on his shaft and feel Aiden growing with arousal in my mouth. I dig my fingernails into his firm, muscular ass cheeks, and draw him deeper down my throat. I feel the wide tip of Aiden's cock grazing the back of my throat and control my gag reflex so I can take him deeper. I feel him about to cum, but Aiden slowly removes himself from my throat before finishing.

"Stand up and turn around," he says. "I want to discuss our wedding while I fuck you."

I rise to my feet and shake my head at Aiden's ridiculous suggestion.

"I can't plan a wedding with a dick inside me."

Aiden stares at my breasts, completely incapable of thinking clearly with me naked in front of him.

"I'd like to try."

"No," I say to him firmly. "Sex first, then wedding planning."

"The way you're acting, I hardly want to wait," Aiden says, turning me around and clutching me against him so my butt slides against his crotch. I feel his dick slapping against my ass cheeks and my desire for him trickles down my thighs.

"You have to have patience for once," I suggest to Aiden, who pushes the head of his cock against my entrance. I don't think there's going to be any patience from him tonight. Aiden scoffs and pushes an inch inside me. He is *huge*.

I moan as Aiden withdraws slowly and then thrusts the rest of his cock inside me with one big thrust. It hurts at first, but my natural instinct causes me to push back against Aiden. My hips thrust backward against Aiden and he grunts as he buries every inch of his dick inside me. He feels so good.

He runs his palm over my baby bump and grunts with pleasure as he touches me.

"I love how you feel," he murmurs into my ear and nibbles on my ear lobe. "I love everything about you, Valentina."

He eases his hips forward, causing me to moan in response. I call out Aiden's name and he wraps his arms around me possessively as he pumps into me from behind. Once his hips begin moving in a steady rhythm, his hands slide between my legs and he massages my clit so I have stimulation in every part of me.

I want to cum so badly that I push my hips back and thrust back against Aiden at my own pace. I'm soaking wet for him and need to finish so badly.

"I'm gonna cum," I gasp, bracing myself against the wall as Aiden makes love to me from behind. He pushes his hips forward, pinning me there with his weight and as I climax, I feel Aiden's dick tense and then he climaxes hard. He grunts and his weight pushes me into the wall.

He's so large. So protective. I don't want to leave his warm embrace ever again. I would follow him to the ends of the world. He keeps his arms wrapped around me, making me feel so tiny and protected. He's the first person I've ever felt completely safe with. We belong to each other and something about the hell we've been through makes our love so special.

"Fuck, you are convincing," Aiden whispers, sucking on my neck until I moan. He still has his dick inside me, making it impossible to think straight. Gushes of his hot cum coat my inner walls. "I have to listen to you. I have to give them a chance, don't I?"

"Boston," I whisper, leaning into Aiden's grasp and letting him nibble my neck. "We can get married in Boston in the backyard of that big pretty house of yours. I liked that house."

Aiden grunts, running his tongue over my neck and tickling me with his gold piercing. That piercing feels fucking good in so many places, especially running along the length of my neck. I shiver and lean back against his chiseled chest. I don't want him to take his dick out of my pussy. I don't want him to move at all.

I'd be perfectly happy if Aiden kept his dick inside me and made love to me again. He moves masses of curls away from my neck and kisses all the way up to my ears. His lips are so soft. I squirm against him and slosh around the thick spurts of cum he placed between my legs. He loves claiming me that way. *Caveman.*

"We'll go," he says firmly. "But you are my happily ever after, Valentina. If anyone or anything threatens that, I'm putting us on a plane to the other side of the world and we are never coming back here."

"You're my happily ever after," I say to him, leaning back so I can indulge in more of Aiden's sexy, sweaty man-scent. "And nothing will change that."

"Let's hope my idiot brother is worth it," he says, stroking my hair with gentle, curious fingers. "Now... get in the shower. I want to fuck you there too before I come to my senses and change my mind."

THE END

Darragh & Kamari's story, *Mafia Property,* will be released on April 20th 2023.
Click here to order the book:
bit.ly/bostonirishmafia2

Click here to receive text message updates when the next Jamila Jasper book releases:
bit.ly/textjamila

About Jamila Jasper

The hotter and darker the romance, the better.

That's the Jamila Jasper promise.

If you enjoy sizzling multicultural romance stories that dare to *go there* you'll enjoy any Jamila Jasper title you pick up.

Open-minded readers who appreciate **shamelessly sexy romance novels** featuring black women of all shapes and sizes paired with smokin' hot white men are welcome.

Sign up for her e-mail list here to receive one of these **FREE hot stories**, exclusive offers and an update of Jamila's publication schedule: bit.ly/jamilajasperromance

Get text message updates on new books: https://slkt.io/gxzM

Dark Mafia Romance
Preview #1

Sample these chapters from my Amalfi Coast Brotherhood Italian mafia romance series while you wait for the next mafia romance series.

If you enjoy dark & twisted mafia romance stories, you can binge the entire completed series on your eReader.

Enjoy the free chapters.

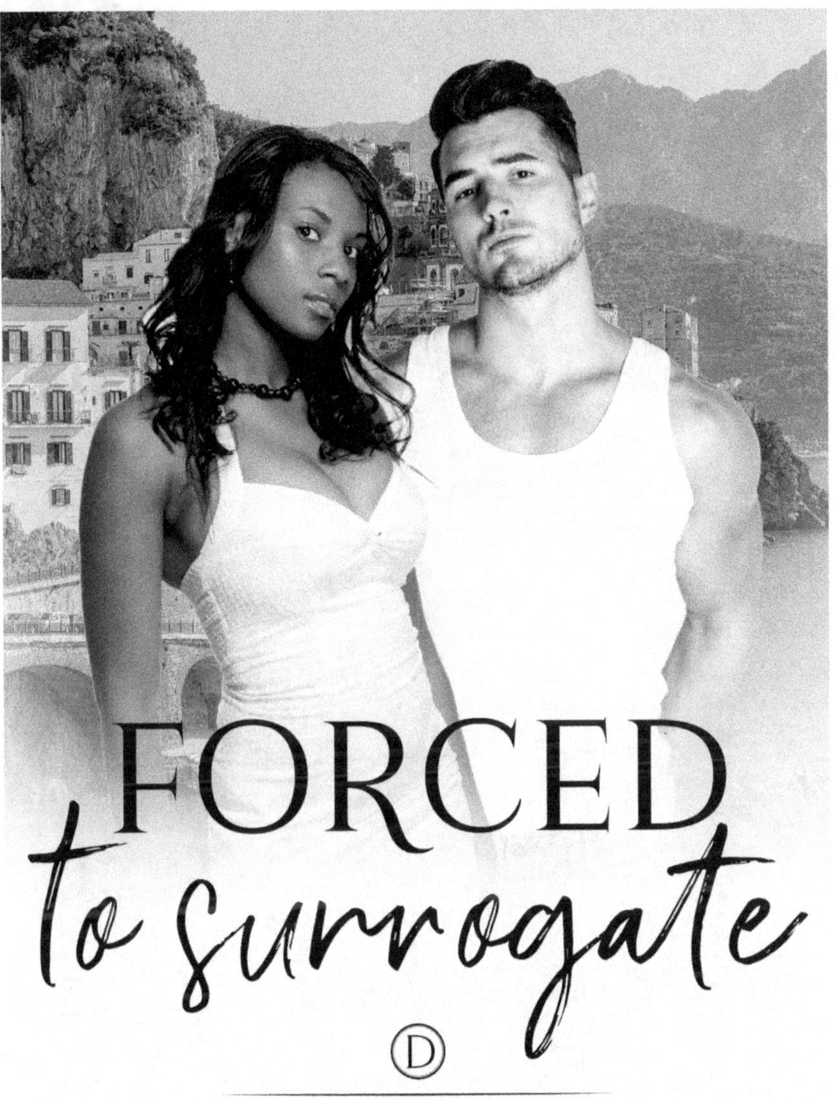

FORCED to surrogate

the amalfi coast mafia brotherhood #1

JAMILA JASPER

Description

The last thing Jodi remembered was a shot of tequila.
Next thing she knows,
Italian sociopath Van Doukas has her chained in his basement...
And he's claiming she agreed to become the mother of his child.

There's a detailed contract and everything... with her signature.
Jodi will do whatever it takes to get away from him...
But she doesn't count on the 6'7" Italian Stallion being skilled with his
tongue and excellent in bed.

Series Titles

Forced To Surrogate
Forced To Marry
Forced To Submit

Content Awareness

dark bwwm mafia romance

This is a mafia romance story with dark themes including potentially triggering content, frank discussions and language surrounding bedroom scenes and race. All characters in this story are 18+. Sensitive readers, be cautioned about some of the material in this dark but extremely hot romance novel. The character in this story is *forced by circumstance* into her situation.

Enjoy the steamy romance story...

Chapter 1
Produce A Pure Italian Heir
Van Doukas

There aren't enough cigarettes in the world for meetings with my father. The boss. Tonight, I meet with him to discuss something 'very important'. He calls everything 'very important', but tonight, I know exactly what he wants from me.

He wants me to kill again, this time for my foolish sister, who can't seem to keep herself out of trouble. Everyone in the family heard about what happened to Ana by now. That idiot Jew was foolish enough to put his hands on her with witnesses and expect nothing to happen? That's not how the Doukas family works, which he'll soon learn.

You mess with the Doukas family, we retaliate. If the Jew had any wits about him, he would disappear from the Amalfi Coast and head for the mountains or Sicily, or somewhere we don't have ears. He could go to Albania like Matteo. Maybe then we wouldn't find him. But fuck, I don't want to carry out another hit. Why can't that lazy fuck Enzo do it? Or better yet, Eddie. I carried out my first hit when I was two years younger than him. We spoil the new generation and wonder why our family falls apart.

None of this would be my responsibility if Matteo would get over himself and come down off his fucking mountain.

I stop my motorcycle and approach my father's front door. The all white old European style mansion sits on an excessive and opulent lot on the coast, right above the cliffs with a long path to the beach, a 'fuck you' to the tax collectors and the government who want to stop us from doing business.

Most of my siblings still live here, but I prefer keeping myself far away from papa and his... associates.

I can hear the party from the entrance. Seriously? On a fucking Tuesday afternoon? I assumed he called this meeting because he was working for once. He's intertwined in a different business based on the noise filtering outside. Please, Lord, let me not walk in on my father having sex with a model... *again.*

I open the front door to our old family home without knocking and immediately regret it when a completely naked foreign woman runs giggling toward the door, too high and drunk to feel self-conscious, exposing her completely nude body to a stranger. At least I didn't find her twisted in bed with papa, although this isn't much better.

"Oh! Good afternoon, sir!" she teases me in crude Italian, spinning around to show off her assets. *Whore. Foreigner. Her tricks possess little interest to me.* My brothers Lorenzo and Matteo would sway more easily.

"Where's my father?"

She giggles and spins around again. Fucking hell, I wish the ground would swallow me up. My father's prostitutes do not interest me.

"Your papa?" she says, standing to face me with her legs slightly apart, daring me to ogle more of her body. I have no interest in whores and I want her to answer my fucking question.

Before I can answer, another one of my father's toys saunters into the foyer, naked. This one is young—she looks eighteen just about— far too young for my father. I grimace and keep my gaze firmly fixed away from the nude females. Just because the men in my family are bastards doesn't mean I have to follow suit.

If we don't conduct ourselves with respect, how can we expect the respect of the Amalfi Coast?

"Yes. My father. Sal," I grunt, failing to hide the irritation in my voice.

The woman ignores my irritated tone with her response.

"Oh, he's in the back with Boyka. I can take you there after we take you to bed upstairs."

How much is he paying these women? We're still struggling to get Jalousie off the ground and he spends all his money on Slavic hookers.

"Not interested. I have a meeting with him."

"Are you sure?"

I don't dignify them with a response. I walk past the girls, keeping my eyes away from their bodies. Where the hell is my father? I pass the long hallway with the family portraits and follow the loud music and the louder giggling from near the pool. The familiar sound of pool jets betrays papa's location.

He's in the fucking hot tub again, I know it. He spends all fucking day in the hot tub, dishing out orders and expecting work to happen without him lifting a fucking finger. It's a fucking miracle anything gets done around here.

My father chuckles loudly, and I brace myself before approaching him. He's the boss and you don't question the boss, even if he's your father and even if he cares more about partying and women than our family — than our future.

When I enter the back patio, the pungent smell of tobacco and marijuana surrounds me. Judging by the bottles of vodka on the ground, the piles of cigarette butts and the other piles of detritus, they've been at this fucking party since last night.

Fuck. I put the cigarette tucked behind my ear into my mouth and approach my father's outdoor speakers, unplugging them and stopping the little dance party happening around his hot tub. Three women, each wearing next to nothing with their tits out belly dance for him while he chuckles loudly, his fat stomach causing waves in the hot tub. When the music stops, they stop too and look up at me indignantly.

They don't have to ask who I am. The ones who don't know Van

Doukas can tell that I'm related to Sal. I have my father's eyes, but thankfully, I don't have his overweight body or his bald head. The girls make booing sounds at me, but I brush them off.

"I'm here for our meeting," I say sternly to papa.

He chuckles and nods. "Yes. The meeting. I almost forgot."

Almost? He doesn't look like he's fucking prepared for a meeting.

Papa dismisses the girls, except for one — Boyka. She slides into the hot tub next to him, twirling his thick plumes of chest hair around her fingers and sliding his freshly cut cigar between his lips. Nauseating. Papa coughs after a puff and taps the cigar over the edge of the hot tub.

"You're early."

"I'm twenty minutes late."

"Oh?"

"Papa, you said it was important. Shouldn't we conduct this business alone?"

None of the girls are dumb enough to rat on Salvatore Doukas, but unlike my father, I don't see the sense in taking risks.

Boyka's hand moves down my father's chest and I don't want to imagine what sorry shriveled part of him she touches next. I just want my orders so I can get the fuck out of this bachelor pad.

"I'm getting old, Van," he says. "I'm getting old."

He didn't call me down here to bitch about his old age. I furiously puff on my cigarette, waiting for him to get to the fucking point. Papa grunts as Boyka touches something… sensitive. Cristo…

Watching my father grunt through a hand job might be the only thing worse than watching him stick it to a woman.

"Do you mind postponing your fucking hand job until later?"

Boyka's hand rises guiltily from the water and I choke down bile. She really was touching the old fuck. I shouldn't swear at him or set him off. Papa might seem old, but he can have me killed. Any of my brothers would do it if he gave the command. Tread carefully, Van.

"Maybe I should leave," Boyka says, giving me a flirty glance as she plays with her tiny pink nipples.

"Yes," I snap. "Please get the fuck out of here."

Papa scowls. "Be respectful, Van. Boyka is a very dear—"

"I said please."

Papa smirks. "Boyka, return in thirty minutes. If we're not done…"

"We'll be done," I interrupt, glowering at my father. I don't have all afternoon for his games when I have the club to attend to.

Boyka reluctantly leaves.

"Are the women in this house allergic to fucking clothes?"

"None of them are allergic to fucking anything."

I'm not doing this with the old man today.

"Why did you call me here?"

I start another cigarette. I keep swearing I won't touch another, then I spend five minutes around papa and change my mind.

He leans back in the hot tub, displacing several pints of water over the edge.

"I'm tired, Van," he groans, leaning back and rubbing his forehead.

"From working?"

My father doesn't pick up on the sarcasm. He hardly leaves his fucking hot tub anymore, and he hasn't done anything even remotely resembling working at either of the nightclubs, restaurants, apartment complexes or construction sites around town.

If it wasn't for me and Enzo, he wouldn't have the fucking time to boink Boyka or whatever the fuck he does with all these young Slavic women.

I still have to tread carefully around him. He's still my father, my boss, and I must obey him.

"Yes," he says, coughing. "From working. I need someone to take my place and lead the family soon. I want to retire, Van. You and I both know I need a break."

He spends every fucking day on vacation while his sons and nephews run his businesses. Vacation? We're the ones who need a fucking vacation.

"Perhaps you should contact Matteo about that."

My older brother spent his entire life preparing to be the boss. It's not my fault he fucked off, leaving his worthless children with us, I might add. I'm already halfway through my fucking cigarette and he hasn't closed in on the point.

Papa scoffs. "Matteo hasn't left Albania in four years. He left his children, his business, his fucking money, and he's not coming back. Give up on him."

"You're the one who trained him for the role. Send Enzo after him. Better yet, send his fucking son."

I don't want to go into the mountains to bring my jackass older brother back and I don't want to have this conversation with my father.

"Why don't you go to Albania?"

"Every time I'm in the same room as Matteo, he tries to kill me," I remind papa. I love Matteo, but he isn't exactly easy to get along with.

I'm surprised a woman tolerated him long enough to allow him to give her Eddie.

"Fair. But I need a replacement, Van. I don't want to be the boss anymore. I can't take the stress much longer."

Stress? What stress? Does my father seriously think sitting in his fucking hot tub banging whores counts as a job?

"Have you considered the role?" He asks before I can spew something disrespectful in my father's direction.

"Why would I want to be the boss of this fucking family? It's filled with degenerates, fuck-ups, people who need more violence to be kept in line. I kill enough as it is. You don't want me to be the boss and nobody in this fucking family wants me as the boss."

"People respect you, Van."

"People fear me. There's a difference."

Papa nods. "Exactly. Personally, I think you would make a good boss."

"I disagree."

But I don't completely. Yes, the job would be horrific and I'd have even more blood on my hands than I do now by the end. I could bring honor back to our family, clean the streets of our scum, stop the Jews from fucking with our shit... but I can't. Not with Matteo gone. Even in the fucking Albanian countryside, he would find out what I did and Matteo would kill me.

"No," Papa replies calmly. "You don't. But I agree with your assessment that you're not quite ready."

"I never said that. I said I didn't want the job."

Nobody smart wants my father's job. He spent twenty years walking around with a target on his back before he built up enough trust, enough loyalty, enough captains in the streets of Italy to ensure his safety. I don't want to lose my freedom.

"You didn't have to say anything. I know my son."

"Hm."

Arguing with my father is entirely senseless.

"You need an heir, Van."

"What?"

"I will give you the leadership of this family without the ritual, without the sacrifice and without the financial investment required. All I want is an heir."

"Why don't I go up to fucking Albania, then? Because I can't produce a child out of thin air."

Papa chuckles. "Don't you have women? If you want a woman... I filled this house with them. I have very young ones too. Eighteen. Nineteen. They make good mothers."

"I am not interested in fucking teenagers."

"Then find a whore like that old Greek Pagonis fuck. I don't care how you get the heir. You can prove how serious you are by giving me a child. I'll be generous. I'll give you a year."

"I don't want this role," I snap. "So the likelihood I'll produce an heir is slim."

Papa laughs, which only infuriates me further. There's nothing funny about bringing a child into the world.

"You can't lie to me, Van. You were always the most ambitious child. Maybe it's because you were smack in the middle and we didn't pay any attention to you. Who fucking knows?"

My father spent little time raising any of us, except for Enzo, and look how that fucking turned out.

"Thank you for the psychoanalysis."

Every time I visit my father, my desire for alcohol increases expo-nentially, along with my cravings for nicotine. He brings the worst out of everyone, especially me.

"No problem," he says, again ignoring my sarcasm.

"What happens if I don't produce an heir? Eh? You still need someone to take your place."

"I make this offer to Lorenzo if you don't produce what I want."

"What?" I would have at least expected him to mention one of our cousins, one of the very obedient captains from the northern coast, or even fucking Eddie, Matteo's 18-year-old son, would be better than my irresponsible fuck of a brother. That old fuck really knows me well because he just said the only thing that could get me to reconsider his stupid fucking offer.

"You heard me."

"Lorenzo would ruin this family. For fun."

"I know. And it would become your responsibility to save it. You would have to act as the boss to save Lorenzo from himself. You might as well earn the position."

Fuck this old man...

"I don't want a family life, papa. I don't want the fucking wife or the fucking family. I want this life. It's what I'm good at. Business. Killing. More killing. That's who you taught me to be."

I'm not a man who can picture himself kicking around a football with my children or taking them to the beach. I'm not built for seducing women for more than a night and dealing with the danger of introducing them to my life or worse, hiding it the way papa did with our mother.

He can pretend it's not his fault what happened to her, but we all know the truth. No woman deserves our life. I can't afford to react. He loves when he can draw a reaction out of me.

Papa continues, as if my reaction is irrelevant. "Part of this life means having a family. I can't expect my other children to carry on my bloodline."

"Matteo has a son. You have a fucking bloodline. Why don't you make him the fucking boss?"

"Eddie? Eddie will not survive long the way he lives."

"That's a way to talk about your grandson, eh?"

"Have another cigarette, Van."

I'm already on my fucking third. But I'm not in a position to turn down his offer, considering the shit he wants me to deal with right now. An heir? I thought he wanted me to kill someone. Producing an heir in a year… It's just fucking impossible. I stick the cigarette in my mouth and light it.

"You can't let the family fall apart. We aren't the only people who would suffer. What would happen to our people, good Italian people, when the only people around they can get money from are the fucking Jews, who hate our guts?" He says.

I can't let his guilt trip work on me.

"I want an heir."

"Hm."

"Consider what you would sacrifice by turning down my offer, Van. It's not just about the family. It's power. You act like you're a fucking saint, but you are my son. You enjoy power. You're just too much of a stuck up cunt to let yourself enjoy it."

"Thanks papa."

"You're welcome. Now, onto the matter of the Jew."

Fuck. I hoped my father would only piss me off one way today, but if we're discussing the matter of the Jew, I won't leave here tonight without an assignment. Someone else could easily do this job, but he wants me to kill. Because I'm good at it.

"I suppose none of my other brothers have the free time to do this?"

"I don't care. I need you to do it. The cunt offended this family."

"Perhaps we waste too much time retaliating for every offense. Ana told you to drop it."

I'm taking a risk just questioning his order, but he's pissed me off so much that I stopped caring.

"Decision making isn't women's work. It's our work. The man

signed his own death warrant. I want it done soon. Call me when you finish the job."

"Hm."

"If you don't like the way I run this family, Van, you know what to do. I want to retire. Make an old man happy."

Drugs and whores are the only things that make my father happy.

"An heir," I scoff. "You want me to have a fucking bastard child to continue your bloodline? A bastard won't have any loyalty to his family. Children have a mother and a father, a mother they spend all their time with. If I fuck some poor woman, you won't have an heir. You'll have a problem on your hands."

"Then get creative. If you need to get the baby and kill the mother, do what you must."

What's happening to this family? When did we lose our way and talking about murdering women for our own ends? Papa... This life changed him. It was slow, but it changed him completely. Too bad there's no getting out.

"Thank you for the advice."

"You're welcome. Now get Boyka back in here and get the fuck out. I need relief."

"Good evening, papa."

I drop my cigarette on the ground without bothering to step on it. Maybe my father's right — it's time for him to retire. But how the fuck will I get an heir? I need help.

There's one person I can call on for assistance in these matters. I don't like involving the Greeks in Italian business, but... they're our cousins. She answers after a few rings and it sounds like she's at a nightclub. She has an inordinate amount of time for parties...

"Ciao?"

I can barely hear her over the sound of the music.

"Miss Pagonis. It's Van."

She giggles. "Duh. What's happening? You finally have work for me?"

"How soon can you come back to Italy?"

Chapter 2
Single AF On The Amalfi Coast
Jodi Rose

I'm the last single woman in my family.

Three months in Italy, and I haven't had so much as a kiss, but my younger cousin Raven gets married to her college boyfriend and he looks like a dream. I drop a congratulatory comment on her photo, but my heart sinks.

You ugly, Jodi. Get used to it and stop chasing all these men out of your league. Settle with Kyle. He's the best you can do. Maybe mama was right. I'm not the marrying kind, anyway. I spent all my dating years focused on school and look at where that got me…

"Edo!"

The bartender gives me a sympathetic look. Ugh. Edo is so hot. Too bad all the hot guys are gay, especially in Italy, apparently.

"What happened?"

"Look at this."

I show him my phone and Edo cracks a smile. "Beautiful! Is she your sister?"

"No, my cousin. She's getting married and here I am… single… again."

And I'm running away from my problems with a one-way ticket to

Italy. When my family finds out I'm not coming back, they're going to lose their minds. Everyone already thinks I'm crazy for leaving Kyle...

"Fuck your ex, Jodi. Seriously, fuck him," Edo says with all the passion of a best friend, even if we barely know each other.

I have major regrets about getting drunk my first night here and spilling all the drama about my ex-boyfriend to a bartender, but at least it made us fast friends. Although I'm not sure if Edo just likes the fact that Americans tip, unlike our Italian friends. He always has a way of scamming some extra euros out of me. At least he's a damn good listener.

I groan and dramatically lean against the bar as I make a proclamation that I wholeheartedly believe.

"I'm never going to get with another guy again. This is it. I'm dying alone."

I've read the statistics. Or at least I've read what women on Lipstick Alley say about the statistics. I'm a thick, well-educated black woman who is tired of the dusties and has real ass standards — according to the internet, I'm dying alone.

Edo grins and shakes his head. Since he learned I was American, he's done everything in my power to take me under his wing since I got here. I just hate getting too far out of my comfort zone, so I've ditched all his invitations to visit the local clubs in favor of spending my nights drinking cocktails alone and checking social media. I'm in Italy. I should have daily adventures and bread. I can't forget the delicious ass bread.

"You will not die alone," Edo says. "At least not without trying... my latest cocktail creation."

Edo does a dramatic dance before revealing some clear beverage that looks like some horrible mix of vodka, vermouth and orange juice.

Good. I want to get completely fucked up.

"That looks... clear."

"You'll love it, I promise."

"Will drinking really make the pain go away?" I muse, twirling the glass around so the little orange peel swirls inside it. Kyle. Why do you always miss the ones who fuck you up the most?

Hopefully, this drink will get my ain't shit ex off my mind, but let's be real. What I really need is a summer romance. Ha. Like that's going to happen in a country where half the people think I'm a prostitute because of my skin color.

"Yes. It will. Absolutely." Edo replies with a wink.

"Cheers." I swirl the drink around despite Edo's repeated claims I ruin his creations by doing that. I pour it down my throat and taste a pleasant citrus flavor before a powerful vodka burn. It takes everything in my power to get the rest of the drink down my throat. Whew! That was a damn burn.

"What the hell did you put in that?"

Edo winks, but offers no response. Tricky ass Italian.

"My shift ends in ten," he says. "I'll take you out tonight to Jalousie. No getting out of it this time to watch *Empire* in your apartment."

How the fuck does this skinny ass white boy know me so well already? I shake my head, prepared to reject his offer to take me to the club, but Edo won't let it go. He wriggles his brows suggestively.

He loves regaling me with stories about all the shenanigans that go down at the Amalfi Coast nightclubs. I'm not really a nightclub girl. Small bars like this one fit me better, but didn't I come to Italy to have fun? Meet someone? I should put in some effort.

The only men who give me any attention are the creeps on the beach who say so much nasty shit to me in Italian that I'm glad I don't understand.

Maybe I'll meet better men at the club, especially a club with a fancy ass French name like this one. Jalousie. Wait… Edo's mentioned Jalousie to me before in the past.

"Ain't that the club with the mafia shootout you told me about?"

I don't believe half the shit that comes out of Edo's mouth, but he loves regaling me with stories about the real Italian mafia, which he claims is apparently far worse than any mafia in Long Island or Staten Island. How could anyone who lives in one of the most beautiful parts of the world hurt and kill other people? I think he likes telling tall tales to impress tourists.

I get people on Staten Island killing each other, but the Amalfi Coast? Hell fucking no. The sea is perfectly blue, the air smells fresh constantly, and it's plain peaceful out here. Italians have a rich culture, amazing food, better wine and the guys here are hot.

Not every guy, but when you walk down the streets here, you definitely encounter more than a few hotties. They all dress like supermodels, too. I've never seen so many regular ass people sporting Gucci and Fendi.

"Yes," Edo says. "But you're here for 9 more months, right? Have a fling. Don't tell him your real name... and disappear. You can find a hot and incredibly rich man to spoil you during your trip."

"Wait... is this a gay club or my type of club?"

Edo chuckles. "The guys are hot. I didn't say they were gay. You haven't earned your way into going to a gay club with me yet."

"Wow, Edo. I thought we had something going here."

Edo shrugs. "My private life is my private life. That's how it is in Italy. Your private life, on the other hand, is my playground. I'll introduce you to people. I know people who frequent Jalousie."

"Hot guys?"

"Eh..."

"Hot straight guys?" I correct myself before he answers. I don't want Edo tricking me into going out for nothing.

"Not exactly... I have a girl friend in town who goes all the time — Cassia Pagonis."

He says the name like I'm supposed to know who the fuck that is.

"Who the fuck is that?"

Edo chuckles. "A very fun girl with very hot brothers."

I perk up a little until Edo tells me they're all married. Great.

"Great. They're married..."

Before Edo can reassure me (again) more customers wander into the bar and Edo scurries to the other end of the bar to take orders.

I gaze into my phone again, looking at pictures from Raven's wedding. My cousin looks gorgeous, but I can't help a twisted pang of envy. I know it's wrong but… will that ever happen for me?

My homegirls from college keep sending me articles about the sorry state of marriage for black women. Alyssa says that we need to divest completely from marriage and just have fun.

My idea of fun isn't keeping a collection of all "my dicks" in a private folder on my phone. I want the real fucking thing! Even if the world loves reminding me that 'the real thing' only happens for white women or black women with the lightest dusting of melanin… I want to believe in love.

I scroll past Raven's pictures and my feed is all babies, new puppies, new jobs, new houses, new apartments, new husbands… new everything. Before Italy, I was just doing the same old shit. I wanted to shake things up. I don't know why my life hasn't transformed entirely. I'm in the prettiest place on earth — the Amalfi Coast.

Edo's shift ends, and he calls my name from the other end of the bar, beckoning me over to the cash register.

"Any tip for me today?"

"I saw you slip that five euro note out of my wallet. I think we're good."

Edo shrugs. "Sorry, this job doesn't pay well."

"I get it. I'll pay for our drinks tonight. Happy?"

"Incredibly."

I shouldn't be offering to pay for anyone's drinks, honestly, but I tell myself that I'll worry about all the damn money I'm spending once I get back to America. I have nine months of freedom and then I can worry about these damn bills and loans and everything else.

Edo drags me off my stool, and we step outside into the cobblestone street. I'll never get over how beautifully blue everything is here. The streets smell like the ocean, pastries, wine and cigarettes, of course. People sell jewelry and fruits on the streets and the Italian accents are… gorgeous. My Italian's still crap, despite Edo's best efforts to teach me a few phrases.

At least I don't have to hear all the street harassment thrown my way, which is plentiful. Edo replies defensively to a grey-haired man who calls something lewd in my direction and grabs me tighter. "Fuck these guys," he says. "You aren't that fat."

I swear, I'll never get used to how fucking blunt they are. But I appreciate Edo doing his best to defend me. We can hear the music from Jalousie echoing down the street before we get close.

"Isn't it early for the club?"

"Why are you so fucking American?" Edo asks, linking arms with me. "Relax."

"EDOARDO!" A shrill voice with a strange accent calls from across the street. I know Italian accents by now, at least how people from the Coast sound when speaking English, and this girl sounds different.

"That's Cass," Edo says to me, a smile breaking out across his handsome face. "Chin up. She'll love you."

Edo waves to the girl across the street and she struts over to us, sticking her hand out to stop the cars making their way down the cobblestone streets. They don't even honk as she passes.

The first thing I notice about her is how striking she is. She's tall, with curly dark brown hair pinned up out of her face and flowing down her back. She's wearing crazy high heels, like all the European girls do, a short leather skirt and a tight black leather crop top.

With her dark red lipstick, she looks like a film noir femme fatale… and she stares like one.

"Edo… is this your American friend?"

She turns to me and smiles. Shit, her accent might be strong, but her English is perfect. Cass's hair falls over her shoulders, her curls carrying a soft eucalyptus scent.

"Jodi Rose," I say, happy to have some female company around here, not like there's anything wrong with Edo. "Nice to meet you."

She takes my hand, three silver Cartier bracelets sliding down her wrist. Wow. Her bracelets aren't the only expensive item of clothing she has.

"Cass Pagonis. I'm sure Edo has told you all sorts of horrible stories about me."

"I did not!"

Edo definitely did. But Cass doesn't seem like a crazy party girl. She rolls her eyes and brushes him off.

"I'm here on the Coast working for my cousin's family," Cass says. "I'm from Thessaloniki. My idiot brothers want me back next week, unfortunately. But I could use a night out before I go."

Edo claps his hands. "Yay! Party time. Too bad Jalousie only caters to the most chauvinistic mafia pigs you can imagine."

"I thought you said they were hotties?!"

"They are," Edo says. "But they might be assholes."

Now he tells me. Edo would have said anything to get me out of my damn apartment. I hope I don't regret it.

"Watch it," Cass cautions, an impish smile on her face. "Those chauvinistic mafia pigs are my cousins and brothers."

Edo shrugs. "Fine. Fine. But I need dick too. Gay rights."

Cass swats his shoulder.

"Edo, why don't you let me take her for the night? There's no one at Jalousie for you, and you can go meet up with Klaus or... that other one."

Edo suddenly straightens his back and reminds both of us that just because he's gay doesn't mean he's given up on old world chivalry.

"I can't send Jodi off with a stranger," he says.

I appreciate the sentiment, but I don't know if Edo would do much damage against... any man who weighed more than his slight 108 lb frame.

"I'm fine," I tell him. "Seriously."

"I'm armed anyway," Cass says. I think she's joking, but neither of them laughs. Is she serious? She doesn't look armed, and she looks more like a model than someone who knows how to use a weapon.

I could use a female friend in my life over here. I've got plenty of female friends back home, but they all want to talk about Kyle and my "healing journey". They don't want to hear that I'm still lost after all these months.

Edo shrugs. "If you insist."

"I insist," I tell him. "You've done enough taking care of me. Plus, I'll get to know my new friend... Cass."

"Exactly," Cass says. "Jodi… I think we can become wonderful friends. We can swap stories about Edo."

"There are no stories about Edo," he chimes in. "Because Edo is an incredible friend and a better bartender."

"Shoo," Cass says. "I can handle things from here."

Edo doesn't quite walk off, but he checks his phone and begins texting furiously to plan his next move.

"It's the last time they have DJ Fat Camel playing here. We'll dance, drink and later, I'll take you home, yes?"

"That sounds good to me."

"Well, you have my number if Cass abandons you on the top of a Ferris wheel," Edo says as he swipes four times quickly across his screen and then shoves his phone into his pocket.

Cass rolls her eyes. "I have done nothing of the sort. Get out of here, you big drama queen."

"Ciao!"

Cass and I say "Ciao!"

Edo walks down the cobblestone streets and lights a cigarette before disappearing around the corner. Cass breathes a sigh of relief and turns to me.

"I just think you're perfect," she says.

Weird comment to make, but I mumble a gracious thank you, assuming something got lost in translation.

"Do you have friends with you?" Cass asks, taking out a hand mirror and fixing her bright red lipstick.

"No. I'm here solo tripping. Had a quarter life crisis and… here I am."

"Do you like Italy?" she asks genuinely. Her eyes are so intense.

"It's beautiful."

"Not as pretty as Greece," Cass says. "But I agree. Shall we go in?"

"We should head to the back of the line," I say, my stomach knotting as I see the line stretched around the block. I hope we can even get into the club.

Cass grins, unperturbed by the growing line outside Jalousie.

"My cousin owns the place. Come on, we go in through the back."

Before I can protest, she takes my hand and we walk around a back alley that smells like trash, vomit and again — cigarettes. Cass drags me over to a door and surveys me once before touching the handle.

"Very proper outfit. Excellent. Let's go. Ready to dance?"

I nod, even if I'm nervous. Sure, I'm trying to have an adventure tonight, but I just met this chick. How do I know she isn't crazy? Well, she has Edo's backing, so at least she'll be a good time. Edo definitely knows how to have fun if his clubbing stories are even 55% true.

Cass punches in a six-digit code and the back door to the club opens. I can smell the club before I hear the music and Cass drags me in through the back before I can second guess myself. What am I really doing? I don't know this chick at all and I agreed to go clubbing with her? Is Edo's word really enough?

Once we're in the back door, a man appears. He's tall, with dark brown slicked back hair, tattoos all over his arms and grey eyes. He has broad shoulders, but is otherwise lean and very muscular. He's handsome, but it's too bad he smokes. I can smell the cigarettes from a distance.

"Cass? What the fuck are you doing here?" he asks, seeming genuinely upset.

"Shut the fuck up, Enzo," Cass snaps, her expression changing suddenly into a disapproving scowl. "I have business here."

The man smirks. He's around Cass' height, but he looks… greasy.

"Is that her?"

"Mind your fucking business."

Cass pushes him hard so we can get past him. The grey-eyed man's eyes land on me and he runs his hand over his jawline before snickering.

"He's going to kill you."

"Shut up," Cass snarls. Enzo laughs and raises his hands in defeat.

"Enjoy your night," he says to me in a sing-song voice. For the first time, I feel real hesitation. But Cass grabs my hand and drags me inside of the club.

Cass drags me all the way to the tables and chairs surrounding the dance floor, chatting excitedly and peppering me with questions about

America. I struggle to understand her accent at first, but then I get into the rhythm of her voice and it's easier for us to communicate.

I have to listen in so hard that I barely scan the room we enter. At least the nightclub has a nice interior, and it doesn't seem like any ghetto shit might pop off. Another Edo exaggeration, it seems. I relax as Cass sets me up at a small, two-person table.

"I'll get you a drink. Wait here. If anyone comes to talk to you, tell them you are with Cass Pagonis. That will shut them up."

Before I can protest, or offer to come with her, Cass disappears. Shit. I guess I have to wait here. I already have five texts from Edo about the hotties he met at the club a few doors over. Damn, he moves quick. I've been here for weeks already and I still haven't met a heterosexual male who hasn't been an incredibly old and excessively horny man offering for me to be his 'African prostitute' — offers I have obviously declined.

Cass returns quickly, before I have any time to worry with two shots, each one with some blue flavoring at the bottom.

"Okay, Jodi. This is to a long and beautiful friendship between us, starting with one crazy night, yeah?"

I nod. "Hell yeah. I've never done anything like this before."

I blurt out the last part nervously, but Cass has a way of soothing me. She just smiles and nods. "Don't be scared! I'm a good Greek girl. Now come on… we'll take the shots together."

She counts us down.

"1… 2… 3…"

I take the shot — and it's the last thing I remember about that night.

Click here to keep reading:
https://bit.ly/amalficoast1

Extremely Important Links

ALL BOOKS BY JAMILA JASPER
https://linktr.ee/JamilaJasper
SIGN UP FOR EMAIL UPDATES
Bit.ly/jamilajasperromance
SOCIAL MEDIA LINKS
https://www.jamilajasperromance.com/
GET MERCH
https://www.redbubble.com/people/jamilajasper/shop
GET FREEBIE (VIA TEXT)
https://slkt.io/qMk8
READ SERIAL (NEW CHAPTERS WEEKLY)
www.patreon.com/jamilajasper

JAMILA JASPER

Diverse Romance For Black Women

More Jamila Jasper Romance

<u>Pick your poison...</u>

Delicious interracial romance novels for all tastes. Long novels, short stories, audiobooks and more.

Hit the link to experience my full catalog.

FULL CATALOG BY JAMILA JASPER:
https://linktr.ee/JamilaJasper

Thank You Kindly

Thank you to all my readers, new and old for your support with this new year.

I look forward to making 2022 an INCREDIBLE year for interracial romance novels. I want to thank you all for joining along on the journey.

Thank you to my most supportive readers:

Cortney, Yolanda S., MonaGirl, Dianna, Mary, Nysha, Fayola, Ty, Shyra, Andi-Mariee, Keisha, Jennett, Fredericka, Candece, Lydia, Sabrina, JM, Jackie, Mo, Ashaunte, Tolu, Lori, Dionne, ZLB, Nicol, Elbert, Jesi, Brenda, Desiree, LaShan, Only1ToniD, Debbie, Tiffanie, Shawnte, Lisema, Christine, Trinity, Monica, Juliette, Letetia, Margaret, Dash, Maxine, Sheron, Javonda, Pearl, Kiana, Shyan, Jacklyn, Amy, Julia, Colleen, Natasha, Yvonne, Brittany, June, Ashleigh, Nene, Nene, Deborah, Nikki, DeShaunda, Latoya, Shelite, Arlene, Judith, Mary, Shanida, Rachel,Damzel, Ahnjala, Kenya, Momo, BJ, Akeshia, Melissa, Tiffany, Sherbear, Nini, Curtresa, Regina, Ashley, Mia, Sydney, Sharon, Charlotte, Assiatu, Regina, Romanda, Catherine, Gaynor, BF, Tasha, Henri, Sara, skkent, Rosalyn, Danielle, Deborah, Kirsten, Ana, Taylor, Charlene Louanna, Michelle, Tamika, Lauren, RoHyde, Natasha, Shekynah, Cassie, Dreama, Nick, Gennifer, Rayna, Jaleda, Kimvodkna, Jatonn, Anoushka, Audrey, Valeria, Courtney, Donna, Jenetha, Ayana, Kristy, FreyaJo, Grace, Kisha, Stephanie E., Amber, Denice, Marty,

LaKisha, Latoya, Natasha, Monifa, Alisa, Daveena, Desiree, Gerry, Kimberly, Stephanie M., Tarah, Yolanda, Kristy, Gary, Janet, Kathy, Phyllis, Susan

Join the Patreon Community.
www.patreon.com/jamilajasper

Patreon

Instantly access all six seasons of *Unfuckable* (Ben & Libby's story) with 375 chapters.

For a small monthly fee, you get exclusive access to my all this & my recently completed serial Despicable (275 chapters) ⬇

www.patreon.com/jamilajasper

Patreon has more than the ongoing serial and previous serial releases...

⚡ INSTANT ACCESS ⚡

- NEW merchandise tiers with **t-shirts, totes, mugs,** stickers and MORE!
- **FREE paperback** with all new tiers
- **FREE short story audiobooks** and audiobook samples when they're ready
- #FirstDraftLeaks of Prologues and first chapters **weeks** before I hit publish
- Behind the scenes notes
- Polls and story contribution
- Comments & LIVELY community discussion with likeminded interracial romance readers.

**LEARN MORE ABOUT SUPPORTING A
DIVERSE ROMANCE AUTHOR**
www.patreon.com/jamilajasper